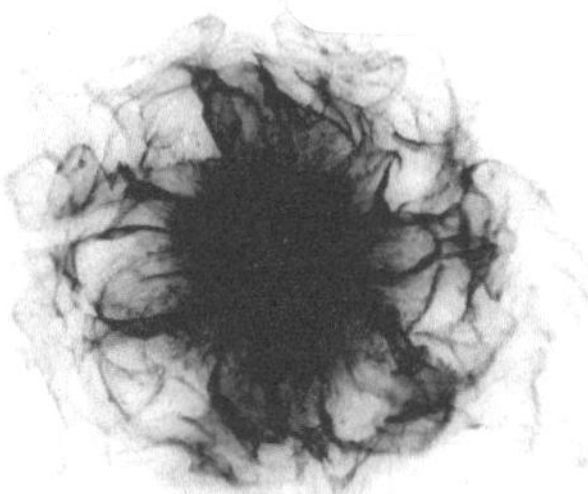

THE LAST SENSOR

BOOK FOUR OF THE ECOSYSTEM SERIES

JOSHUA DAVID BELLIN

The Last Sensor

Cover and interior design by Damonza

Map by Jessica Khoury / Lizard Ink Maps

Paperback ISBN: 978-1-7321859-7-5

eBook ISBN: 978-1-7321859-8-2

For life

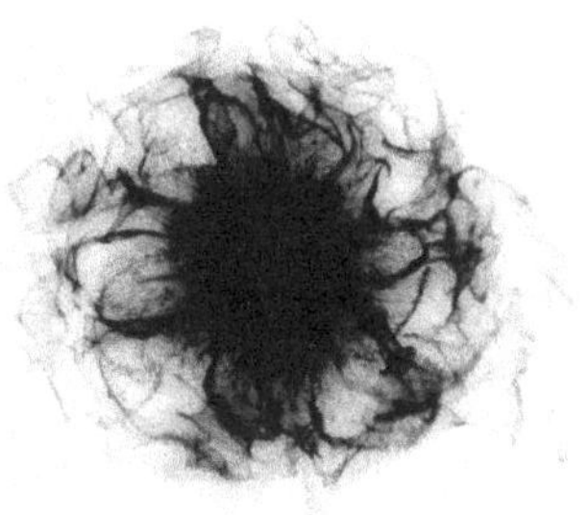

BOOK ONE
WORD

If nature were about to end, we might muster endless energy to stave it off; but if nature has already ended, what are we fighting for?

—Bill McKibben,
The End of Nature (1989)

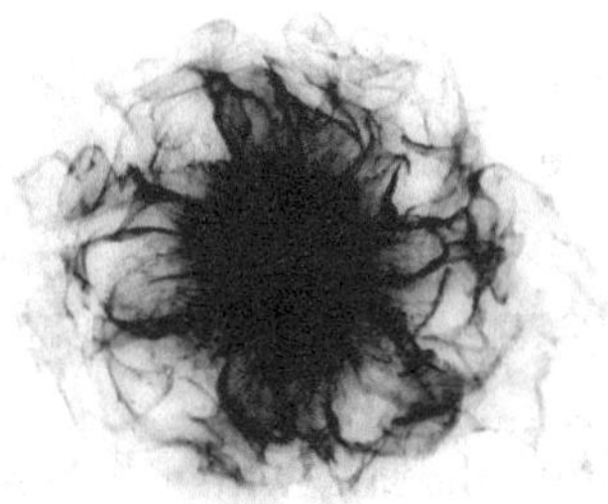

She comes to me at night, and slips away before dawn.

I never know when to expect her. She crawls in my open window, padding silently on bare feet, bringing the scent of mushrooms and fresh air. We talk softly, she telling me about her latest journeys while I catch her up on my studies, my siblings, my fights with Mom. When I grow sleepy, she kisses my forehead and climbs out the window, vanishing into the night. In the morning, I ask myself if she was real or if I dreamed her. But then something catches my eye—the shape of her body in the blankets at the foot of my bed, the seed she left on the nightstand for me to plant when the sun rises—and I know she was truly there: my secret visitor, my only friend.

Sarah.

Tonight it's been almost a year when I feel her hand on my cheek, hear her whisper in my ear. I smile and start to sit up in bed, but she hushes me with a finger to her lips, then sits on the edge of the mattress beside me. Her skin is hot, her cheeks flushed. She smells like soil after a rainstorm, as if she's traded her flesh for the aroma of the earth itself.

"Hadassah," she says breathlessly. "I found it."

"Found what?"

"The tree," she says. "I found the tree."

I shake my head. "What tree?"

"*The* tree. Daniel's tree."

She's mentioned Daniel, a man who lived a long time ago in the village where she and my parents grew up, but she never said anything about a tree. "Tell me about it," I say, knowing that when Sarah's in a mood like this, she can talk all night.

"It's beautiful," she says, with a dreamy look in her eyes as if she's standing in front of the tree right now. "Slim and graceful, and covered in bark that shimmers like gold. Fruit hangs heavy from its branches, sweet red globes that glisten in the sun. The leaves are veined in silver. The trunk pulses like a heart, and the light in the branches shines down on you as if you're standing beneath a starlit sky."

She's silent for a long time, gazing into the dark. "Is it far away?" I ask.

"As far as I've ever gone."

"Would you… could you take *me* there?"

Her laughter washes over me. "When you're ready. If your mother lets you."

"I'm ready now."

"You're only thirteen," she says teasingly, touching my cheek with her fingertips.

"I'll be fourteen in three months."

"When you pass the trials," she says. "You'll be ready then."

I'm about to say something to that, but I decide better of it. What I wish I could tell her is that I don't think I'm cut out to be a Sensor, that I'm as far from passing the trials as anyone in my class. Having me join the Queen's Corps is Mom's dream, not mine. For as long as I can remember, my dream has been to explore the Ecosystem with Sarah—to leave the City of the Queens, to trace the paths only she knows. I want to be free like her: living the life I've chosen for myself, not the life someone else has chosen for me.

But I can't tell her that. I'd sound like a child. And when she passes her hand over my forehead, my eyelids grow heavy, as if she's played some queen's trick on me. The last thing I see is her smile, and the dance of blue in her deep brown eyes.

"Soon, Hadassah," she says in a fading whisper. "I give you my word that soon, you'll be ready to come to me, to see the world as it truly is..."

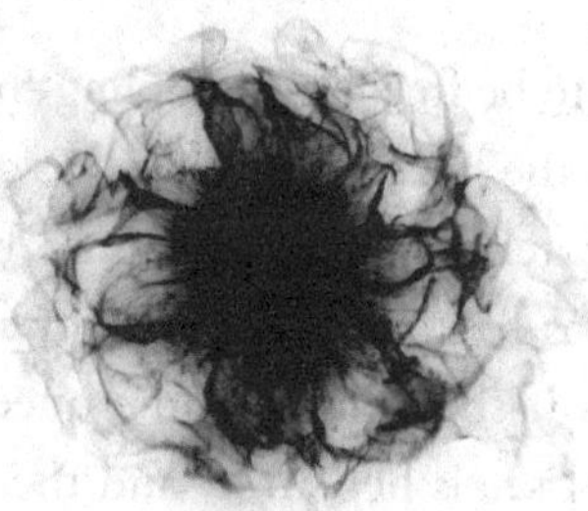

Voices wake me. Mom and Dad, in the kitchen, talking in hushed whispers. The most I can pick out is a word or two.

"…last night…"

"…the Queen…"

"…tell them…"

I slide from bed, glance out the window at the wakening dawn. The bloodbirds are screeching in the garden that grows all the way around our house as they hunt for dry stalks to build their nests. The dream-feeling of Sarah's visit hangs over me, only this time, there's nothing in my room to show me she was really here. But when I remember her words from last night, it's as if I can see the tree standing in front of me just the way she described it. As if she planted its seed in my mind, and I could almost reach out and pluck the fruit from its branches.

I tiptoe down the hallway in bare feet and sidle up to the kitchen door. This won't work for long; Mom will Sense me, and I'll be scolded for eavesdropping. But for now, I lean close and listen.

It's her voice I hear first. "I can't believe it. I just can't."

"Mimi…"

"I can't!" she says sharply, and I pull back. Mom never raises her voice at Dad. "How could the Ecosystem let this happen?"

"We don't know how it happened," Dad says in a calming voice. "It could have been an accident..."

"For everything in the Ecosystem, there is a purpose," Mom says, sounding like she's reciting one of her lessons. "There has to be an explanation for this... this..."

Her voice breaks, and whatever she was going to say is swallowed by the sound of her crying. I hear someone move, probably Dad, but whatever he's doing doesn't help. She cries and cries, in big gulping sobs, more like my little sister than my mom. I'm about to go back to my room when her voice freezes me where I stand.

"You can stop hiding, Hadassah," she says. "We know you're there."

I take a deep breath and try to compose my face. When I step through the doorway, I see Mom sitting at the table Master Gideon carved for her and Dad as a wedding present, with Dad standing behind her, his hands on her shoulders. Daylight floods the kitchen, shining off the floorboards, the wooden cabinets, the brand-new metal ice chest. Mom looks terrible, with red eyes and tear-stained cheeks, though she's not crying anymore. Her black hair is a mess, the tight curls I inherited from her even more tangled than usual. The threads of gray seem to have multiplied too, unless that's just the morning light.

"Come on in, sweetie," Dad says.

I edge into the room, keeping well clear of the table. That would have been impossible in our old kitchen, but with the additions we built when Tovah was born, there's plenty of space. The two follow me with their eyes. I can't help noticing how puffy Mom's look.

"Your mother and I have gotten some bad news," Dad says. "But you probably figured that out."

"I didn't hear what you said…"

He smiles. Mom's hand has crept up to her shoulder, her fingers twining with his. He squeezes them before stepping away to pull a chair out for me. I don't want to sit, but his eyes aren't taking *no* for an answer. He sits across from me and folds his hands on the table.

"We were planning to tell you later," he says. "Once Chaim and Tovah are up. There's going to be a lot of talk in the city, and some of it might be… surprising to you. So you should always know you can ask us anything you want."

I nod, lower my eyes. I'm sure he thinks he's doing a great job, but all he's doing is making the knot in my stomach tie even tighter.

"There will also be a number of ceremonies," he says. "And you'll be expected to attend. As the eldest child in the family, and an apprentice to the Sensor corps…"

I swallow, and look at him. "Why?"

"Isaac," Mom says. "*Tell* her."

"I'm trying to," he says. "I'm just…"

He looks helplessly at Mom. Something deep and terrible opens up inside me as I realize that whatever they're talking about, *he's* the one who can't handle it. Mom is crying, sure. But Dad is breaking apart.

"What is it, Daddy?" I say.

He gives me a smile as tears trickle down his cheeks into his beard. Mom lays a hand on top of his.

"It's our friend Sarah," he says. "She died last night."

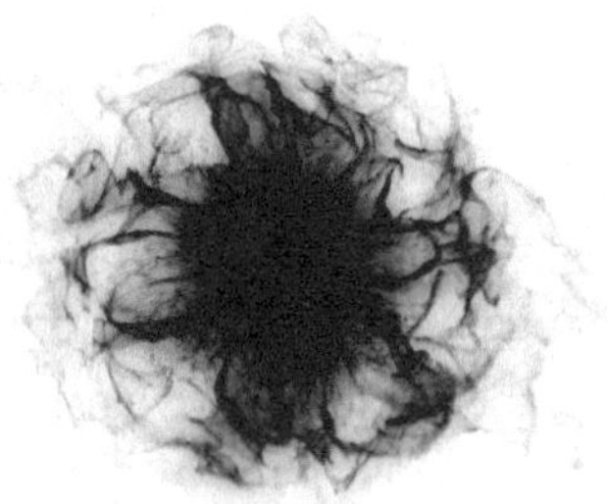

His words make me flinch. I shake my head.

"No," I say. "She can't have died. She can't."

"It was a shock to all of us," Mom says. "We still don't know what happened, but..."

"*No*," I repeat. "I just... I just saw her."

They trade a look. Not like they're surprised. Like they're communicating in that secret language only they speak.

"Everyone saw her," Mom says when she turns back to me. "All of the Queen's Sensors and healers. Captain Angelica and Lieutenant Leah, too. The Queen communicated her death to everyone who was close to her. She thought it would be better if we—"

"*No!*" I say. "I *saw* her. Last night in my room. She was *there*, and she told me... she told me..."

I stop, though I don't know why. Sarah's story about the tree is in my mind, as clear as the memory of her face. But I can't tell them what she said. I just can't.

"Hadassah," Mom says, letting go of Dad's hand to reach for mine. "The Queen's messages are powerful, especially for someone who's never received one before. They seem real, but they're only visions. Sarah didn't visit you last night. She hasn't been within leagues of the city for years."

I yank my hand away and push myself from the table. I feel like screaming at her, but I know that if I do, I'll end up crying instead.

"She was alive," I say. "I saw her in my room last night, and she was alive. Why would the Queen send me a vision like that? To make me think I'm going crazy?"

They exchange another look, and I can't stand the thought of what they're sharing, what they're shutting me out from.

"She was my friend!" I say. "She's been coming to my room for years. And this time, she told me she would take me with her when she left, but then..."

My voice chokes, and I can't say anything else. I can't even remember if what I'm saying is true. *Did* Sarah tell me she would take me with her? Or did she say I wasn't ready yet? Was it her ghost, trying to trick me into joining her?

"If she stayed away from the city all this time, it's because no one would let her live the way she wanted to," I say to the two of them. "Because her so-called friends turned their backs on her!"

"Hadassah!" Mom says, rising from her seat. Her eyes, which are violet like mine, have turned as black as her hair. I face her for a moment before spinning away and running from the kitchen.

"Come back here, young lady!" Dad calls out, but I keep going. If it's gotten to the *young lady* stage, there's nothing he could say that I'd want to hear.

The wooden floors echo my steps as I fly past the nursery. Tovah is wailing as usual. I throw open my door and slam it shut. I don't know why I'm bothering, since the door doesn't lock. Mom will just follow me here, and then I'll get the same lecture as always, with minor adjustments for age. *Your father and I expect better of a candidate for the Queen's Corps. You're almost fourteen years old. It's time you learned to deal with your feelings instead of acting out every time you don't get your way.* I almost wish she would hit me instead. At least then it'd be over quickly.

I fling myself facedown on the bed and listen for her footsteps coming down the hall. I hold my breath and wait for the door to spring open, and I prepare the words I'm going to spit at her when it does.

But no one comes. I wait and wait, but the only thing I hear are Tovah's screams. When Mom goes to hush her and the screaming stops, I hear a new sound, one that's even worse. I pull my pillow around my ears, but I can't shut the sound out.

That's because it's the sound of my own sobbing, and when I hear it, I know at last that my friend is truly dead.

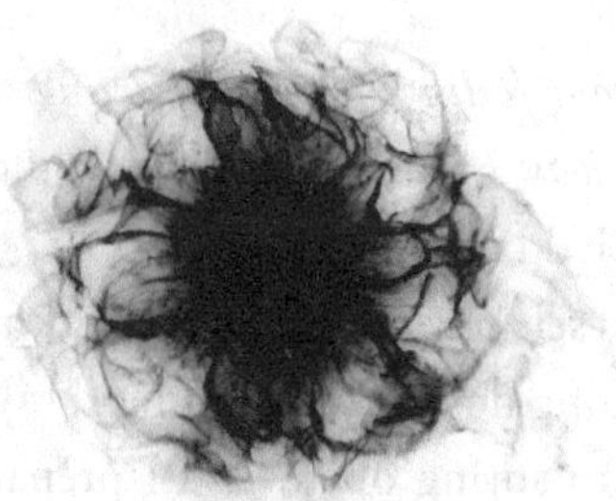

I'M WEARING AN itchy black dress and sitting in the front pew of the council house. Dad sits to my right, with Mom holding Tovah beside him, then Chaim next to her. The place is as full as I've ever seen it, more full than on Commemoration Day, more full than it was when Master Gideon or Captain Aurelia died. Everyone in the city knew Sarah. Even the people who'd never met her.

Even the ones who thought she was some kind of freak.

Sarah didn't have any family except for Queen Rebecca, who's something like a third cousin, so I guess we were the next best thing. We stood stiffly in an anteroom beside the front entrance while the entire population of the city shuffled past, giving Mom and Dad hugs and Tovah and Chaim cheek-pinches and me something in between. They looked at us with pity in their eyes, and mumbled the same words over and over again. *I'm so sorry. My condolences. May her memory be a blessing.* But I heard the things they said when they thought I wasn't listening, things like *peculiar* and *dreamer* and *couldn't seem to settle down, poor thing.* Having to listen to them talk about her like that and not be able to defend her made my throat tighten with anger. I hated every minute of it, and it lasted for hours.

But that part, at least, is over. Only the funeral remains.

The council house is quiet except for the rustle of bodies and a few half-smothered coughs when Queen

Rebecca comes up the aisle in her wheelchair. She's wearing black like everyone else, a high-necked gown with long sleeves. Somehow, the black doesn't look totally depressing on her, which must be because her eyes are so piercing and bright. Her crown of black vines sparkles in the glow from the stained glass windows that line the right-hand side of the council house.

I've tried to avoid looking at those windows, which portray all the queens from Dominica down to Rebecca herself. Just before Rebecca's window, there's a half-window dedicated to Sarah, showing her kneeling on the ground in a cream-colored dress and cupping a seed in her palm. Even though it's been almost fifteen years since the windows were installed, the image looks so much like her, so much like my memory of her from my room two nights ago, my eyes sting every time they fall on it. When I look away, I see that almost everyone else in our row is crying too, Lieutenant Leah hardest of all. The only exception is Celestina, who to tell the truth looks a bit miffed to have a funeral get in the way of her beauty sleep.

The Queen reaches the altar and wheels herself up the ramp, where she's saluted by Captain Angelica in her ceremonial uniform. The ramp is only one of Master Gideon's inventions, along with the doors that open by pull-chains instead of handles, the smooth wooden sidewalks that are easier for wheels to roll over, the chairs with sturdy armrests to help a person climb in and out. He made all of those things for Queen Rebecca, though now they're so much a part of the city, everyone uses them. When I asked Dad how anyone could rebuild a whole city for one person, he told me the story of how Queen Rebecca lost the use of her legs when she was seven years old, and how Master Gideon spent the rest of his life making the city a safe place for the little girl he'd once carried in his arms.

Thinking about that makes my eyes sting even worse, so I'm thankful when the Queen turns to face us and begins to talk.

"Sarah was my first teacher," she says in a voice that's soft but clear in the hushed silence of the room. "In the early days of my apprenticeship, that meant she was something of a babysitter, something of a mother. Later, when I lost my own mother and my own legs during the same terrible journey, she taught me how to heal. When I became queen of this city, she taught me how to read, and how to rule. And when she left the city, it was because she had spent enough time as *my* teacher, and she had resolved to devote her life to becoming the teacher of us all."

There are some murmurs at that. I wish I could look around the cathedral to see who they're from, but Mom drilled into my head that I have to *comport myself properly* today, which included *not fidgeting*. I focus on Captain Angelica instead, who stands erect in her shining uniform, her hair flowing in a red wave over her shoulders.

"Most of you don't know this, but Sarah stayed in touch with me no matter how far she traveled," the Queen goes on. "There are some who might think of her as a wanderer, but Sarah never wandered in her life. Every step she took was filled with purpose. For the past fifteen years, she was charting the life of the Ecosystem at my behest, chronicling its terrain and its creatures. She never stopped searching for human communities, and though she failed to find them, she kept alert for the traces they left behind: their relics, their lore, their history. She was my eyes in the field, my link to a much wider world than I could compass on my own. She knew the deep places of the Ecosystem better than any person alive—yes, even better than I—and she shared her knowledge unstintingly, for the good of our people and the growth of our city in peace and prosperity."

Even though it ruins my perfect posture, I lean forward to listen. Every apprentice to the Queen's Corps knows about the changes in our relationship to the Ecosystem that have made life so much easier in the years since the War of the Queens: plants we know how to use, animals we can communicate with, ecozones we're no longer afraid to enter. But nobody told me Sarah had so much to do with those changes.

"There are scientific advances we owe to her research," the Queen continues. "Previously unexplored territories she's mapped for us, lost arts of building and healing she's helped us to reclaim. Even more than this, there's an entire history of the earth dating back millions of years that she's studied and transcribed, step by step, day by day, so that the world might never again be a mystery to us, and we never again feel ourselves alien to it. If the story of our planet is ever to be written in full, it will be because Sarah lived that story, and died in order to pass it on to us."

A moan breaks out from our pew, and I turn my head to see Lieutenant Leah with her face buried in her hands, while her spouse Beulah and their daughter Huldah wrap their arms around her and hold her tight. When I touch my fingers to my cheeks, they come away wet. I look up at the Queen, and it seems as if her wise, gentle eyes are gazing right back at me, though her words are spoken to everyone.

"We will never lose the memory of our friend Sarah," she says. "For she lives forever in the Ecosystem she loved, and the Ecosystem lives forever in us."

She turns and bows her head to Sarah's window. Everyone else does the same, all except for Leah, who's crying loudly while Huldah rocks her and makes hushing noises. At a signal from Captain Angelica, people rise from their seats, and the Queen's husband, Caleb—her *consort*, Mom says is his official title, since there's no King of the city—comes forward to meet Rebecca as she wheels down the ramp. Dad nudges me in the back, and I start down the row to the center aisle, where we take our places behind the Queen's chair. Dad puts one arm around me and one around Mom, his hand trailing down to Chaim's. We all move in an awkward huddle as the Queen leads the congregation from the council house.

She sets a pace the rest of us can keep up with. It's a long walk to the cemetery, past the reflecting pool with its bridges and wharves designed by Master Gideon, along the lanes that curve around the monument where the Cathedral used to stand, then through the most populated part of the city with its newer brick and traditional stone houses, and finally over the hills to the wrought iron gates that lead to the burial grounds. At the top of the tallest hill, there's a spot for the most important people in the city; it's where Master Gideon and Captain Aurelia are buried, where the shrines stand for Sarah's mother and father and great-grandmother Delilah. The three of them died before I was born, and none of their bodies were ever found. Now that Sarah's about to join them, it feels wrong to erect another monument over another empty grave, to have nothing but words chiseled in stone to remember her by. But according to my dad, she was so far from the city when she died, not even the Queen could bring her body back.

I think about her out there in the wild, alone, suffering the kind of death only the most distant parts of the Ecosystem can dream up for you. *Our friend,* Rebecca called her. *Our* friend. Maybe she never was *my* friend. I've heard the story from my parents, how Sarah was the first person other than the Queen to know that Mom was pregnant, how she showed up out of nowhere the day I was born, as if she knew when that day would be. How Mom and Dad named me *Hadassah* because Sarah told them it was another name for Esther, a woman who'd been Chief Sensor back in their village. Maybe hearing those stories over and over from when I was little is why I've always thought of Sarah as my special friend. Maybe everything I've ever believed about her is because of things that happened in other people's lives, not mine.

The marker is in place, a white marble headstone with the figure of a woman sprouting from the top of it, her hands spread wide as if she's planting seeds. Whoever did the carving—probably Beulah, she's the sculptor around here—added some touches that are totally Sarah: bloodbirds nesting in the woman's long wavy hair, a tiny smile on her lips as if she's keeping a secret. There's no way a stone this fancy could have been carved in the two days since the Queen sent out her vision; Beulah must have been working on it for a long time before. The only part that looks rough and unpolished is the inscription on the pedestal beneath the woman's bare arms:

Ruth, known as Sarah
Born AD 156
Ruled AD 174
Died AD 189

My family stands beside Queen Rebecca as she leans down to place a spray of white blossoms at the base of the monument. No words are spoken while other mourners step up to the grave and leave their offerings. Leah falls to her knees before the marker, covering her face with her hands and crying so hard Huldah has to help her to her feet and hold her as she hobbles away. When everyone else is gone, Dad signals for me to place a sprig of witch hazel on the upturned grass at the foot of the tomb. My hands have taken on its smell from clutching it so hard through the day.

Dad says something in a language I don't understand, then goes to offer his condolences to the Queen. The crowd has broken up, but I stay behind, staring at the grave, trying to picture Sarah's face in the stone woman's. When I turn, I find Mom there, with Tovah at her hip and Chaim by her side. She holds a hand out to me, and I take it. A moment later, Dad joins us, and we walk down the hill for home.

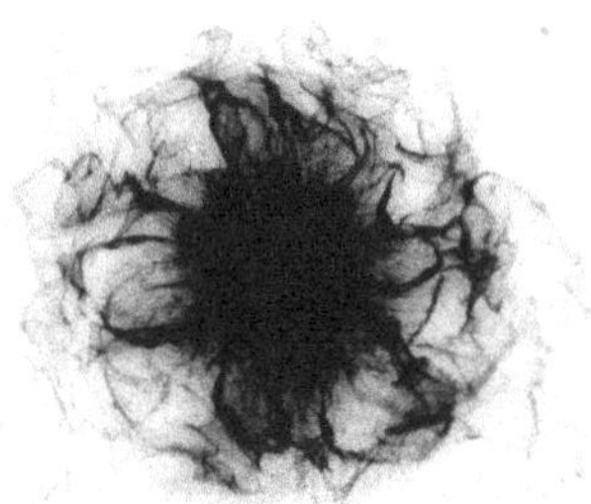

It's way past bedtime when there's a knock on my door. I shove the funeral card into my dresser drawer and jump into bed, pulling the covers up to my chin. At the last second, I remember to blow out the candle sitting on the nightstand. "Come in."

Dad leans into the room, holding a lantern that casts his tall shadow against the ceiling beams. I'm sure he can smell the smoke from the candle I just blew out, but he doesn't say anything about it. "I wanted to see if you're all right."

"I'm fine."

"Would you like to talk?"

"I'm pretty tired."

"I'll say goodnight, then," he says, and turns to go.

"Dad."

He stops.

"What was it you said? At Sarah's grave?"

"It was part of a song," he says. "One I learned a long time ago. In our language, it means: *Follow to its repose your resting spirit: go to whatever spot of earth you love best.* I thought Sarah would like that."

I roll the words around on my tongue, testing their sound. "Was everything the Queen said about her true?"

He doesn't answer right away. A small smile forms

beneath his beard, though it doesn't make him look any less sad.

"Yes," he says. "But it wasn't the whole story."

He comes into the room, setting down his lantern and squeezing himself into the chair at my desk. The light makes his face seem more deeply lined than it is. He leans forward, resting his elbows on his knees as he begins to talk.

"When you were first born, Sarah visited us every month or two," he says. "Always unannounced, always unexpected. We'd be at home, and a knock would come on the door, and there she'd be. Once or twice, we came home to find her already here. In the house." He grins. "She must have gotten in through a window."

I smile back. So that wasn't anything new.

"She'd usually stay the night," he continues. "We'd talk until late, your mom and I catching her up on events in the city while she told us where she'd been since we last saw her. She was a bit cagey about that, though. Wouldn't give us many specifics. But she was always excited to see you."

"Me?"

"Yes, you." He reaches out to touch one of my curls. "She was so proud of you."

I lower my eyes, the pleasure and ache of his words mingling in my chest.

"As time passed, her visits became less and less frequent," Dad goes on. "We wouldn't see her for months, then a year, then two. At first, we thought that only meant she was traveling farther from the city, but then we started to think there was more to it than that. She'd seem edgy the whole time she was with us, as if she couldn't wait to leave. In the middle of a meal, the middle of a conversation, she'd jump up and walk out the door without so much as a goodbye." He sighs. "And then, finally, she stopped coming at all."

"Was something wrong with her?"

"I wish I could tell you," he says. "The best your mother and I could figure out was that the more time she spent on the road, the less comfortable she became around her own kind. She never married, for one thing…"

"There's nothing wrong with that."

"Of course not," he says. "It just seemed as if she'd grown to prefer the company of the Ecosystem, and she found it harder to connect with people, even with her oldest friends. That was tough on your mother and me, and even tougher on Leah. She and Sarah used to share everything, but from what your mother can tell, the two of them must have had a falling out somewhere along the line." He sighs again. "The last time any of us saw her in the flesh was close to ten years ago, the day before your fourth birthday. After that, it was only because of the Queen's reports that we knew she was alive at all."

"That's when it began," I say.

"Hm?"

"When I was four. That's when she started coming to my room."

He stares at me in silence. His mouth opens once, twice, as if he's trying to come up with an explanation but can't think of one that works. *That's just a coincidence. It must be because you heard us talking about her. You couldn't have remembered something from when you were so young.* Except he knows that's not true, because people with Sensor genes get their memories much earlier than other people.

Mom says that's because the Ecosystem calls out to us and wakes us up.

"Sarah told me something," I say, though I find myself hoping Dad won't ask me what it was. "When she… when I thought she came to my room two nights ago. Something I couldn't have known by myself. So if what she told me is true…"

"Then it wasn't a dream."

"Do *you* believe me?"

He stands, looks out the window, though there's nothing to see but the dark. Finally, he turns back to me.

"I don't know what to believe," he says. "I believe you're not lying. Your mother does, too. *Something* happened two nights ago that none of us can explain. Maybe the Queen will have an answer."

"We're going to see the Queen?"

"First thing tomorrow," he says with a nod. "I talked to her after the funeral, and she's as troubled by this as I am. Her brood chamber showed her a vision of Sarah's death, and she had no reason to doubt it was true. If that vision was flawed in some way, we need to know how and why."

"So really," I say, "*I'm* going to see the Queen tomorrow."

"Is that all right?"

"Sure," I say, more confidently than I feel. "And Daddy?"

"Yeah, kiddo?"

"I'm sorry," I say. "About Sarah. I know how much she meant to you. Mom, too."

He leans down to hug me, which might be a way to hide his tears. I feel them on my cheek, along with the scratchiness of his beard. For the first time ever, I wonder if Sarah was more than just a friend to him.

"I'll tell your mother that," he says. "She'll want to know."

He presses his lips against my forehead. Then he stands, takes his lantern, and goes to the door. He blows me one last kiss before he leaves the room.

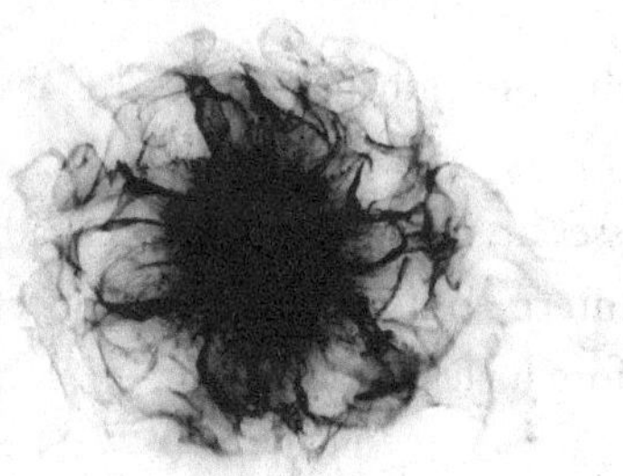

THE QUEEN'S COTTAGE sits across the courtyard from the council house. Though many of the buildings in the city were destroyed during the War of the Queens and many of the houses, like ours, were rebuilt over time for space and comfort, the Queen's house is still the same as it was when Dominica made it her home: a low-roofed stone dwelling with shutters on the windows and bright flakes of quartz flashing from its walls. I've only been here once, nine years ago, during the induction ceremony for apprentices to the Queen's Sensor Corps. I was too little then to understand much of what was going on, except Mom told me it was a very important day and a great honor.

Caleb lets me and Dad in. He's big and burly, much broader than my dad, but he's always got a smile that puts me at ease. Dad told me that when Caleb and his six-minutes-younger brother Noah were kids, they used to switch places with each other to trick everyone in the village. Except that won't work anymore, because even though they're twins, Caleb has a thick head of hair and Noah is going bald. The Ecosystem does strange things with genes sometimes, Mom says.

"Make yourself at home," Caleb says, showing us to a parlor next to the Queen's bedroom. "Rebecca will be out in a minute." Then he leaves us and hustles off to do whatever the Queen's consort does all day.

The room's cozy, with comfortable chairs and a big stone fireplace, though it's too warm today for a fire. Everywhere I look, I see Master Gideon's handiwork: wooden rails to help the Queen move from place to place, a wider-than-usual writing desk so she can roll her wheelchair right up to it. Dad smiles when he sees me looking around.

"I wish you'd had a chance to get to know Gideon better," he says. "He was something else."

I don't know what to say to that, so I simply smile back.

"Hadassah, Isaac, welcome," the Queen says as she wheels into the room.

We stand, and I curtsy the way I was taught while Dad kisses her hand. The Queen is much younger than Mom, and she's beautiful, with smooth brown skin and curly hair pulled back in a braided chignon, a few loose strands hanging artfully around her ears. Her sleeveless pink dress shows the bulging muscles of her shoulders and forearms, but her legs have shrunk to doll-size in the fifteen years since she lost the ability to walk. She's been queen most of that time, ever since she was eight years old, the same age Chaim is now. It's hard for me to imagine my little brother walking to school by himself, much less being in charge of the entire Ecosystem.

"Hadassah," she says, holding out her hands for me to take. The black bracelet that matches her crown gleams on her wrist. "I'm so grateful to you for agreeing to meet with me."

I didn't think I had a choice, but I drop another polite curtsy.

"Isaac, if you wouldn't mind waiting here," she says to Dad. "I'd like to talk to Hadassah privately."

"Of course," he says. Which, whatever he's really thinking, is how you talk to the Queen.

She spins sharply and leads me down the hall to her bedroom, which I've never seen before. My eyes take in the huge canopy bed with its pink coverlet and drapes, while my nose twitches at the heavy scent of potpourri. I worry that we're going to have our conversation here, in the same room where she sleeps with Caleb, but she turns to the glass door that opens onto the garden. A ramp takes us to ground level, where I stop to look around in wonder.

The Queen's garden is the second most secret place in the city, right behind her brood chamber. It's the place where Sarah's grandmother and grandfather fell in love, the place where Celestina, when she was queen, made the silver rose bushes that shine outside her and Angelica's mini-mansion. It's where Sarah herself was trained to be queen, and where Rebecca will train her own daughter when she has one. The garden is overflowing with flowers Rebecca grew in her favorite colors: little pink balls climbing long stems, yellow strands blowing from wooden trellises, orange lilies with swirls of pink and yellow on their petals. Brightly feathered birds flit among the branches of the flowering plum trees that line the garden path, and the shockingly pink creatures that used to be called poison arrow frogs—until Dad and his healers found a way to neutralize their poison—hop from trunk to trunk. A stone fountain in the middle of the garden gushes water in a series of patterns too complicated for me to follow, while a high green hedge woven with pink-and-yellow honeysickle and orangish virago creepers borders the whole, keeping it hidden from the rest of the city. In all, it's more beautiful than any place I've ever seen, and I can't help wishing Sarah was here to see it with me.

I turn to find Rebecca gazing at me. The Queen can read minds, Mom says, but she doesn't like to do it unless she has to. She reaches for my hands again, and when we touch, I feel her power surge through me like a warm wave.

"Sarah never told me," she says. "In all the years she traveled beyond the city, she never let on that she'd been coming back to visit you."

"My dad told you that?"

"In a manner of speaking," she says. "He told me that you've been having dreams of Sarah coming to your room. But to my mind, there's no difference. Sarah was a queen of this realm, and if she chose to, she could project herself anywhere in the Ecosystem—not her physical self, but her thought and will. That dream-self could have visited you many times, spoken to you, heard your replies, even if Sarah herself was hundreds of leagues away."

"It couldn't have been her… dream-self," I say. "She left things in my room—things like seeds, and flowers. And also…"

"Yes?"

"I would find the shape of her body on my bed. So that couldn't have been a dream."

Her eyes twinkle. "Are you certain? As certain as you are of that prowler monkey?"

She points at the creature swinging from the nearest plum tree. It drops to the paved path, shakes itself, and hoots at me. "Of course," I say, turning to her.

"Then look again."

I turn back to the monkey, only to find it gone. In its

place, I see nothing but a pile of pink petals. My mouth opens in shock as I face the Queen.

"Child," she says. "A queen has many powers, and Sarah had years to perfect them. You were so young when you began to receive her visits, what wouldn't you have believed of her? A courier from the Ecosystem could have delivered her gifts. A bloodbird could have flown in your window to drop seeds on your nightstand, or a sting-tailed lemur could have settled itself on your bedsheets then swung away before dawn. None of this matters. What matters is that you were the last one to see her—in any form—alive."

"Then you don't think she's really dead?"

A line crosses her forehead. "I received a vision of Sarah lying in a formless space, unbreathing, with darkness all around her. Ordinarily that would have given me pause, for the Ecosystem tends to ignore the dead. But I'd asked it to keep an eye on her, so I never thought to question what I saw. Now, though, I can't help wondering why you've been receiving secret visits from her all these years, and why, three nights ago, some part of her made a final visit to show you something that was kept from me."

"But show me *what*?" I say, flustered.

"I think you know," she says. "It's the thing you couldn't tell anyone else, the thing you sensed, deep down, was for my ears alone."

Her eyes hold me, their dark depths flickering. The words leave my lips as if drawn from my tongue.

"She said something about a… a tree," I say. "She called it Daniel's tree, and she described it to me. She never said anything about it before, not in all the times she… visited me."

The Queen's eyes take on the same dreamy expression Sarah's did on her last visit. "Daniel's tree..."

"Do *you* know about it?"

She nods, though the dreaminess doesn't leave her voice. "Chief Warden Daniel spoke of it years ago, in the village. He told us the story of a tree that grew at the end of the world, a tree that was planted at the dawn of time. He said that it stood in the center of a garden—not like this garden, but a garden that *was* the world. But the tree was lost, and the people who lived there were cast out of the garden forever." She shakes her head. "I'd nearly forgotten that story. I was only seven years old when I heard it."

"But is it... was the tree *real*?"

"The way Daniel spoke of it, it sounded like make-believe," she says. "In all the years I've cared for the Ecosystem, I've never encountered anything remotely like it. But now..."

She wheels closer, looks up at me. I find myself bending toward her without meaning to. Her hands rest on either side of my head, not even touching my hair, but I feel their power all the same.

"May I?" she asks. "This won't hurt."

I close my eyes and feel the Queen probing my mind, reaching inside me the way Mom tells us to reach out to the Ecosystem. Her power is so strong it's as if there's nothing of *me* left, as if I'm no more than the creation of her thought. Maybe that's what I am, what all of us are. It's almost comforting to float along like that, knowing that she's the one in control, that no harm can come to me as long as she holds me in her hands. What would happen if she ever let go is something I can't begin to imagine.

"Open your eyes, Hadassah," the Queen says, and I come rushing back to myself all at once. I do as she says, and no sooner do my eyes open than I gasp in amazement.

The tree is there, standing in the Queen's garden just the way Sarah described it. The golden trunk gleams like a lantern, the silver leaves flash among the branches. It's not very tall as trees go, only about ten feet from foot to crown, so it would be easy to grab one of the ripe red globes that hang at head height. I reach out to touch one, but as I do, something tugs at my mind, warning me against it. It's as if a voice in my head whispers that if I touch that fruit—or, worse, taste it—nothing will ever be the same again. But even though the voice tells me not to, my hand itches to find out for myself, and I have to fight to keep my arm at my side.

The Queen circles the tree in her chair. I'm pretty sure by now that it's only a vision she pulled from my mind, but when she passes behind the glowing trunk, I lose sight of her. When she comes back into view, her hand stretches out, and a branch bends down to bring a piece of fruit within her reach. Her hand closes around it as if it's as solid as the plums of her own trees, and the voice in my head cries out for her not to pluck it. But before I can say the words out loud, her face twists in pain, and she lets the fruit go, the tree flickering once then vanishing in a shower of golden mist.

I run the few steps to the Queen, who's slumped over in her chair, breathing in short gasps. I'm afraid to touch her, afraid not to. I lay my hands on her shoulders, feel her shivering as if her blood's been turned to ice. I'm trying to decide what to do—am I allowed to slap the Queen?—when she draws a long breath and pulls herself upright, her eyelids fluttering open. She smiles at me, but tears sparkle on her cheeks.

"Hadassah," she says weakly. "Oh, my dear, I fear for our Sarah now. I fear for her more than I ever have before."

"She's alive?"

"She was," she says. "Only a living queen in full possession of her powers could have planted such a strong vision in your mind. When she spoke to you last, did she seem… anxious? As if she believed herself to be in danger?"

"She sounded excited," I say. "She talked about how beautiful the tree was, and she said…" My mouth falls open when I remember her words. "She said, *Fruit hangs heavy from its branches, sweet red globes that glisten in the sun.* Do you think she…?"

"That's precisely what I fear," the Queen says. "Sarah was wary, but she desired knowledge above all else—knowledge of the hidden world that might be used to help her people. I fear she might have given in to the tree's power, and now…"

Now she's dead, I think. *She's dead, and she's never coming back again.* "What can we do?"

"Find her," the Queen says. "And find the tree."

Her moment of weakness has passed. She cruises up the garden path, while I try to keep up with the wheels that blur beneath her hands.

"I'll need to search for her," she says. "The vision I received from the Ecosystem was incomplete—I saw Sarah's body, but couldn't guess where she was or what had happened to her. Now that I know she kept the tree's power to herself, I'm all the more certain that something went terribly wrong. She would never have withheld such important information from me of her own free will."

"Unless she was trying to…" I swallow the words before I'm finished. What could I possibly say that the Queen hasn't already thought about ten times?

She spins to face me. "Yes?"

"Trying to… to protect you," I say. "If she knew the tree was dangerous, she wouldn't want anyone else to get hurt, least of all you."

I expect her to scold me for speaking out of turn, but instead, she nods. "That would explain why she dispatched the memory to you, not me," she says. "To preserve a record of what she'd found without putting the Ecosystem itself at risk. I wonder, though, if she calculated the risk to *you*?"

The way she says that makes me shiver in the warmth of the sun.

"There's much we need to discover," the Queen says after a pause. "If the tree is dangerous, what is the danger, and how did Sarah hope to protect us from it? If knowledge was what she sought, is it too late for us to learn it for ourselves?" She sighs, looking much older than she is. "I will have need of you, Hadassah. The city will have need of you. I ask you not to fret for now, but to return home, and tell your parents only as much about our meeting as they need to hear."

I hesitate for a single second before dropping the lowest curtsy I can. She rests a hand on my hair, and for a moment, I'm not afraid.

"How will I know when you need me?" I say.

She lifts me from the ground, gazes at me somberly. Her finger tucks a strand of hair behind my ear.

"When I need you," she says, "you'll know."

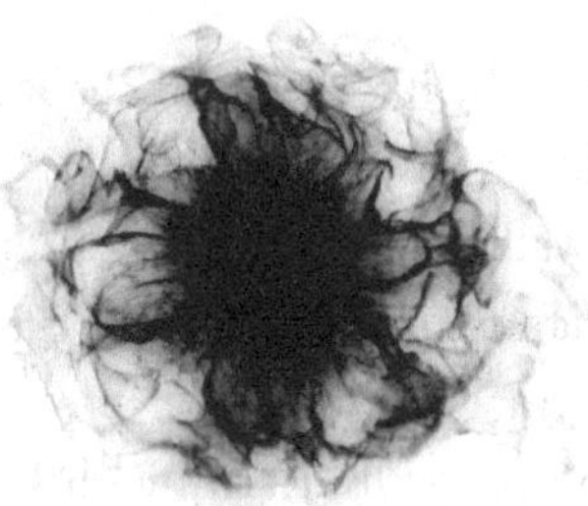

THE LAST THING I want to do the day after my interview with the Queen is go back to school. But it's not like I have any choice.

That's the way it works when the teacher is your mom.

My stomach is as full of butterflies as the field she's taken us to for today's lesson. Excitement that the Queen chose me, nervousness about what she's going to ask me to do, worry about Sarah—all of them make it impossible for me to concentrate. My mind drifts even worse than usual, and I become distracted by everything around me: the grabgrass tickling my feet, the towering trees touched by warm breezes smelling of pine and saffron, the shrieking bloodbirds and shouting blurjays, the pigdeer and warhogs rooting in the loam. The only part of the Ecosystem I can't seem to focus on is the one part I'm supposed to, which has something to do with—

"No, Hadassah!" Mom says, stomping straight toward me despite my best efforts to disappear. "Do you have any idea what that is?"

My face grows warm when I realize that everyone in the group has stopped what they're doing to stare at me. Everyone, that is, except the oldest boy in class, Peter, who's two years older than me and has blond hair and unnaturally pale blue eyes. The most acknowledgment I ever get from him is an insufferable smirk every time Mom singles me out, which means he has plenty of chances to practice that particular skill.

"That's a swallowtale," Mom says, standing in front of me with her hands on her hips. "It'll burn a hole right through your skin."

I watch the yellow butterfly with blacks spots dance away from me. My blush deepens when I realize I was about to touch it.

"How do you tell the difference between venomous butterflies and their mimic twins?" Mom asks.

I stare at her, try to come up with a response, but my mind is a blank. She gives me a few more seconds to feel stupid before sighing in frustration.

"Peter?" she says. "Can you explain the difference to the class?"

I scowl. Peter hardly ever says anything and never volunteers, but he's the one Mom always calls on when she wants to show me up.

"The swallowtale's numerous mimics lack a distensible proboscis," he says. His voice has a tinny sound, like he's reading from a script. "And their flight pattern is notably less erratic than a true swallowtale's."

Mom turns back to me with a look on her face like that should settle the matter. But I have no idea what a distensible pro bossy is, and I don't remember ever learning that butterflies have flight patterns. So all I can do is stand there like an idiot until she sighs again and walks away.

I spend the rest of the afternoon watching everyone else—including the five-year-olds—run circles around me. I wish I could blame today entirely on my talk with the Queen, but the truth is, I've had the same problem for the past nine years, ever since Mom decided I was going to become a Sensor. The others can Sense what I can't, and they can put into words what they Sense. Me, on the other hand, I always seem to be somewhere else—in the clouds, or way out in the Ecosystem with Sarah, searching for something without knowing what it is we're searching for. Mom thinks I don't try, but that's not true. When I'm alone, I *can* Sense the things that are right in front of my face, can faintly see the golden threads she always tells me to look for. But when I'm in class, when I'm supposed to be proving myself to the only person that counts, the threads become so tangled I can't see anything at all.

The worst part about this—Mom aside—is that Sarah herself was a Sensor before she became queen. She was a great Sensor, from what Lieutenant Leah and Captain Angelica tell me. So when I make a total mess of things, I'm not only disappointing Mom. I'm spoiling Sarah's legacy, too.

"Come, Hadassah," Mom says after everyone else has gotten their daily report and returned to the city. "It's late."

I look around to see that dusk has fallen on the woodland clearing. Something moves among the trees, and my heart jumps when I realize it's a huge pandalion, its black-and-white coat camouflaged by the shadows. Mom doesn't seem concerned, though. I help her gather up her equipment, the blindfolds and drinking gourds and stopwatch she uses to time our exercises. She shoulders the supply bag, and we head for home.

We walk without speaking, the only sound our bare feet crunching on the grabgrass. Nighttime is supposed to be best for Sensing, because the loss of light awakens the inner Sense. That's what Mom says, anyway. You couldn't prove it by the way I stumble through the meadow like a lame jackalass.

She sighs for what must be the fiftieth time today. I tense, preparing for my fiftieth lecture.

"Did I ever tell you about the time Sarah trained me and your father?" she asks.

"Dad was a Sensor?"

"He was a nuisance, mostly," she says with a short laugh. "He interrupted our training so often, Sarah decided to include him in the lesson. You'll never guess how."

She's right, I won't, so I wait for her to tell me.

"She walked us into a swarm of cicatrix," she says, smiling in a way that looks almost devious. "Neither of us was paying attention, and we'd have been picked to pieces if Sarah wasn't keeping an eye on us."

"Picked to pieces? By cicatrix?"

"They used to be much more dangerous than they are now," she says. "They bred all year round, not just in the warm season, and their swarms numbered in the millions. That's how they got the name *cicatrix*, from all the scars they left."

The thought of a cicatrix swarm that size makes me shudder. I know I'll never look at those beady-eyed little bugs the same way again. "Then how'd you escape?"

"Sarah controlled the swarm," she says. "As you know, the Sensors of past generations were different from us in one critical respect: they saw themselves as warriors fighting against the wild, not as acolytes charged with interpreting the Ecosystem so that all might live according to its will. But they never forgot the importance of their calling. And after that day with Sarah, I never forgot either."

I don't say anything to that, because really, what am I supposed to say? *Great syllogism, Mom. Sarah was to you as you are to me. It's time for me to start taking being a Sensor seriously, because that's the best way I can honor Sarah's memory.*

Except there's one thing I don't quite get. "Who does the calling?"

"I beg your pardon?"

"Who does the calling?" I repeat. "If it's a calling, you have to be called to it, right? So who calls people to be Sensors?"

"Sensors call themselves," she answers. "Or the Ecosystem calls out to them, and they respond. That's the way it was for me. And for Sarah."

"Really?" I say. "Because it seems to me that the only one calling me to become a Sensor is you."

She stops. It's almost fully dark by now, so her eyes are hidden beneath her brows. But I can imagine the daggers flying out of them.

"Perhaps I didn't make myself clear," she says. "When Sarah sprang the cicatrix trap on your father and me, it was because she knew I could do better. Because she had very high standards, and she demanded that I meet them. She's the one who trained me, and I'm the head of the Queen's Sensor Corps. She's also the one who trained the Queen. Don't you think she was successful?"

"I—"

"You ask who called you to the Corps," Mom keeps talking. "And I suppose it makes sense that you'd think it was me. But I had nothing to do with it. Neither did your father."

"Then who was it?"

"It was Sarah," she says. "She visited the city on your first birthday, and she told us she detected the strength of the Sense in you. That's much earlier than usual, as you know. With each subsequent visit, she told us she saw it more and more clearly. When she came to us the final time, she stayed only long enough to tell us that you were ready to start the training. Then she was gone."

"That's the last thing she said to you?"

"The very last."

Of all the things I can think of that Sarah would want to say to Mom and Dad before she vanished from their lives forever, telling them I was ready for Sensor training would have to be the furthest from my mind. "But I didn't start until the next year," I say. "When I was five."

"That's because your father and I didn't want to push you too fast," she says. "You had never talked about your connection to the Ecosystem the way most young children with the Sense would have, but we did notice that you had an interest in the outdoors and in living things. So we talked it over, and finally decided to let you become the Sensor Sarah saw in you. The Sensor, she told us on that final visit, that you were destined to become."

"She *said* that?"

"You can ask your father if you don't believe me," she says. "Unless, that is, you want to preserve the illusion that I've forced you into this."

I can't see her face, but I can hear her breathing in the darkness, short breaths as if she's holding inside what she really wants to say. She's never told me any details about her training with Sarah; I knew about it, but it wasn't something she or Dad talked about. Now I wonder if the reason she kept it from me is because she didn't *want* me to join the Queen's Corps, to train under her the way she trained under Sarah. Was she angry at Sarah for pointing me in that direction? Is that why she's so impatient with me every time I fail?

"Sarah was one of my oldest friends," she says. "But that doesn't mean I always understood her. I don't know what she had in mind when she told us about your gift, but I had enough faith in her to believe she only wanted what was best for you. I try to hold on to that faith, even when I see more evidence with each passing day that this isn't the path you would have chosen for yourself."

Before I can say anything to that, she turns and makes her way down the lane toward our house, leaving me alone in the dark.

Totally in the dark.

Sarah picked me to be a Sensor? All this time, when I told myself I wanted to be like her, when she kept hinting that one day I could join her, *she* was the one who first spoke the words that trapped me in a life I can't see myself living? A life that will keep me in the city forever, working a job I'm no good at, with my mom giving me orders day in and day out? While the life I've dreamed of becomes nothing but a more and more distant memory?

Sarah. My friend. My jailer.

And now she's gone, and I don't know if I'll ever see her again. If I'll ever be able to ask her *why* she chose this life for me.

Or if I'll ever be able to forgive myself for letting her down.

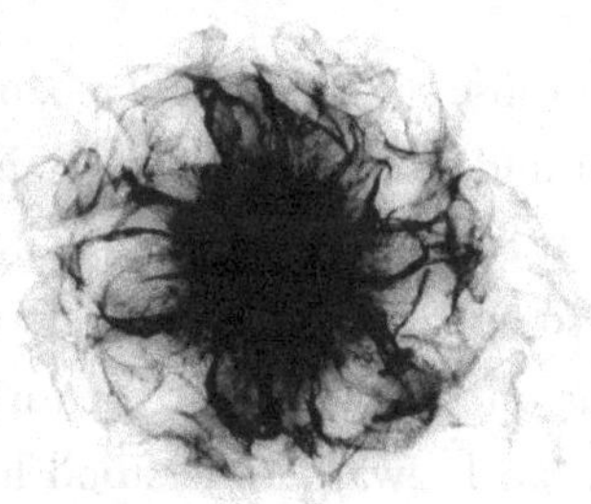

Hadassah!

The voice jars me awake. I jump up in bed, my heart pounding, my eyes flicking around the darkened room to see who cried out my name.

But there's no one there.

Hadassah, I hear the voice again, though softer this time. *Come to me…*

The voice fades, and the night is silent.

I take a shaky breath, try to calm myself. I've figured out that the voice came from inside my head, not from anywhere in the house. I just never thought that when the Queen called for me, it would be like this.

"I'm coming," I say, and hope she can hear me. Just in case, I add, "I'll be right there."

I rise from bed, throw a jacket over my nightdress, and slip into a pair of moccasins I hope won't make too much noise. I crack my door and listen to the house, but all I hear are Dad's snores coming from the room two doors down. There's no moonlight leaking through the curtained window at the end of the addition, but I'm afraid to risk a candle, so I glide down the hall in darkness. The kitchen table and chairs look like grotesque squatting beasts that crawled into our house from the Ecosystem. I edge past them, into the foyer, then gently ease the door open and closed.

Once I'm outside, I run.

Lampposts line the city streets. They cast eerie shadows over the cobblestones, long bars of darkness that put me in mind of deadly tree branches from nursery tales. It's strange to think how seldom I've been out in the city at night, and never by myself. Streets that seem so straight and open in the daytime appear like crooked, zigzagging lanes whose houses crowd me from all sides. There's not another soul out walking at this time of night, and that makes me feel even more lonesome, and frightened. If the Queen needs me right now, something must be wrong. She'd have waited until morning, unless...

Unless she found Sarah.

The thought lends speed to my feet. My nightdress flaps behind me as I race through the city, finding my way as a Sensor would: by hints and feelings, not memory or logic. Mom tells the apprentices that when we're ready for the trials, we'll be able to complete them with our eyes closed and our ears plugged with wax. I wonder if she'd be proud to see me now, or if she'd ground me for the rest of my life for leaving the house without permission.

I skid around the edge of the council house and look for the Queen's cottage across the pitch-dark courtyard. There's nothing to show me the way, not even a pinprick of light to suggest that Rebecca is wheeling through her home with a lantern, waiting for me to arrive. I aim in the direction my heart tells me her house lies, but no sooner do I set foot on the pavement than I jump back in alarm.

The stone feels like it's covered with something soft and sticky—something that tried to hold my moccasin the way swampy ground would. My heart pounds as I stand at the edge, wishing I'd brought my own lantern, knowing I can't afford to delay while the Queen's expecting me. What could have happened to her courtyard, which is always kept spotless year-round, free of the muddy tracks that are left in the streets by carts carrying lumber and produce from the forest?

I'm debating what to do next when a huge shadow rises from the ground in front of me, and I choke off the scream that's about to leave my throat.

The shadow grows taller and taller, much too tall to be a human being. It sways back and forth, dark against the night's darkness, and I hear a sound like new shoes squeaking on stone. Other than that, the thing in front of me is perfectly quiet; I can't even hear it breathe. Maybe it's not a living thing at all but a machine of some sort, one of Master Gideon's cranes or scaffolds, and it's unfolded out of the ground to block my way to the Queen's house.

I gather my wits and reach out with my shaky Sense toward the dark mystery. Before I can lock onto it, the thing leans close enough for me to see what it is, and I receive an even bigger shock.

It's an urthwyrm, the kind I've only seen in picture books. Dad has told me stories about the thirty-foot-long monsters that fought on Delilah's side during the War of the Queens, as well as about the single heroic wyrm that gave its life to help Sarah win the war. So far as I know, no one's seen an urthwyrm around here since those days, and I thought they were either extinct or hiding deep in their burrows underground. Is *this* why Rebecca called me to her home? Has the Queen's cottage been invaded by a horde of wild urthwyrms, and does she expect me to help her fight them?

I haven't begun to work through that question when I find myself sailing into the air, somersaulting end over end. The scream I kept inside my mouth comes bursting out, and I hold my hands in front of my face so I won't have to watch myself disappear down the monster's gullet.

I land, not hard, on something that feels like slime-coated rubber. When I grip the thing I'm sitting on, my hands touch the same sticky stuff from the courtyard, and I realize what happened: the wyrm used its snout to flip me onto its back. I scramble to climb down, but my legs are stuck. The next thing I know, we're moving so fast I have to wrap my arms around the wyrm's body for dear life. It's too dark for me to see where we're going, but wherever it is, it's on the back of an out-of-control urthwyrm.

Then it's even darker, and the air grows cold.

Wind blows in my face, carrying an earthy smell. I'm completely blind, but I feel something brushing against my arms where they're wrapped around the wyrm. With a sickening feeling, it comes to me that we're underground—inside one of the wyrm's tunnels, which is so narrow that even if I could risk jumping off at the speed we're going, there'd be nowhere for me to jump. The wyrm is taking me to its burrow to feed me to its wyrm-brood. I'm about to become a meal for creatures that can chew through rock and spit what they eat out the other end, and I'll never see the Queen or my parents or anyone ever again.

With a lurch, we come to a dead stop. It's not until I open my eyes that I realize I had them squeezed shut the whole ride. Even with them open, I don't understand what I'm seeing: a long tunnel whose floor is tiled with six-sided plates that glow golden in color. At the end of the tunnel, there's a golden wall, thick and waxy-looking, with a hole in the middle shaped like one of the tiles. Golden light spills from the hole, and as soon as I see that, I know where we are: the entrance to the Queen's brood chamber. But it's what I see lying in front of the doorway that makes me throw myself from the wyrm and race down the tunnel.

A woman in a pink nightdress is slumped on the ground, her hair loose and her doll-legs splayed awkwardly behind her.

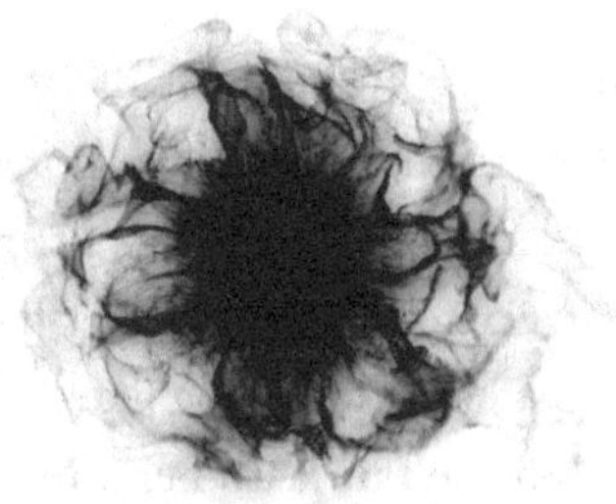

I KNEEL BESIDE Queen Rebecca, whose head rests on the golden tiles and whose hair covers her face. Her wheelchair is nowhere to be seen, and neither is her crown. I can't tell if she's breathing, but I carefully lay a hand on her neck to feel for a pulse.

When I do, I jump back. Her skin is hot, nearly burning. In the glow of the golden tiles, I can almost convince myself she's on fire.

A squeaking sound comes from down the tunnel, and I turn to find the wyrm approaching, its body rippling like a wave. Now that I see it fully, I'm terrified by its inky black skin, its wide open mouth with row after row of jagged teeth. Other than that, it has no more face than a regular earthworm. The thought flashes through my mind that it brought me here to devour me along with Rebecca. I freeze, unsure whether to run for my life or try to protect the Queen.

The wyrm reaches us, but it doesn't attack. Instead, it pushes me aside with its nose—if it has a nose—and nudges the Queen as if it's trying to get her to stand up. When that doesn't work, it lays its head next to her cheek and holds it there. I don't know if wyrms breathe, but I feel a vibration in the floor that's something like a cat purring, except on a much larger scale. The wyrm's mouth stays open the whole time, its teeth poking in and out of its pale gums like a colony of fearkats trying to scare off a predator.

All of a sudden, the Queen stirs, lifting her head from the floor. Her eyes are half-closed, her hair matted to her cheek, so she must have been lying like that for a long time. She tries to push herself up with her arms, but ends up collapsing into my lap.

"Your Majesty," I say, remembering how my mom told me to address Rebecca. "Are you all right?"

She raises her head again. She's sweating, and her eyes don't seem to be able to focus on my face.

"You're… here," she says unsteadily.

"I came as fast as I could," I say. "What happened to your wheelchair?"

"I… don't know." She gazes at me with wide eyes, then says something I never expected to hear. "Who… who are you?"

"I'm… Hadassah," I say. "Don't you know me?"

She tries to answer, but the sounds coming from her lips are too soft for me to hear. In a moment, her effort at words stops altogether, and her head rolls back onto my lap.

I look down the tunnel, and that's when I see that the wyrm has backed off a few feet but hasn't left, staying close to the Queen as if it's a rescue warhog. Its silence is creepy, but I'm sure by now that it isn't going to hurt us. In fact, I'm beginning to think its touch revived the Queen, and that gives me an idea.

"Can you hear me?" I say out loud. "Can you go for help?"

The wyrm makes no sound, but its head swings back

and forth like the pendulum of the grandfather clock in our kitchen.

"Does that mean yes?" I ask it, and the head does the same thing, which doesn't really answer my question.

"I can't carry her," I say, and pantomime tying to lift the Queen's body. "But I could probably put her on your back."

The wyrm's head movement is more energetic this time, but I still don't know what it means.

"Listen," I say. *Do wyrms even have ears?* "I'm going to try to pick her up. You hold still, and I'll—"

The wyrm surprises me by slithering closer and lowering its head all the way to the ground. Either it understands me, or it's figured out the solution on its own. Either way, it seems eager to help.

I hook one of Rebecca's arms over my shoulder and put my hands under her legs. Her head flops against me, and I can feel her breath on my neck, so hot it steams against my skin. She's mumbling something again, but I don't waste time trying to guess what it is. Lifting her is surprisingly hard, considering how small her legs are. I manage to get to my feet, but then I lose my balance and the Queen almost falls from my arms.

Almost, but not quite. The wyrm is there to catch her on top of its flat head. Slimy as its skin is, once I get her settled, she looks as if she's resting on a soft bedspread, her eyes closed and her head cradled on an outstretched arm. Her black bracelet reflects the light of the golden tiles.

The wyrm leads the way back, moving slowly as if it's concerned about the Queen taking a tumble. I am too, so I keep a hand on her burning skin. The tunnel stretches ahead of us for a long time, the golden tiles on the floor eventually giving way to bare dirt. Torches in metal brackets emit much less light than the tiles did. The wyrm makes no noise at all, and big as it is, I have to touch its side to convince myself it hasn't vanished into the darkness. When I do, I feel vibrations coming through its sticky skin. The sensation is oddly calming, considering I was worried the creature was going to eat me just a half hour ago.

In another half hour of walking, we find the Queen's abandoned wheelchair, tipped on its side as if she fell out of it. Her crown lies in the dirt beside the chair. I'm beginning to figure out what happened: she must have come down to the brood chamber to search for Sarah, but she got too dizzy or too weak to stay in her chair, and once she fell, she was too confused to pull herself back into it. When I lean close to look at her hands, I see that they're scuffed and dirty, the nails cracked. The thought of her dragging herself all the way down the tunnel makes my heart ache. But the thought that confuses me most is how an illness this bad could have stricken Rebecca down in the first place. What could the queen of the city have caught that she wasn't able to cure herself?

Maybe, I think, I can ask someone else when I get her back to bed. One of the healers. Someone like Dad.

Dad.

Of course. He's the Queen's chief healer, the most powerful healer in the city next to her. If anyone can help Rebecca, it's him. A huge wave of relief washes over me as I realize I don't have to do this alone. As soon as I get her into bed, with Caleb to watch over her, I'm going back home to bring Dad.

It's not much longer before we come to the end of the

tunnel, where twin braziers glowing with fire give me plenty of light. Instead of a staircase, the tunnel ends in something I've never seen before: a wooden platform with two sides and a top, basically a box except with an open front and back. Heavy chains attached to the top disappear into the darkness overhead, and there's a giant metal gear beside the box with more chains running from above to connect to it. I get the idea immediately: when the gear moves, the chains pull the box up and down. The only problem is, there's no way I can turn the gear, which looks like it must weigh hundreds of pounds.

The wyrm sticks its nose into the box, then turns toward me in what seems to be a request for me to step inside. I shake my head, trying to get it to see that even if I lower Rebecca onto the platform and join her there, there's no way we can return to the surface.

"Listen," I say. "It's too heavy for me. I can't—"

The wyrm swings its head back and forth, though more slowly now that Rebecca's resting on top. I wish I could read its mind, but as usual, my Sense fails me when I most need it. If, that is, a wyrm even has a mind to read.

"Please," I say. "Tell me—"

With a rude shove, the wyrm noses me into the box. Before I can step out, it pokes its head the whole way in, blocking my escape. It flattens itself against the platform until Rebecca starts to slide off, and when I catch her in my arms, her weight drags me to the floor. Something clatters into the box after her: the wheelchair, which the wyrm must have dragged along with its tail. Only when the two of us are inside the compartment, with me trapped beneath Rebecca's body, does the wyrm retreat.

It moves much faster now that there's no risk to the Queen. With the speed it showed on our journey from the courtyard, it wraps its body several times around the gear, then locks its mouth onto the metal teeth. Its entire body tightens, and with a creak and a jolt, the box inches upward. The wyrm holds us in place while relaxing its body back to its normal length, only to telescope again and pull the box another few feet higher. It repeats the movement again and again, faster and faster, until it settles into a rhythm so smooth there are no more stops or starts in the platform's rise. We're gliding upward at a rate of five or more feet per second, and when I gather the nerve to peek over the edge of the platform, the wyrm's body is so far below it looks as tiny as one of its harmless cousins.

Wyrm power. The creature must have lived here during the whole of Queen Rebecca's reign, ready to raise and lower her to her brood chamber using the machine Master Gideon designed.

"Thank you!" I call out, but there's no answer from below.

It feels like a long time that we travel upward, the platform swaying slightly and the chains clanking like distant bells overhead. I can't see anything except darkness through the box's open front or back, and I can't see Rebecca either, though I can feel her body's heat and the unnatural warmth of her breath on my neck. With nothing else to do and no idea when we're going to reach the top, I try to Sense the cause of her sickness, but I come up empty as usual. It makes me wonder what power Sarah could have seen in me when I feel helpless compared to the truly powerful beings in the Ecosystem.

The box comes to a stop so smooth, it's a second before I realize we're no longer moving. Darkness is all around us, but I see the outline of a doorway just beyond the rear opening of the box, lamplight shining around the edges. I make sure the Queen's chair is locked before lifting her from me and hoisting her onto the seat. She's gone entirely limp and feels like she weighs a ton; when I finally wrestle her into position, she slumps forward and nearly falls. I balance her with one hand, then reach behind the chair with a toe to release the foot brake. Using my other hand to move the wheels and my body to keep Rebecca from sliding out, I back toward the door and push it open with my butt, and then I see where we are.

It's the front hallway of the Queen's cottage, the same place where Caleb let me and my dad in the day before. A single candle gleams in a brass holder on the floor, the wax melted down to nearly nothing. I wonder if Rebecca was using it to light her way and for some reason left it here. I can't pick up the candle without losing my grip on the Queen, so I continue backing down the hallway, toward her bedroom. When I get there, I pause, breathing hard. I'm about to open the door when I come to my senses.

This is the Queen's bedroom, and it's the middle of the night. Caleb's got to be accustomed to her coming and going at all hours, so I doubt he'd wait up for her. What is he going to think if I barge into his bedroom dragging his unconscious wife behind me? What am *I* going to think if I find him in bed?

My face warms with embarrassment. No matter how hard I try to talk myself into it, I can't bring myself to take the final two steps.

I rest the Queen in her chair in such a way that I'm pretty sure she won't fall. She mutters while my hands move her this way and that, and I take that as a good sign, since these are the first sounds she's made for an hour at least. Her skin is terribly hot to the touch, but there's nothing I can do about that. There's only one person in the city who can help her, if she isn't already beyond everyone's help.

I leave her there, a slumped shadow in the light of the sputtering candle, and speed for home.

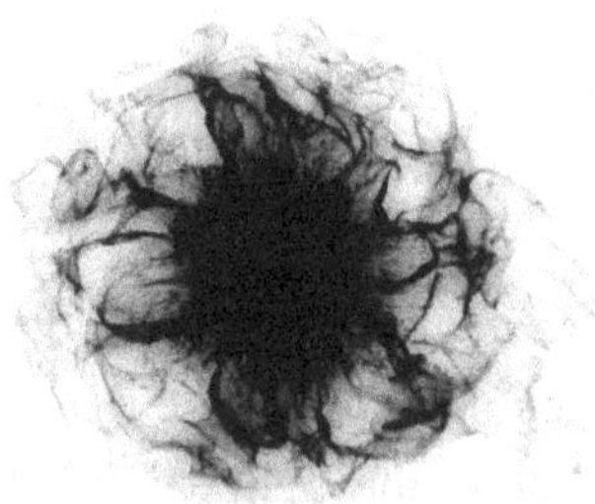

It's daylight when I fling the Queen's front door open. People are out in the streets, going about their business as if today is just like any other day. I pull my jacket around me to hide the fact that I'm wearing my nightdress, but no one seems to notice. At most, I get a smile or a nod from some of the grownups as they pass by. I guess they have more important things to worry about than why Miriam and Isaac's daughter is running around town half-clothed at the break of day.

I reach home, out of breath, and burst through the front door. "Dad! Dad!"

There's the sound of a door opening and closing quietly. Mom steps into the kitchen, shushing me with a finger.

"Where have you been?" she loud-whispers.

"At the Queen's." I can barely catch my breath. "She's sick. I need Dad."

Mom walks to the pump-handle sink that was installed in our kitchen last year. She's got a bucket with her, and she starts to fill it with forceful strokes of the pump.

"Your father's not feeling well," she says. "I need you to stay here with Tovah while I go get Michael."

"What's wrong with Dad?"

"Just a touch of fever." She lifts the bucket from the sink, grunting at the weight. I rush over to help her, but she waves me away. "Tovah needs a change. I'm going to take this to your father, then I'm going to go. I don't want you in our bedroom in case it's catching."

"But—"

Her eyes turn to me, and the objection dies on my lips. The fact that she's not reading me the riot act for leaving home in the middle of the night tells me she's more worried about Dad than she's letting on.

Mom drags the bucket into her bedroom while I go to where Tovah is standing in her crib. She reaches out to me, and my nose wrinkles when I get a whiff of her. I put her on the changing pad and take a clean cloth diaper from the shelf, a moist washcloth from the basin. She plays with my hair while I lean over her to wipe up the mess. I try to listen to what's going on in the room next door, but all I can make out is the sound of Mom's voice, not the words she's saying. Then the bucket clatters, the door opens and closes, and Mom sticks her head into Tovah's bedroom just as I'm pitching the dirty diaper into the pail.

"I'll be back as soon as I can," she says. "I need you to give Tovah breakfast and help Chaim when he gets up."

"Why don't you just send Michael a bloodbird?"

She frowns, and for a second I think she's going to let me have it. Then the weariness creeps back into her face, and her shoulders slump.

"I already sent one," she says. "Almost an hour ago. I'm going to go search for Michael myself." She brushes a strand of hair from her eyes. "Breakfast. And let your father sleep."

She leaves without saying goodbye.

I carry my little sister into the kitchen and buckle her into her high chair. From the cabinets, I collect her cup and bowl, the spoon with the extra-large handle, some dried oat flakes. When she sees what I've got, Tovah bangs the spoon on the chair and squeaks, "bekfess!" I try to shush her, but she starts fussing, so I quickly open the ice chest and take out a flask of milk, mixing the oatmeal mush and sliding it in front of her. At the last second, I remember to tie a bib around her neck before she digs in.

Over the sound of Tovah's slurping and splatting, I listen for any sign of movement from my parents' room. The house feels unnaturally quiet, like it's holding its breath the same way I am. Even the birds outside seem to have stopped their songs while I wait for the least hint of my dad's voice, the sound of his big feet on the floor. When Tovah's finished and I've wiped most of the slop from her cheeks, I take advantage of the fact that she's strapped in and creep down the hall, cracking the bedroom door as quietly as I can.

"Dad?" I whisper, but there's no answer.

I tiptoe into the room, where I'm instantly hit by a stale smell—not the same as Tovah's stink, but like the air hasn't moved for weeks. The windows are closed and the drapes drawn, but I can see the shape of Dad's body huddled under the covers, the very top of his hair poking out like a roaster's crest. Mom's even put an extra blanket on him, the heavy quilt that Lieutenant Leah sewed for the two of them as a tenth anniversary gift. I listen for the sound of his breath, and at last I hear it, though it seems much too fast and shallow, as if he's the one who ran from the Queen's house instead of me.

I approach the bed, fold back a corner of the quilt. Tovah calls out her mangled form of my name—"Dafah!"—but I ignore her. Dad's eyes are squeezed shut. The moist washcloth lies across his forehead, and when I lift it to touch him, I notice that the cloth isn't cool anymore. His skin has the tight, dry feel of someone running a high temperature. It's possibly not as bad as the Queen's, but it's much worse than Mom said.

I take the cloth and rush back to the kitchen to wring it out and wet it again with cold water from the pump. Tovah bangs her spoon and reaches out to me, but I ignore her again. She starts to scream when I enter my parents' room, so I close the door to shut out her tantrum as much as I can. I hope her shrieks don't wake up Dad.

He hasn't moved since I left, not even to pull the covers back up. I lay the cloth on his forehead, molding it to his shape so it won't fall off. He's started to shiver, and his teeth are chattering. I touch his burning hot cheek, and at that moment, his eyes open.

They roll around before finding me. Even when they're on my face, they don't seem able to focus, just like the Queen's. He tries to smile, though with his teeth chattering so badly, he can barely manage it.

"Hey, kiddo," he says in a weak voice.

"Hi, Dad," I say. "How… how do you feel?"

"A little under the weather," he says with his usual lopsided grin. Except with the shape he's in, the expression looks forced. "Where's Mom?"

"She went to get Michael."

"That's great," he says, but his voice is fading and his eyes closing, as if he's slipping back into sleep. "Tell her…"

He doesn't say anything else, not that I can hear, even when I lean close. He's shivering so badly, I'm afraid he might fall out of bed.

Before I can decide what to do, Tovah lets out a scream that seems to shake the whole house. The bedroom door opens a crack to show Chaim's face, his eyes sleepy, his hair as mussed as Dad's.

"What's going on?" he mumbles.

"Nothing!" I tuck the covers as tightly around Dad as I can, then push past Chaim to where Tovah is screaming and flailing her arms, trying to free herself. My fingers shake as I undo her straps and swing her from the chair. She continues to scream and squirm against me.

"Tovah, be still!" I order.

"She wants her cereal," Chaim says from the doorway.

"She already *got* her cereal," I say. "What she's *going* to get if she doesn't settle down is a smack right across the rear end."

Apparently, that doesn't work either.

There's a loud rap on the front door, which makes everyone—including Tovah—freeze for a second. Then she starts to cry even louder than before. I practically throw her at Chaim.

"Get her out of here," I say, hating the quaver in my voice. "And keep her away from Mom and Dad's room."

"What's wrong with—"

"Out, Chaim!" I say. "I mean it."

He retreats meekly, pulling our screaming sister down the hallway. There's only one thought in my head as I take two jerky steps to the door.

Please let this be Michael. Please please please.

But it's not.

Instead, it's a woman I recognize from Sensor training, the mother of one of the little kids who made me look like a fool at yesterday's session. I can't remember her name. She seems surprised to see me, or maybe to see me in nothing but my jacket and nightgown.

"Is your father here?" she says, in a way I might consider rude if I cared about things like that right now. Tovah's screams keep coming from down the hall, and every time she lets out a blast, my nerves feel like they're about to snap.

"He's not able to come to the door right now," I say with an attempt at manners. Then, since she's not being polite either, I add, "What do you need him for?"

She looks over my shoulder as if I might be hiding him somewhere. She even seems like she's about to push past me into the kitchen, but I block her with the door. At that, she half-smiles, in a way that looks more like she's about to cry.

"My Stephen has a temperature," she says. "I thought your father could help."

The tremble in her lip makes me soften. "My mom went to get Michael," I say. "You can come in and wait for them if you'd like."

I open the door the whole way and step back. She looks undecided, but takes me up on it. Miracle of miracles, Tovah's screams have stopped. Silently, I thank my little brother for removing that source of irritation.

I sit at the table with Stephen's mother, who keeps looking at me as if she's waiting for me to say something. The grandfather clock ticks away the time, the only sound in the entire house.

My mind, though, is racing. *First the Queen, then Dad, and now one of Mom's apprentices.* All in a single day, and all of them coming down with what sounds like the same thing. Did Dad catch some kind of bug from the Queen when we visited her? Did it get passed on to others in the day since? As chief healer, he's always in and out of people's houses. I still can't believe the Queen could get sick at all, and I can't erase the image of her sitting where I left her, alone in the dark. Surely Caleb found her by now, or one of the maids—but if so, wouldn't they have called for my dad? And when in the Ecosystem is my mom ever going to get back with Michael?

The clock has struck the ninth hour before there's a jiggle on the doorknob and Mom enters the kitchen.

Alone.

She takes in the scene, her face shifting from what I can't help thinking of as defeat to determination when she sees Stephen's mom. The woman has already risen from the table with a question on her lips when my mom stops her.

"Michael is unavailable," she says. "It seems he's not feeling up to making house calls. I hunted for Flora, but I found her in bed as well. The report is that many of the healers are sick, possibly all of them."

"*All* of them?" the woman repeats.

"And some of the Sensors, too," my mom says. "Is Stephen...?"

"He's burning up," the woman says with panic in her voice. "He doesn't... he doesn't know me..."

Mom rushes over and catches Stephen's mother as she crumples. I stare as the woman covers her face in her hands while Mom hushes her and pats her back like she does with Tovah. I can't hear the words Mom's saying, but I get a sick feeling at the sight of a grown woman falling to pieces in her arms.

Mom's eyes meet mine, and for the first time in I can't remember how long, I see that we share the same thought.

Whatever the Queen has, it's spreading like lightning through the city, but it's not making everybody sick. The only ones coming down with it are people who, like the Queen herself, have an especially strong connection to the Ecosystem. Sensors. Healers.

Everyone except the two of us.

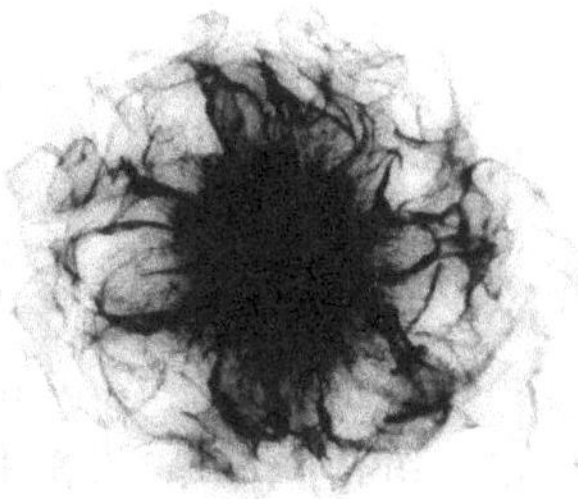

After Stephen's mother has left and Mom has checked on Dad to make sure he hasn't gotten any worse, she calls a bloodbird to the window and scribbles a quick note for it to take to the Queen's house. Bloodbirds were one of the first creatures to appear in the Ecosystem, when the birds called robins developed a taste for human blood. They're perfectly safe now, though. They eat worms and bugs, and some people say they're a sign of winter ending and warm weather coming back.

Once the bird has winged away with the note tied to its leg, Mom jots down another note, her handwriting even messier than usual. Like everyone from their village, she and Dad didn't learn to read and write until they moved to the city.

"This is for Angelica," she explains to me as she ties the slip of paper to a second bird's outstretched leg. "As captain of the Queen's guard, she'll need to know what's going on."

"What are we going to do?"

"We're going to wait," she says. "And take care of your father. There's no point in running off in a panic until we know the extent of what's happening."

She probably doesn't mean that as a scolding for what I did last night, but it feels like one.

So we wait. Now that it seems clear that she and I aren't going to catch whatever Dad has, she lets me into their room to give him water from one of Tovah's sipping cups. He can't hold the handles or open his mouth on his own to drink, but I make sure the water goes down his throat just the same. Mom gets Tovah dressed and helps Chaim with his breakfast. The pangs in my stomach make me realize I haven't eaten anything all day, but it's likely that Mom hasn't either. And I'd rather be here with Dad than sitting at the breakfast table staring at lumpy oatmeal and worried faces.

I'm in the middle of exchanging washcloths for what must be the twentieth time—he sweats through each one in a matter of minutes—when a rustle of wings announces the return of one of our birds.

"It's from the Queen's housekeeper," Mom says, scanning the note. "Chaim, can you take Tovah to play?"

He looks at her with fear and resentment mixed in his face, but he holds Tovah's hand as she toddles down the hall to her bedroom. Chaim might only be eight years old, but he's not stupid.

When we're alone, my mom gestures for me to sit at the table. She joins me, spreading the note out between us.

"Queen Rebecca is in a coma," she says. "They were about to send for your father when they received my note. And it seems Caleb is sick, too."

"Caleb?" I say. "He's not a healer."

"But he was," my mom says. "Before his marriage to Rebecca, he and his brother Noah trained first as Sensors and then as healers. So it's obvious this illness isn't affecting only those who are active members of the Queen's Corps. It's attacking anyone with a greater-than-normal concentration of *A. impunita* genes." She looks at me. "The genes from the original Ecosystem hive."

"I know what they are."

"Then you must understand what this means, too."

"No," I say. "Not exactly."

"Neither do I," she admits, which makes me wonder if she was hoping I did. "You said that the Queen was even worse than your father?"

"She had a higher fever. And she seemed… weaker. More confused."

"Hm." She squeezes her eyes shut, as if she's calling out to the Ecosystem. Her face looks pained, not relaxed the way it would if she was hearing the Ecosystem's response. "The Queen has the highest concentration of *A. impunita* genes of anyone alive," she says. "Her genes are derived from the queen bee herself, from *Apis dominica*. If she sickens…"

The caw of the second bloodbird interrupts her thoughts. It lands on the table between the two of us, but I snatch at it first. I glance at Mom guiltily before unwrapping the note from its leg.

"It's from Lieutenant Leah," I say. "Captain Angelica was too sick to report to duty this morning. It sounds as if Celestina is even worse. She's—"

"Read it," my mom says. "Word for word."

"I am reading it," I say. "*Angelica unfit for duty. Celestina gravely ill. Acting in my capacity as lieutenant to the Captain of the Queen's guard, request your immediate presence at the guardhouse.*" I look up at Mom. "Captain Angelica was never a healer! She told me herself that she's always been a fighter. So it's not what we thought!"

Mom rises from her chair and goes to the kitchen

window. She wraps her arms around herself as if she's cold, and my heart skips a beat at the thought that she's coming down with something too.

"Angelica was a healer," she says in a dead voice, looking out the window instead of at me. "She nearly died during the War of the Queens, and that seems to have broken her connection to the Ecosystem. Celestina tried to restore her partner's powers, but she concluded that it posed too much of a risk. Angelica hates to talk about what she went through, which must be why she told you what she did."

I wait for her to say something else. When she doesn't, I jump up and run to the window, my chair clattering to the floor. Mom surprises me by spinning and catching me in her arms, pulling me close. It's been so long since she held me this way, I don't remember if her body always felt this thin and sharp.

"Is Daddy going to die?" I ask.

"Not if I can help it," she says. "But this is larger than us, Hadassah. As the Queen sickens, so does the Ecosystem she commands. Rebecca is young, without a daughter of her own. If she dies without an heir…"

"What?" I ask. "Mom, what?"

She pulls back, holds me at arm's length. "If the Queen dies, the Ecosystem will not survive."

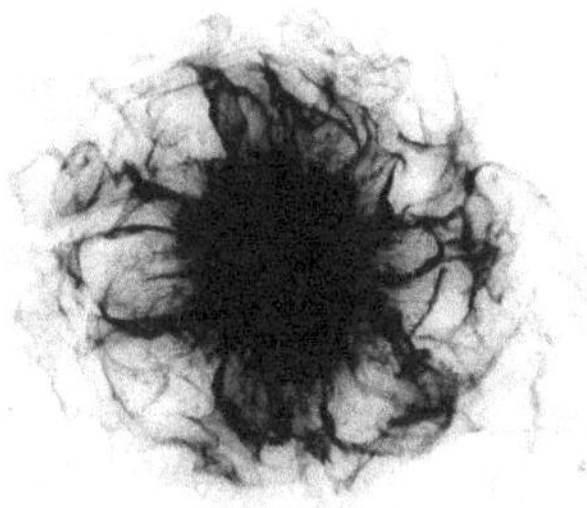

THE GUARDHOUSE IS one of the oldest buildings in the City of the Queens. It used to be student housing, which explains the way it looks: an ugly three-story box made of rough brown stone. Inside it's even worse, with beige-colored cinder-block walls, threadbare carpeting, and identical doors that lead to cramped rooms. People say the basement is where Delilah was imprisoned all those years ago by Queen Leonida—the place where Delilah's tongue was cut from her mouth to keep her from telling anyone about her cousin's treachery. I've wondered more than once why a witch like Leonida gets a window in the council house. Mom says she did a lot of good for the city despite her cruel ways. Dad says it's important to learn to forgive.

Thinking about that story doesn't help my mood as I settle into a chair in the guardhouse conference room, with Mom by my side and four members of the guard, plus Lieutenant Leah, seated around the table. We left Dad under the care of one of the Queen's handmaidens, a woman who knows something about nursing even though she's not a trained healer. He was still conscious, but his fever was alarming, even to Mom. Chaim and Tovah are at a neighbor's house. Mom sent bloodbirds all over town to figure out how many people were sick and to find others who could care for them. Then she grabbed my arm and, before I had a chance to kiss Dad goodbye, dragged me across campus to Leah's meeting.

I've always liked Leah, who was Sarah's best friend before I was born. I like her energy, her warmth, and most of all how she makes you feel like she's paying a hundred percent attention to you, even if you happen to be a teenager. It comforts me to know that she'll be running this meeting instead of Captain Angelica, who can be too intense at times. But thinking unkind thoughts about Angelica makes me feel bad, since she's being cared for right now by one of the Queen's other handmaidens while both she and Celestina fight the same sickness as the Queen and my dad.

Leah doesn't waste time getting things started. "Thank you for coming," she says. "Miriam, can you provide us with a report on the spread of this disease?"

Mom folds her hands on the table. Unconsciously, I brace for a lecture, but she doesn't even look at me as she begins to speak.

"So far as we know, the disorder began with the Queen," she says. "Isaac, Celestina, and others with comparable concentrations of hive-genes have fallen next." The word *fallen* makes my heart stop, but she doesn't seem to notice. "From there, the illness appears to be spreading among members of the Queen's Corps, though it's not affecting everyone to the same degree. Every healer of whom I'm aware is exhibiting at least some symptoms, and most of the Sensors are as well."

"And you think there's a direct correlation between the illness and the hive-genes?" Leah asks.

"There's not a doubt in my mind," Mom answers. "If the Queen weren't among the sick, she could scan each affected person to determine the concentration of *A. impunita* genes in their blood. But even without her, the proof lies in the fact that the few Sensors who remain unaffected are the ones who volunteered for the corps rather than being recommended on the basis of prior affinity."

"Translate that for me," Leah says with a tight smile.

Mom doesn't smile back. "As you know, when Rebecca assumed the throne, she put me in charge of a new program that allowed common citizens to apply to the Sensor corps. Prior to that point, candidates were nominated by an acting Sensor who saw promise of the gift within them. Rebecca's reasoning was that everyone possesses a degree of connection to the original hive, and so everyone should, in theory, be able to develop Sensory skills to some extent."

"And was her hunch right?" Leah asks.

"In part," Mom replies. "The volunteers take significantly longer to train than the traditional recruits, and they don't develop the same degree of Sensitivity as those who are 'born' with the Sense. But over the past fifteen years, they've proven quite valuable in supporting roles."

"And so the absence of sickness among them..."

"Suggests that only individuals whose concentration of *A. impunita* genes crosses a certain threshold have been struck down so far," Mom says, ignoring the face I make at the words *struck down*.

"So far?" Leah asks. "Will others sicken in the future?"

"I believe so," Mom says. "If I'm right that this disease originates with the Queen, it'll spread until it affects every member of her hive, which means not only human beings but every organism within the Ecosystem."

There's dead silence after she says that. It's broken a

minute later by Luke, one of the senior members of the guard. His spouse, Michael, is second only to Dad in the healer corps. Mom told me that he's in worse shape than most.

"I'm not following this," Luke says. "You keep calling what's happening a *disease*, but it doesn't sound like it's spread by contact. Is it, what, in the air?"

"I wish it were," Mom says. "If that were the case, we could initiate quarantine procedures, or abandon the city if all else failed."

"Where is it, then?" Luke insists.

"It's in the code that shapes all living things," Mom answers. "That's the nature of the Ecosystem: everything is connected, the entire hive, through the genetic material of *Apis dominica*, the original queen. It's what gives the current queen her power, what enables Sensors and healers to plumb the mind of the wild. The lines of connection are invisible to anyone who hasn't been trained in the Sensing or healing arts, but when you learn to see them, they're everywhere: golden threads that link us to all that lives. We can't escape those connections, and we can't sever them to prevent the disease from spreading. Not without destroying the very thing we're trying to save."

"But *you're* a Sensor," Luke presses. "Why aren't you sick, too?"

"Luke," Leah says.

"Sorry," Luke mumbles.

"It's all right," Mom says. "The truth is, I don't know why I've been spared. My daughter, who's a Sensor in training, hasn't been affected either. Both of us were identified for the corps in the traditional way, so I can't explain why we seem to be immune to this outbreak."

All eyes in the room turn my way. Maybe, before Mom mentioned me, people thought I was just tagging along because there was no one to watch me at home. Now I feel the pressure of their hopes and fears, as if I'm supposed to come up with an answer to the mystery that baffles the city's Chief Sensor. As if I know some secret that's been kept from everyone else.

And the thing is, I do.

"I met with the Queen," I say. "On the day after Sarah's funeral. I had a… a dream about Sarah three nights before, where I thought she came to my room and told me something. I couldn't tell anyone else about it, but I told the Queen."

"What did you tell her?" Leah asks, her voice soft yet probing.

I swallow. Though I know how important this is, I feel strangely reluctant to talk about the tree, as if it's supposed to remain a secret. But with everyone staring at me, I don't have much choice. I tell them the whole story, from the time Sarah came to my room to the day in the Queen's garden. I can see my mom out of the corner of my eye, her face showing surprise, then shock, that I never mentioned any of this to her before. When her expression turns to anger, I falter, looking to Leah for help.

"Go on, Hadassah," she says gently.

"The Queen touched the tree," I say. "Even though it was only a vision. And it seemed like… it hurt her. And then, last night, she called to me while I was asleep, and when I went to her house, I found her outside her brood chamber. She was already sick, and I helped her get back to her bedroom, but I didn't know what else to do..."

No one says anything, but I can guess what they're thinking. That I'm responsible for all of this. That I was the one who brought the sickness to the city through the vision Sarah planted in me, and then through my conversation with the Queen. I want to say to them, *My Dad's sick, too,* but I doubt they'd listen.

"The tree must have made Queen Rebecca sick," I say at last. "I don't know how. All I know is, after she touched it, she told me we had to find it."

I lower my head and shrink into myself the way Mom tells me not to, especially in public. There's some random shuffling of chairs and clearing of throats, but no one says anything. I don't look at Mom, mostly because I don't want to see the expression that almost always follows anger: disappointment. The same expression I see day after day in Sensor training, and that, ever since the story she told me yesterday, I can't help thinking is coming not only from her but from Sarah, too.

Then I feel a hand on my shoulder, and I look up to find Leah standing beside me. The tears she sheds so easily brighten her eyes.

"I know of this tree," she says. "Miriam does, too. Do you remember?"

Mom's face twists as if the question causes her pain. "Of course."

"Do you remember when Daniel told us about it?"

"At my wedding," Mom says, or more like gasps. "In the village."

I look back and forth between the two of them. This

is news to me: I've always been told that Mom and Dad were married after they moved to the city, not in the village where they were born.

"And do you remember the name of the place?" Leah goes on. "Where Daniel told us the tree stood?"

Mom shakes her head.

"You do remember, Miriam," Leah says. "You have to."

"It was… *edinnu*," Mom says in a whisper.

"That's right," Leah says, as if she's just remembering the strange word herself. "*Edinnu*."

She leans down and gives Mom a hug. When she pulls away, I see that Mom's eyes are teary, and her hands shake.

"Everyone in our village heard Chief Warden Daniel tell the story of *edinnu*," Leah says to the rest of the guards. "The way he talked, I assumed his tale was little more than a nursery rhyme about magic lands that never existed. And so I let it fade from my memory, as did we all. Only one of us who heard that story seems to have believed the tree might be real. And it sounds to me as if she set out to prove that she was right."

She bustles around the table while everyone absorbs her words. When she returns to her seat, her eyes are shining. She leans forward and speaks with barely controlled excitement.

"Everything's connected," she says. "The tree, Hadassah's dream, the Queen's sickness. The story of *edinnu*, which Miriam and I had nearly forgotten. If we want to discover the cause of this disease and its cure, we need to comply with the Queen's wishes and find that tree." She winks at me. "*Sarah's* tree."

All of the guards explode into talk at once. Luke

volunteers to join the expedition, and he shouts so loudly the others have to shout even louder to be heard over him. A tall, pretty guard named Catherine raises her voice the loudest, saying that it's a lot to place on the Queen's supposed instructions, and that we need to investigate further before we venture without adequate preparation into the wild. When she says *supposed instructions*, I know she means *instructions reported by a teenager*, and when she says *without adequate preparation*, I'm pretty sure that's supposed to be a dig at Leah. Another man, I don't know his name, says that the guard's duty is to defend the Queen, not to run off on a wild gnoose chase after an imaginary tree spoken of by some vagrant. I shoot him a dirty look on Sarah's behalf, but he's not paying attention to me.

"And in any event, we don't have the slightest idea where to look!" he wraps up. Catherine crosses her arms and nods, obviously thinking that puts an end to the discussion.

Then my mom stands. She's the smallest person in the room except for me, and she looks even smaller standing behind the conference table. Her eyes are still teary, but her hands have stopped shaking. She faces the others with her head held high, less like the Queen's assistant than the Queen herself.

"It's true that we don't know where to find the tree," she says. "Either we never knew, or we've long since forgotten. It's possible even Rebecca couldn't have taken us there." She rests a hand on my shoulder. "But I've a feeling Hadassah can show us the way."

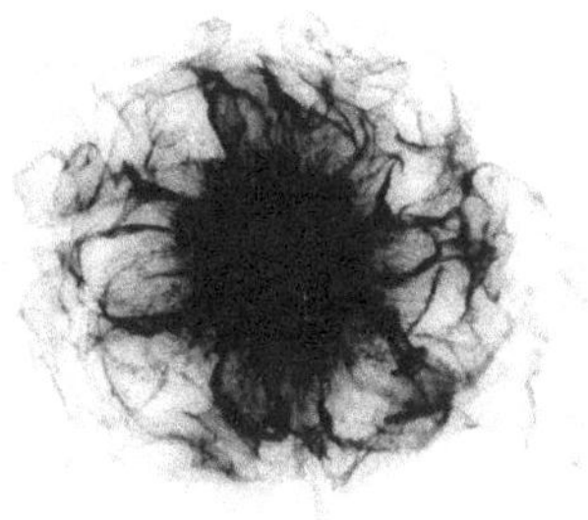

BOOK TWO

WORM

At the same time that we are earnest to explore and learn all things, we require that all things be mysterious and unexplorable, that land and sea be infinitely wild, unsurveyed and unfathomed by us because unfathomable. We can never have enough of Nature.

—Henry David Thoreau,
Walden (1854)

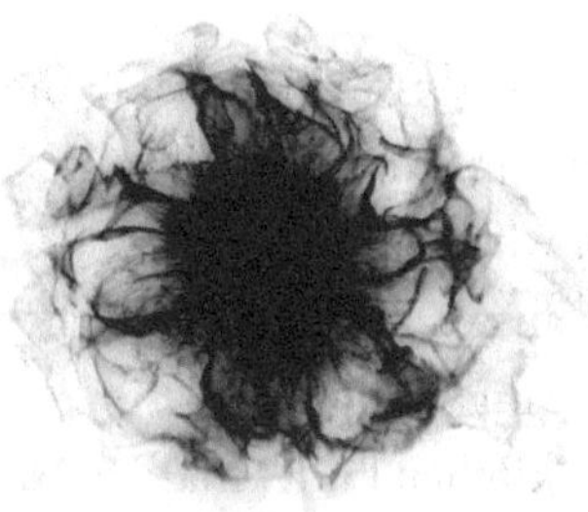

I'M MOSTLY PACKED.

There wasn't much to throw into my bag: a couple of changes of clothes, a jacket, a water flask. I'm wearing heavy boots, which isn't the Sensor way, but I might need them for marshy ground. Mom insisted I take some clean pads in case what she calls *my time* comes while I'm away, but after nearly fourteen years, I'm not convinced it's ever going to come. Not that I want it to. I have enough on my mind without having to worry about that.

I can see the tree Sarah planted in my memory as clear as anything, but I have no idea how to get to this *edinnu* place, if it's a real place at all. The tree seems to float free of the earth, a spiked dangerlion puffball drifting on the breeze. When I tried to explain that to Mom, she told me she was sure I'd find the way. It's so unlike her to show confidence in me, I decided not to spoil the moment. But whenever I think of myself out there, supposedly leading the team when I don't know where I'm leading them to, I feel like curling into a ball and hiding in a dark corner. Except with the curtains open and the sun shining, there's no corner to hide in.

We're looking around the room to see if I've forgotten anything when Mom presses an object into my palm. I flinch when I see what it is.

"Sensors used to carry knives," she explains. "Knives of

stone, since we couldn't work metal in the village. Keep this one close to you, just in case."

"In case of what?"

Instead of answering, she leaves the room. I hold the knife up, watching squiggles of sunlight bounce off the blade. It's not a kitchen knife, that's for sure: it's longer and sharper, and it looks ugly and cruel in my hand. A knife for slitting throats, for gutting killdeer. Sensors haven't needed knives like this since before the War of the Queens, and it makes my stomach churn to think that my own mother wants me to return to those days.

She comes back into the room while I'm trying to bury the knife at the bottom of my bag. Without comment, she holds out a rolled-up tube and gestures for me to help her spread it on the bed.

When it's unrolled, it takes up most of the mattress. It's a map, the old-fashioned kind that's printed on a cured warhog hide to make it last. It shows a part of the Ecosystem I've never seen, a dense tangle of black forest as thick as me or Mom's hair sprawling halfway up the hide before ending where three blue stripes come together at a point. According to the compass rose in the corner, one of the stripes runs northwest, the second northeast, the third southeast. The triangle between the northeastern and southeastern stripes is dotted with mixed forest and grasslands, but above and to the west of the place where the three stripes meet, there's nothing except pale brown hide. Mom runs a hand over the blankness, smoothing out creases.

"This map is based on reports Sarah sent to Rebecca," she says. "It depicts an area far to the west of us, beyond the site of the village where your father and I were born.

Rebecca had several copies made so that Sarah's friends would have some idea where she was."

"Why isn't there anything here?" I ask, pointing.

"We assume because Sarah hadn't explored that far when the map was made," Mom says. "Either that, or she hadn't reported her journeys to the Queen. This area is what mapmakers used to call *terra incognita*, unknown land. Land that's a blank space in people's consciousness, just as it is on the map."

"And you think Sarah went there?" I say anxiously. "That that's where she found *edinnu*?"

"I think it's the best place to start looking," she says. "If Sarah was concentrating her research on this area, she must have felt it was important. And if she did find *edinnu*, it might explain why she was unable to return."

The way she says that scares me, and I stare at the map, as if just looking at it will solve the riddle. "Rebecca told me that queens can project themselves anywhere in the Ecosystem," I say. "So how could there be blank places for them?"

She rolls the map up, ties it with one of my hair ribbons, and sets it on the desk. Then she sits on the bed and pats the covers for me to sit beside her. When I do, she surprises me by taking my hands in hers.

"Sarah told me years ago that there were blank places in the Ecosystem even for her," she says. "Some of those blanks were the ruins of cities, where dead stone prevented her mind from penetrating. Others were guarded by powerful spells, so strong they could wrap even a queen's vision in night. I suspect *edinnu* is one of those places. In fact, I wonder now if it's the place Sarah was trying to tell me about. It seems to exert a power of forgetfulness over people, as if it doesn't want to be found."

"How can a place *want* something?"

"Places are alive, the same as we are," she says. "They're infused with the Ecosystem's will, and they possess memories and desires just like people. The only difference is that places live much longer than we do, and so their desires grow much deeper into the earth. The longer a place lives, the deeper its desires become, and the very deepest of those desires is what Sarah meant by a spell. You know the story of Delilah's web."

I nod.

"When she created the web almost a hundred years ago, she meant for it to surround the village as a protective shield against Leonida," Mom says. "But the ground in which her web grew had a will of its own, and it hexed the web into growing beyond Delilah's control. She became its servant instead of the other way around. When her spirit returned years later, it was as if the original desire had grown stronger over time. If Rebecca hadn't been willing to sacrifice a part of her own life to appease the anger of the earth…"

She shudders. I look into her eyes and see a shadow there.

"Mom," I say. "Why didn't you tell me that you and Dad got married in the village?"

She looks away. When she talks, her voice sounds small, like the voice of a little girl trapped in a cave.

"Because we didn't," she says. "We were supposed to be married, and Daniel told the story of *edinnu* to celebrate our wedding. He went back to the beginning, to a time before the Ecosystem's rise, because he had faith, or at least hope, that our people could recapture what we'd lost. But he was wrong. It wasn't until much later, after the War of the Queens, that the marriage took place, here, in the city."

"But why?" I ask. "Why'd you wait so long?"

She turns back to me, and her eyes are as wide as those of the little girl in the cave.

"Something terrible happened," she says. "Something I can't tell you. I'm sorry, Hadassah. Believe we when I say that I *will* tell you, just as soon as I can. When I can say the words without feeling as if they're going to tear me away from everyone I love."

She reaches out to me, and I find myself in her arms, each of us holding onto the other as if to stop ourselves from being swept into the blank space on Sarah's map. She squeezes so tight it hurts, but I cling to her all the same.

"Keep the knife," Mom whispers fiercely in my ear. "Learn how to use it. Leah can teach you. The Ecosystem might seem tame to you, but there are dark places in it still, places full of memory and hurt and longing. That's where Sarah went, and if she's alive, that's where you'll find her."

"I don't want to go," I say. "I want to stay here with you, and Dad, and..."

"You *must* go," she says. "Sarah chose to come to you for a reason, and that must have been because she believed you had a better chance of finding her than anyone. If you stay here, the tree will remain hidden, and the Queen will die, and the Ecosystem with her. Your father will die, Hadassah," she says. "You can't save him by waiting at his bedside."

"Why can't you come with me?"

"Because the city needs me," she says. "Your father needs me, and so do Chaim and Tovah. I'm no queen, but I do have power in my hands, and perhaps I can slow the spread of this illness until you return. I have to try, in any case."

She squeezes me even tighter. I understand how she must feel when she remembers her wedding day in the village: it's too big, too much, and if I think about it or try to talk about it, I'll lose myself. Mom holds me for a long, long time, then she pulls back and takes a look at me. She's smiling, though it's the kind of smile that could crack like a blood-red bloodbird's egg.

"You're a daughter of the Ecosystem," she says. "And a daughter of mine. What you must bear, you will bear. But you won't have to bear it all alone."

She reaches into the pocket of her dress and pulls out a small trinket wrapped in a rawhide cord. When she unwinds the cord and holds the bauble out to me, I see that it's a shard of bone or tooth, highly polished and with blue veins branching across its miniature surface. She pulls back my hair and loops the charm around my neck.

"This belonged to Sarah," she says. "She gave it to me on the day I became a Sensor, just as it was given to her by her grandfather Aaron on the day she joined the order. It passes from master to apprentice in an unbroken line, and you'll pass it on to another when the time comes. I was going to give it to you on the day you completed the trials and received your investiture. But I think that day is today."

She kisses my forehead. I clutch the token in my fist and close my eyes. *Sarah never knew her mother,* I think. *She died when Sarah was only two years old, too early for even a Sensor's memories.* If her mother had lived, would she have been the one to give her daughter this gift? And if she had, would Sarah have found the love she was missing all the years of her life?

I fall into my mother's arms, and she strokes my hair as she whispers the words of her goodbye.

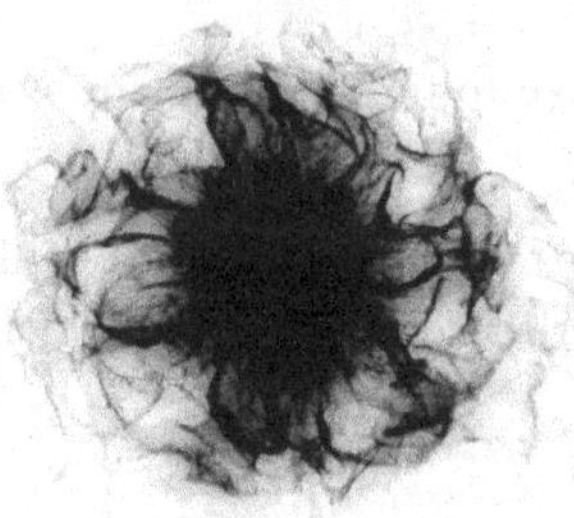

The others are waiting for us at the front gate of the city, just past the memorial where the Cathedral used to stand. I wish I could have been alive to see it before it fell in the War of the Queens. Right now, all that's left to mark it are a stone and a plaque and a brazier that's always kept burning. Even with the Queen and so many people in the city either sick or keeping watch over the sick, the flame is still lit.

Leah is there, wearing a shirt of braided metal under a stiff warhog hide jerkin. Her pants are made of bristly-furred prowler monkey hide, and her boots are even sturdier than mine. A long sword hangs from her belt, and there are other weapons—knives, a shorter sword—strapped to various parts of her body. Next to her fighting gear, my little knife looks pathetic.

Two guards have been chosen to come with us: Catherine and the man from the meeting whose name I don't know. Leah introduces him as Simon, and tells me that he and Catherine have worked as partners for years. They don't look very well matched: where Catherine is tall and graceful, built more like a dancer than a fighter, Simon is short, stocky, and crawling with muscle. His face is ill-tempered, probably because Leah selected him for this mission. I know that he blames me, so I keep my mouth shut when we're introduced. I wish Luke had come instead, but Leah needed him to take charge of the guard while she's gone.

The fifth member of our group comes strolling up while Leah is leading us through a final check of our supplies. I'm shocked and annoyed to discover that it's Peter. He smiles in his typical superior way, then proceeds to ignore me like usual. Mom leans close to whisper in my ear.

"Leah asked me to recommend a second Sensor for this journey," she says. "The other volunteers were too young, so..."

So I'm stuck with him, I think. The fact that Peter's not sick means he must have a low concentration of *A. impunita* genes—which makes it even more embarrassing that he's so much better than me at Sensor training. All I can hope is that he'll continue to ignore me for the entire trip.

Leah finishes her check and hitches my bag more firmly on my shoulders. Even though she looks like she's dressed for war, she finds the time to smile at me. Then she turns to my mom. "Is our transport ready?"

Mom nods.

"Transport?" I ask.

"We're going a long way," Leah says. "And we don't have time to dawdle. Fortunately for us..."

She doesn't get to finish what she's saying before the ground starts to shake so hard, Mom has to grab me to keep me from falling. The eternal flame on the memorial flickers as if it's about to go out. Seconds later, a dark shape bursts through the grabgrass outside the gate. Mom squeezes my arm as if to reassure me, but I've already met the one that comes slithering toward us.

At least, I think I have. Maybe all urthwyrms look the same.

It wriggles through the gate and stops in front of us, inky black and seeming even bigger in the sunshine than it did underground. Its mouth is open, but its teeth are retracted for the time being. Leather cords or straps are looped around the first third of its body, each one connected to what looks like a shallow leather bucket on its back. Leah rests a hand on one of these things, and the memory of last night makes my eyes go wide.

"We're going to *ride* it?"

"Sure are," Leah says. Out of the corner of my eye, I see Peter looking bored, the guards looking disgusted. I'm so amazed at the thought of what we're about to do, I don't entirely care.

"Underground?" I ask.

This time, Leah laughs. "I've ridden urthwyrms both aboveground and below," she says. "Either way, they go as fast as ghosthawks. And they never tire, so they can carry us straight through the night while we're asleep."

"Can they see?" I ask. "I mean, to read the map?"

Leah laughs again. "Never heard of an urthwyrm that could read."

"But then how will it know where we're going?"

Leah turns to Mom. "You're sure about this, Miriam?"

"Absolutely," Mom says.

She reaches for my hand and lays it on the wyrm's flank, against the slimy stickiness of its skin. Deep inside, I feel the same vibrations I did in the Queen's tunnel, as if the wyrm is purring like a fell-cat. Not with its throat—which I don't think it has—but with its entire body. Cautiously, I stroke it, and the purring grows stronger. I'm about to touch its snout, not too close to the mouth, when a deep, rumbling voice speaks inside my head.

We are bundled in the flesh, it says. *Welcome, two-leg-walker.*

I pull back in alarm. My hand tingles where I touched the wyrm as if I'm still feeling its vibrations. Mom puts an arm around me.

"This is the Queen's wyrm," she says. "I've communed with it, and it's agreed to bear you wherever you ask it to go."

"You spoke to a wyrm?"

"Don't act so surprised," she says. "Here."

She guides me back to the wyrm's side, lays my hand on its head. The moment my palm touches its skin, the voice jumps into my mind once more.

We beg your pardon, it says. *We mean you no harm, two-leg-walker.*

"My name is… Hadassah," I say.

The wyrm says nothing back. Maybe, I think, it can only hear me in its head, the same way I seem to be hearing its thoughts. I close my eyes and focus on communicating without saying anything out loud.

I'm Hadassah. Not Two-Leg-Walker.

Hadassah-not-two-leg-walker, the voice replies instantly, so I must be doing something right. *It is good.*

Just Hadassah, I say.

Just-Hadassah. It is very good.

I figure we can work on my name later. With a hand still touching the wyrm, I lean close, as if there's an ear to hear me. *How can you understand what I'm saying? How can I understand what you're saying?*

We do not know the meaning of 'saying', it answers. *We are bundled in the flesh—fellow fibers, with one will and one mind. Just-Hadassah calls, and we respond. We call, and Just-Hadassah responds. There is no separation between us.*

Then am I even talking to you at all?

We know no 'talking,' it replies. *We do not hear what your kind calls 'sound' or 'speech.' We perceive your will, your need. That is the nature of our bond.*

Do you mean I'm Sensing your mind? And you're Sensing mine?

We are bundling, it says. *We are joined in the flesh. 'Sensing' is for your kind, and it is very good. But bundling is better.*

I don't understand what that means, but I ask it the question I most need to know. *Can you take us to the tree?*

A feeling of uncertainty flows through our bond, and the wyrm's head moves back and forth the way it did in the Queen's tunnel.

We do not know which tree Just-Hadassah means, it says. *You must show it to us first.*

How can I… I'm about to say, when a stronger than usual vibration flows through me and my mind floods with light.

Is this the tree? the wyrm asks.

Uh-huh, is all I can manage.

It shimmers before me, drenches my eyes with silver. It's utterly beautiful, so much so that tears blur my sight. The tears become droplets on the ripe red fruit, and the droplets flash like rubies in the sun. I'm not sure if I'm seeing the tree or feeling it with my whole body. Maybe, I think, it *is* my whole body. As if I'm not dreaming of *it*, but it's dreaming of *me*. I shiver, and my shivering becomes the wyrm's as we gaze at the tree together.

Can you take us there? I ask.

Its head moves back and forth again, and my heart falls.

You don't know where it is?

An embarrassed apology flows from it to me. *We are sorry, Just-Hadassah. It is beyond the bundle.*

What does that mean?

It is beyond. It lies in its own place. It does not bundle with us.

Then you can't…

We must follow the path, it says in a stronger voice, as if it's made up its mind. *To the-place-of-which-little-remains. This path we know. There we may learn of the further path we must take.*

Wait. Is that the way the map says to go?

For the first time, it makes no effort to answer me directly. *We will take you there,* is all it says. *We will go fast, Just-Hadassah. Do not fear.*

It's not Just-Hadassah, I say. *It's just…*

I startle as the connection is broken. When I open my eyes, I find myself seated on the front bucket-thing, just behind the wyrm's blunt snout. Leah must have lifted me there while I was talking to the wyrm, or bundling with it, or whatever. She swings herself into the seat behind me, followed by the other three. I wish Peter would stumble or slip for once in his life, but he climbs aboard easily and sits there staring into the forest as if he's done this a hundred times before.

Leah wraps her arms around my middle. "Whenever you're ready," she says.

I look down at my mom. She's smiling, but her eyes are bright. I want to tell her I'm not ready, that I still don't know where we're going, that this wyrm she partnered me with doesn't know either and might be leading us into the middle of nowhere, or a different middle of nowhere than the map shows. I want to say all of that and more, but the main thing I want to say is that I'm afraid I'll never see her again.

"Go," she says, reaching up to touch my cheek. "And hold on tight."

I swallow hard, then grip the reins looped over the wyrm's back. Some instinct I didn't know I had tells me to lean forward and tap its snout. I'm not prepared for how fast it responds to my touch. My fingers have barely brushed against its slimy coating when it rockets through the front gate and into the forest.

I take a long look back, but my mom is already lost from sight.

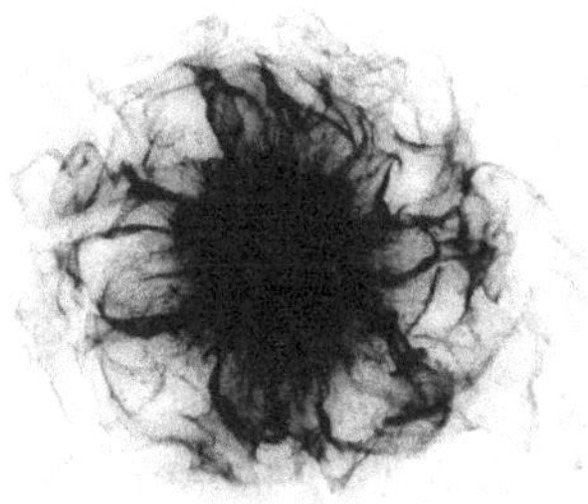

THE FOREST TOSSES trees at my face. That's what it looks like from my perch near the speeding wyrm's snout. Every time I see the branches of an ache or hexlox coming, I duck, but the wyrm zooms past them without a single twig touching my cheek. That doesn't stop the dust from stinging my eyes, which is what I plan to tell Leah if she asks why they're wet.

In no time at all, we're deep in the forest, with just enough sunlight sneaking through the canopy to paint yellow polka dots on the green. I can tell by the sun that we're heading west, but that's the only thing I can tell. I relax my grip on the reins slightly, then lean forward and open my mind to the wyrm.

Hello? I say. *Are you there?*

At first, there's nothing. Then I feel a series of pulses coming from the creature's body, like a heartbeat except much stronger. When I lift my head, I'm startled to see the forest lit up as if with millions of flameflies, the shapes of ache trees and stabbing nettle bushes and Great Horned Howls glowing in cocoons of golden threads the way Mom says they're supposed to. I realize that I'm Sensing, but far better than I ever have before. Hardly believing it, I lay a palm flat on the wyrm's flesh, and the threads glow even brighter. I'm about to ask it what's going on when I feel ripples of amusement surfacing from deep inside it and racing up my arm to my chest, where they tingle like warm soapy water.

What's so funny? I ask.

We beg your pardon, it answers. *Just-Hadassah knows little about our kind, is that not so?*

I haven't exactly had a chance to learn, I say. *And my name is Hadassah, not Just-Hadassah.*

You are Hadassah?

That's right.

You-Hadassah, it says. *This is very good.*

I'm about to correct it again, but I decide *You-Hadassah* is close enough. *You were about to tell me something.*

We were? it asks. *Ah, yes. We were about to tell that since you-Hadassah have not exactly had a chance to learn about our kind, you-Hadassah must not exactly have had a chance to learn that our kind are fiber-bundle. We bundle with the wild-world and all wild-things.*

What does that even mean?

It's quiet for a minute, as if it's thinking the question over. I can actually *feel* thoughts, or whatever is closest to thoughts for a wyrm, running up and down the length of its body, like a chain of static shocks from shaking out a blanket on a cold morning.

The wild-world is fiber-bundle, it says at last. *What your kind call nerves.*

Nerves?

Are we wrong-speaking?

No, I say. *I just never thought of it that way.*

It makes a sign of approval. *Fiber-bundle runs through the wild-world, and through all wild-things. But our kind is all-fiber-bundle. Give or take,* it adds. *We have extra parts for eating.*

So, I try to translate, *the wild-world—the Ecosystem—is like a giant nervous system? And you're a particularly big part of it?*

We are one with the bundle, it answers. *Excuse us.*

I'm not sure what it's excusing itself for until it rears high, then plunges into a huge hole that must have been dug by one of its own kind. I expect darkness, but instead, there are golden threads down here too, wrapped around everything from tree roots to molusks to other wyrms, though none of them are as large or fast as the one I'm riding. As if it can feel my eyes growing wide, the wyrm puts on another burst of speed, and the threads flow past me like sparkling streamers.

As we were saying-not-saying, the wyrm goes on, *the fiber-wild-world is all around us, and there are some of your kind who can—to use the words-not-words of you-Hadassah—'talk' to it. The two-leg-walker your kind call Queen joins the fiber-bundle in the flesh, and so can make it act at will, just as you-Hadassah can make your two-hands lift or your two-legs run. But our kind, we are one with the bundle. And so your kind can reach into the wild-world-fiber-bundle with us and through us.*

I think that over. *So you can strengthen our Sense. Our nerves.*

It nods.

And that's what you did to me just now, I say. *You attuned me to the Ecosystem. You… you made me part of the fiber-bundle that's you.*

It expresses delight that I've caught on so fast. The next

second, my stomach jumps to the roof of my mouth as the wyrm descends to a deeper level. The second after that, my insides reverse course as the creature arrows straight upward and bursts into the sun-and-shade lit forest again. Once my guts have stopped wobbling around, I lean close and whisper to the wyrm with my mind.

Thank you, I say. *For showing me your world.*

Its delight deepens. My heart glows at the simple pleasure it takes in our bond.

I feel like I should ask you your name, I tell it.

We are honored that you-Hadassah should ask us this, it answers. *But we have no idea what you-Hadassah should be asking-not-saying.*

Your name? Don't you have one?

We do not know, it answers. *What is this 'name' that we do not have?*

It's… what you're called, I say. *Like I told you I'm called Hadassah. Don't wyrms have names?*

Our kind are fiber-bundle, it answers. *Strands of a much larger strand. For what purpose would we call one strand something different from another?*

I don't have an answer to that. Still, I don't want to spend this whole trip calling it *the wyrm.*

Would it be okay if I gave you a name? I ask. *I wouldn't forget that you're part of a larger fiber-bundle, but having a name to call you would make it easier for me to talk to you.*

And why is this?

I don't know, I say. *People just like to give things names, I guess.*

The wyrm mulls that over.

Your kind are peculiar, it says. *But we do not object to being given this… name.*

It falls silent, as if it expects me to give it a name this instant. Except now that it's not talking—or thinking, or bundling—I realize that I have no idea what its name should be. We had a pet fell-cat once that I named Mister Suzy-Boy, but I was only a year older than Tovah at the time. It ran off, as fell-cats do, and never returned except to leave the carcasses of much larger animals on our doorstep. This wyrm is no pet, that's for sure, and the thought of giving such a mighty creature a name seems so intimidating I wish I'd never suggested it.

Still, I *did* suggest it. And the wyrm's waiting—twiddling its thumbs, more or less, if it had thumbs to twiddle. A thought pops into my head, probably a stupid one, but it's the best I can come up with.

My dad read a book to me when I was five, I say. *About giant snakes with wings. They were only make-believe, but I thought they were real at the time.*

We are not a giant snake, the wyrm says. *Nor do we have wings.*

No, I know. But you're long and skinny like a snake, and you move so fast, it's as if you have wings. So maybe I could call you…

Giant-snake-with-wings?

Wyvern, I say. *That was my favorite type of winged snake from the book. They had two legs, but I don't think that matters.*

Wyvern? it asks, and I hear the skepticism in every fiber of its being.

Forget it, I say.

Wyvern, it says as if it's rolling the word around on its

tongue, another thing it doesn't have. *You will be Hadassah, and we will be Wyvern. That is what we will name each other.*

I won't be Hadassah, I say. *I am Hadassah. That's what my mom and dad named me when I was born.*

Wyvern sighs through the entire length of its body.

Your kind are most peculiar, it says. *But so it shall be, you-Hadassah-named-by-mother-father. Now sit still, and we-Wyvern will instruct you-Hadassah further in bundling.*

And we're going to the village, right? I ask. *That's where this path leads.*

Wyvern answers with a satisfied nod. *We are bundled in the flesh,* it says. *You-Hadassah know our will, as we-Wyvern know yours. We go to the-place-of-which-little-remains, and there we will seek what we seek.*

I pat Wyvern's flank and rest against my seat-bucket. Though I know the map points us much farther to the west, the thought that we're going to stop over in the village where Mom and Dad and Sarah were born gives me an odd feeling of peace, as if I'm going home. I close my eyes and slip back into the bundle, watching the golden threads spool out in front of us like lanterns lighting our way.

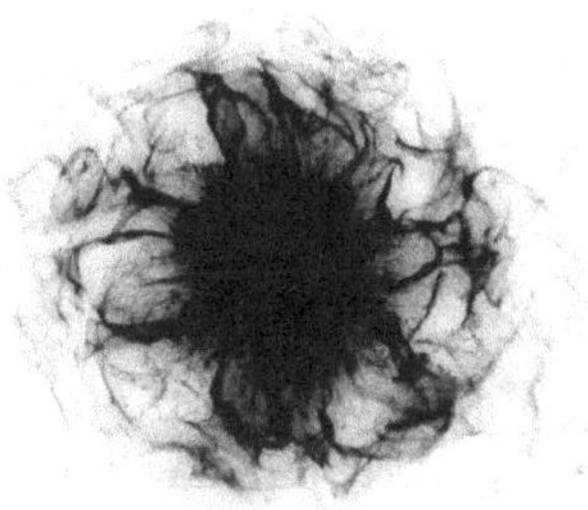

We ride until mid-afternoon, when Leah calls a break for lunch. Wyvern has shown no signs of tiring, but we humans are hungry, not to mention stiff from being crammed into our seat-buckets. As I climb painfully to the ground, I think it wouldn't be such a bad thing to be nothing but a bundle of fibers.

Wyvern disappears into a wyrm-hole while Simon and Catherine start a fire to cook our stew. It doesn't smell anything like the savory dishes Dad makes, but my stomach grumbles just the same. With no job to do, I sit on the forest leaves and try to rake the bugs out of my hair. It would be a lot easier if I had a mirror, but I guess that's one of a thousand things I'm going to have to learn to live without.

Leah approaches me when I'm finished. "You holding up okay?" she asks.

I miss home, and I'm sick to death with worry about Dad, but if I tell her that, I'm sure I'll start bawling. "How far have we gone?"

"Not far by wyrm-measures," she says. "Only about six leagues."

"*Six* leagues? But that's—"

"Almost halfway to the village. Which I assume is where we're headed?"

There's no accusation in her voice, but I feel the need

to apologize anyway. "Wyver—I mean, the wyrm thought this would be the best way to go. I think it wants to look for something."

Leah frowns. "In the village? The tree's not there."

"No," I say. "But maybe..." *Maybe Sarah is,* I want to say, but can't. It sounds like such a little kid thing to say. "Mom's map points west. So at least the village starts us off in the right direction."

Leah studies me silently. I brace for what she's about to say: that the village is leagues and leagues short of the three rivers, that we shouldn't be wasting time searching in a place where we know we're not going to find what we're looking for. I'm getting a response ready when, to my surprise, her eyes grow bright.

"Your mom probably told you about me and Sarah," she says.

"Um," I say. "Not really?"

She sighs deeply. "We had a... disagreement. Or more like a fight. The last time she visited the City of the Queens."

I don't want to butt in, but she was the one who raised the subject. "What about?"

"It was my fault," Leah says. "I'd been asking Sarah for years why she didn't visit more often, and she would never give me a good answer. Finally, I got mad. I told her she didn't know what true happiness was, that she had friends who loved her, but that she was hex-bent on pushing them away." She kicks angrily at the ground. "Sarah left in a huff, and that was the last time I saw her."

I reach out to take Leah's hand. "She's alive," I say. "I know she is. I *feel* it."

"I wish I had your confidence," she says. "But I guess..."

She takes another deep breath, then lets my hand go and reaches for my bag.

"It'll be a while before lunch is ready," she says. "Let's see what you've got."

She opens the pack, rummages around inside. When she pulls out the knife Mom gave me, she fake-winces.

"Miriam's been cooped up in the City of the Queens too long," she says, appraising the blade with her head cocked to the side. "This might be good for poking you in the butt, but not much else."

She wraps the knife in a strip of cloth and tosses it into the bag. Then she pulls her short sword from its sheath and holds it out to me, one hand on the handle while the flat of the blade rests on her other palm.

"The first thing to know about using a blade," she says, "is to keep it where you can get to it fast. I expect you to wear this from now on."

She unbuckles the belt that holds the sheath, then makes me stand so she can buckle it onto me. She has to tighten it to the very last hole before it fits, and even then, it feels loose above my hips.

"The sword goes in like so," she says, showing me. "And it comes out the same way, in one fluid motion. If it gets caught, you're doing it wrong."

I grip the handle and try to pull the sword free. It catches on the leather, and it won't come loose no matter how hard I pull. There's a horrific squeak that makes us both cringe.

"Stop," Leah says. "Let the sword settle back into its scabbard, then pull it out gently, like your hand is reaching for something and you're not holding a blade at all."

I try again. It sticks again. Leah kneels and makes a minor adjustment to where the scabbard hangs at my side, rearranges my fingers around the sword handle. Then she stands and nods.

"Again," she says.

I pull, and the sword comes free so easily I almost swipe my teacher across the belly.

"Whoa, tyger," she says. "How does it feel?"

"Heavy," I admit, because now that I'm holding it, the wickedly sharp point drags my hand toward the ground. "Like, *really* heavy."

"No better way to build muscle," she says, flexing her biceps through her chain-metal shirt. "Maybe we should start with two hands."

I wrap my other hand around the sword handle and hold the blade up in front of me. It still feels heavy, and I don't like the way the point dances right in front of my eyes, as if I might accidentally walk into it. Leah notices at once.

"Eyes on me," she says. "You have to trust the sword to do what you want it to."

"I can't even swing it," I say, which is true, because with both hands holding it, if I try to swing, my arms will get crossed up.

"We are *so* not there yet," Leah says. "First, you have to learn the positions. Technically, these are for the longsword, but you're not ready for that, so..."

She stands behind me, wraps her arms around my waist to hold my hands. Gently, she guides my arms upward until the sword is at shoulder height, parallel to the ground. She freezes me like that and says, "Tox."

My ears burn. "What?"

"It's just a word, Hadassah," she says. "A word for the position."

She lowers the sword until it's at my waist, jutting straight out, and says, "Plow." She lets that sink in for a moment before guiding my arms downward until the sword is pointing at the ground the way it was before and says, "Fool."

"Just a word, right?"

"You got it," she says. "Last one." She raises my arms all the way above my head, so I could basically scratch my back with the tip of the sword, and says, "Roof." She spins me around, waving the blade away before it nicks her. "That's it. Four positions. Easy, right?"

I smile. Weakly, because the sword feels even heavier than when we started. "But what are they *for*?"

"They're the basics of fighting technique," she says. "Defense, offense. They were developed hundreds of years ago, long before the rise of the Ecosystem. Aurelia taught them to me when I was her student."

Now I'm impressed. Captain Aurelia was a legend in the city. "When did she teach you?" I ask, and realize I'm panting from holding the heavy blade.

"You can put that back now," Leah says. "Remember: smooth and easy."

I slide the sword into its scabbard. My arms tremble with fatigue, but it doesn't get stuck.

"I learned to fight during the War of the Queens," Leah says. "I was a seamstress back in the village, so I'd never laid hands on a weapon more dangerous than a needle. No one had except the Sensors. And I guess the threshers, if you count their scythes."

"Like my dad."

"That's right," she says. "But your dad learned how to fight by watching Sarah. Sensor technique was more like mixed martial arts. Aurelia was totally old school: longsword, attack and counterattack, classical stance and footwork. Which we're not even close to covering yet. There's a lot to learn."

"How long did it take you until you got good?"

"Until I could swing a sword without the risk of killing myself?" she asks. "A week. Until I could fight with nobody telling me what to do against an adversary that might have anything from claws to teeth to prehensile stingers?" She shrugs. "Once you learn the basics, your body responds when it needs to. You'll see."

I nod, but I'm not reassured. Sweat is dripping down my face, my arms are quivering from two minutes of holding a pee-wee sword, and I can't remember the name of the second position. Catherine and Simon are studying me over their simmering pot, and I see now why they make such good partners: their mocking smiles are a perfect match. Even worse, Peter is smirking the way he does when I've made a particularly stupid mistake during Sensor training. I wish Wyvern hadn't disappeared to take care of underground wyrm-things. *It* wouldn't smirk at me, and not only because it doesn't have the right kind of mouth to smirk with.

Leah glances over her shoulder at the others, then steps close. "Do you know what Sarah used to say you should do when people stare at you?"

"I know," I say. "Ignore them."

"Nope." She grins. "Stare right back."

And she does, until the guards turn away and Peter gets much more interested in a family of bamboons chattering and grooming nearby. With their nimble fingers and leathery canine snouts, they look both innocent and devilish.

"Soup's on," Leah says. "We have to build up those muscles for tonight's training session."

She gives my hand a squeeze before heading over. With the sword clattering at my side, I follow. The smell of the stew makes my mouth water, but the main thing on my mind is how to sit down in front of the others without jabbing myself in the rear end.

I almost succeed.

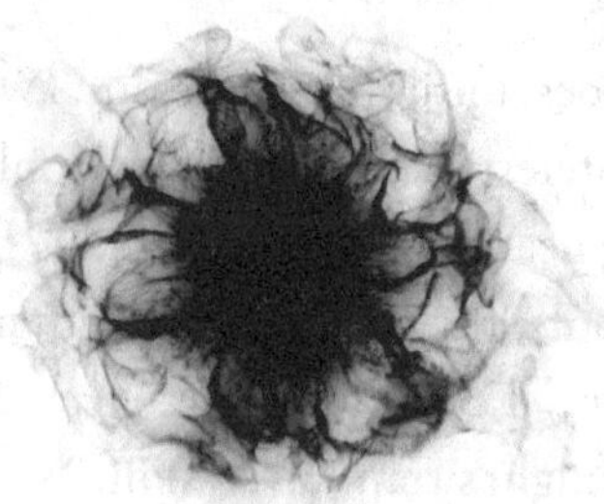

The rest of the day passes in a blur of activity: sword-fighting lessons with Leah when we stop to stretch, fiber-bundling sessions with Wyvern when we climb back aboard to ride through the forest. I'm so busy, I don't have a chance to miss home, much.

Which is probably the real point of Leah's lessons. The sword doesn't get any lighter throughout the day, but she works me so hard at it, I quickly learn to shift positions without her having to guide me. I'm not sure why whoever made up this style of fighting called the first position "Tox," the name of a plodding four-footed animal that used to pull people's plows and wagons. But every time I take a step while I'm holding the sword, I feel as if I've got four feet, so maybe it makes sense.

Bundling with Wyvern is a totally different story. It's effortless, probably because all I'm doing is closing my eyes and letting the wyrm connect me to the Ecosystem. I'm not sure it's as different from Sensing as Wyvern seems to think, or maybe humans, not being all nerve fiber, can't truly bundle the way wyrms can. All I know is that when Wyvern's power flows through me, I'm amazed by how many golden threads of life there are to see: tree roots sucking up water, baby birds developing inside eggs, microscopic life-forms by the millions squirming in the soil. Mom used to tell her class that when we became Sensors, we'd be aware of all of these things at once, but I guess I never truly believed her until now.

The most important thing that happens when we bundle is that I see Sarah's tree even more clearly than I saw it in the Queen's garden. It glows in the darkness behind my closed eyes, and sometimes, when I open them, I see it floating in the air in front of me. I *hear* it, too, which I've never been able to do before: it makes a low humming sound that keeps time with the pulsing of its silver light. Actually, when I stop to think about it, I'm not sure if it's the tree that's making the sound or if something inside *me* is vibrating in response to it, because the vision is so strong I lose track of where I end and the tree begins. Either way, I feel as if the tree is as real, as solid, as the giant aches and mauls that whip past us while we race through the forest.

The only difference is that I know where those trees are, but I still don't have the faintest idea where *the* tree is.

It puzzles me. I can see it more and more clearly with each passing hour, but I can't see anything that surrounds it, anything that might tell me where to find it. It floats like an island in a sea of darkness, and every time I try to pierce through the dark, it's as if a wall comes crashing down in front of me. I can't understand why, if Sarah wanted me to find the tree like Mom said, she wouldn't have just told me how to get there. Maybe she tried to tell me but couldn't. Maybe the tree really *doesn't* want to be found, and the vision in my mind is leading us in the wrong direction. Or maybe—and this is the worst thought of all—the tree isn't real to begin with, and everybody, from Mom to Leah to me, is chasing after a phantom Sarah dreamed up to play some kind of queen's trick on us all.

I wish I could share my worries with Wyvern. But the wyrm seems so joyful whenever we bundle, I don't want to spoil its mood.

You-Hadassah have learned much from we-Wyvern, it purrs while I rock drowsily in my seat after a dinnertime sword-fighting lesson that dragged on into dusk. *Soon, you will bundle without we-Wyvern's help.*

That'll be the day, I sigh.

It is nighttime now, Wyvern responds. *So if we-Wyvern understand you-Hadassah correctly, the day that it will be will not be until morning?*

I decide not to go into a discussion about that. Wyvern is beginning to grasp how human beings think, but its wyrm-mind can be awfully literal.

I've been meaning to ask you something, I say.

We-Wyvern have been meaning to listen.

Okay, I say. *So what I wanted to know is… are you a boy, or a girl? It doesn't feel right to keep thinking of you as an 'it'.*

We-Wyvern are most assuredly not an 'it', the answer comes. *'It'-things are not fibers, and do not bundle.*

So you're a boy? For some reason, I've started to think of him that way.

But Wyvern signals a strong *no. We-Wyvern do not understand what you-Hadassah mean by 'boy' or 'girl'. We-Wyvern would like more you-Hadassah-words, please.*

Well…. I try to come up with an explanation that will make sense to a wyrm. *I'm a girl, and so is Leah, and Catherine. And my mom and the Queen, too. But Simon and Peter are boys. We're… different.*

Your kind are all different, Wyvern answers. *But then, your kind are all the same.*

I'm sorry?

We-Wyvern are wyrm, the words come. *You-Hadassah are human. Different, but all one fiber-bundle. Is 'boy' or 'girl' not part of the same?*

I.... I guess so.

Wyvern's head nods in approval. *Then we-Wyvern are not 'boy' or 'girl'. We-Wyvern are fiber-bundle.*

But it takes both boys and girls to make... you know.

Wyvern chuckles. *Not for our kind. We-Wyvern can make more wyrms without 'boy' or 'girl.'*

Then you mean you're... both?

We-Wyvern are fiber-bundle, is all the answer I get. *'Boy' or 'girl' might be very good to you-Hadassah, namer-of-separate-things. To we-Wyvern, it is all one.*

I'm not sure I understand, but I'm too tired to ask how one wyrm-fiber-bundle makes other wyrm-fiber-bundles, so I simply pat Wyvern's flank, close my eyes, and fall back into our shared thoughts as we plunge ahead through the darkening trees. The last thing I hear before I drift off to sleep is Wyvern's voice, and the last thing I see is the tree shining like a star in the night.

From now on, I decide, I'm going to call Wyvern *they.*

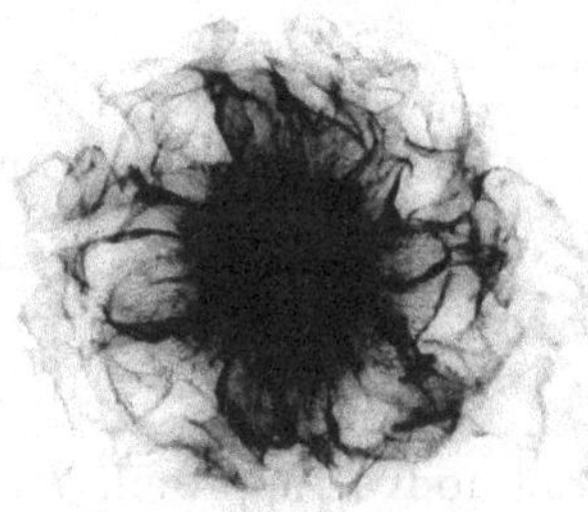

I'm awakened by a gentle shake on my shoulder. I open my eyes to see Leah's face. For a split-second, the image of Sarah's tree seems to form a halo around her hair, but then I realize that it's the bright light of the risen sun. I must have been dreaming about the tree all night long.

"We're here," Leah says, throwing her leg over Wyvern's back to dismount.

"Where?"

"The village," she says. "Come take a look."

She helps me down. The others are making breakfast—or at least, the guards are, while Peter stands by himself staring into the distance. Leah leads me through a stand of young ache trees until we reach a circular clearing a hundred or more yards wide. Sunlight sparkles on a level field that's as black as loam, though it crunches strangely when we step on it. Farther on, there's another circular plot of ground covered in grabgrass. To the right of that, twenty or so crabapple trees are laid out in neat rows. The small wrinkled crabapples open and close their claws to snap at the bugs and breeze.

"Where's the village?" I ask, looking around.

"You're standing on it," Leah says. "There's not much left."

"There's not *anything* left."

"There are a few things," Leah says. "Like this circle:

that's where the firestarters used to burn away the grabgrass so it wouldn't get too close to the village stone. Funny that nothing ever grew over it in all this time."

She stoops and picks up a handful of black earth, then runs a finger through it, tracing trails on her palm. Fine grains flash like buried jewels. She rubs her hands together, the cinders sifting back to the ground.

"Over there is where the town hall was," she says, pointing to a few moss-covered rocks that poke above the grabgrass. "That was the biggest building by far, probably thirty times the size of any of the houses. We gathered there for ceremonies and things."

Like Mom and Dad's almost-wedding, I think.

Leah shields her eyes from the sun as she scans the plain. "I don't see much else. The rest must have been reclaimed by the Ecosystem."

"In only fifteen years?"

She smiles. "That's a long time for the Ecosystem. It's a long time for *you.* All this happened well before you were born."

Thinking about that makes a pang of homesickness shoot through me. I touch the token around my neck and realize it's even more precious than I knew, one of the last pieces of this place that's survived over time.

We stand there for long minutes, not talking, the wind ruffling my hair. Leah starts to say something, stops, smiles instead. A nudge at my elbow makes me look down to find that Wyvern has slithered silently up to us—or maybe under us—and is gesturing with their snout toward the crabapple trees.

It is as we-Wyvern surmised, they say. *This grove belongs to the earth-walker.*

Who?

The one we seek. The one who bundles with you-Hadassah-tree.

Do you mean Sarah?

Their head bobs up and down. *If we are separate-naming things, yes. The seed-planter, tree-keeper. Here.*

Now? I ask with a wild burst of excitement.

No, Wyvern brings me back to earth. *But before.*

I communicate Wyvern's thoughts to Leah, remembering when she doesn't respond that she can't hear me unless I talk out loud. "The wyrm says that Sarah was here. She planted those trees."

Leah turns her attention to the crabapples. Her eyes sparkle with tears, but a small smile softens her face.

"I wouldn't be surprised," she says. "Queens all have green thumbs."

I'm not sure what the color of somebody's thumbs has to do with anything, but I let it go as one of the many strange things Mom's friends say. "If she was here, maybe she left something for us," I suggest. "Some clue."

"Like what?"

My face warms. "I don't know. But I think that's why the wyrm wanted us to come here first."

"Those trees have stood a long time," Leah says.

"Still," I say. "Can I try? Just for a minute?"

She's got the *about to say no* look on her face, but then she lays a gentle hand on my shoulder.

"While we finish making breakfast," she says. "Take the wyrm. Maybe the two of you can figure something out."

I don't tell her I've already spoken to Wyvern. They slink along by my side as I crunch across the gravelly ground toward the crabapple grove.

Where should we look for clues? I ask.

You-Hadassah look above, they say. *We-Wyvern will look below.*

Without another word, they dive snout-first into the soil. Plumes of black dust and rock spray upward while they gobble a tunnel. In a matter of seconds, they've vanished, the quick flick of their tail a goodbye before they're totally gone.

I walk the remaining distance across the grabgrass, not helped by Wyvern's division of labor. There's a lot of *above.* I stop beside a few trees and look for anything obvious: cut-marks in the trunks, upturned soil by the roots. When my ground-level inspection doesn't turn up any evidence, I squint into the trees' thick foliage while the crabapples try to bend the branches they hang from so they can nip at my hair. I jump when I see huge round eyes staring back at me, but relax when I realize it's only a small mammal with feathered front legs and a long, tapering snout. It stares at me for a second before scampering away, moving so fast it looks as if it's flying from branch to branch instead of jumping.

The ground shakes as Wyvern returns, their head poking above the grass a few paces from where I stand.

Find anything? I ask.

Much food, they answer, waves of satisfaction rolling off their body. *But not-much... clues.*

The way Wyvern says that convinces me that they had no idea what they were looking for. My heart falls at the thought that coming here was nothing more than a blind stab in the dark.

Wyvern, I ask, *why can't you bundle with the tree? Sarah's tree, I mean. Not one of these busybodies,* and I swipe at the annoying apples.

Wyvern shakes their head in the way that means confusion or discomfort. The thoughts that flow from them emerge slowly, hesitantly.

We-Wyvern can bundle with you-Hadassah. And you-Hadassah carry the vision of the tree within. Yet the tree is... it is....

Again, they pause. I feel the strain in their wyrm-thoughts as they try to explain.

We-Wyvern cannot separate the tree-bundle from you-Hadassah-bundle. We-Wyvern cannot find the tree without finding you-Hadassah, and there is no need for that, for you-Hadassah are here, bundled with Wyvern. And so the tree is here, and yet it is not. It is beyond, and yet it is not-beyond.

I'm confused, but what Wyvern is saying sounds enough like my own problem that I have to ask. *Do you mean you can see the tree, but not find it? Is that how it's here and not here at the same time?*

Wyvern shakes their head over and over again. I place a hand on their back to try to calm them down, but even my touch doesn't seem to soothe their agitation.

We-Wyvern do not know what we-Wyvern mean, they say. *We-they-Wyvern-bundle know only that we-they cannot find the tree without finding you-we-Hadassah-bundle, which we-they have already found-not-found.*

A part of my mind that I hope Wyvern can't hear thinks, *Huh?* I pat their head, wishing for a moment I was back at home with Mister Suzy-Boy, sitting in a chair by the fireplace while she kneaded my lap with her sharp claws.

That's okay, I tell them. *Maybe we shouldn't talk about this right now.*

Wyvern nods, but I can tell they're troubled. The shining image of the tree floats into my mind for a second, yet everything around it remains as dark as the black field. I close my eyes and the image grows even brighter, so real I swear I could touch it the way Rebecca did. But when I reach for it, my hand passes through empty air.

"Are you coming to breakfast or not?" a voice says by my ear, startling me out of the vision.

I open my eyes to find Peter right beside me. He doesn't sound like he cares whether I come to breakfast; he sounds like Leah sent him to fetch me against his will. I glare at him as hard as I can, but he won't even look at me, focusing instead on the leaping creature that's become nothing but a dot way off in the ache trees.

"Didn't anyone ever tell you it's rude to stare?" he says.

My ears burn, but my anger burns even hotter.

"Didn't anyone ever tell you it's rude to sneak up on people?" I shoot back.

He shrugs, walks off. I reach out to touch Wyvern's back, only to find that they've disappeared into another of their wyrm-holes. It hits me all at once that, even with Wyvern and Leah trying to help, I'm alone out here in the middle of nowhere, with no sign of Sarah and no way to find the tree that everyone's counting on me to find. Maybe the Queen's vision was right after all. Maybe Sarah is dead, and we're no better than a fell-cat chasing its tail, getting farther and farther away from the people who need us, the people who'll die without us.

I watch Peter walk through the ache trees, his hands in his pockets, and I hate him more than ever. Not because he doesn't care about me. Because he doesn't have to care about anything.

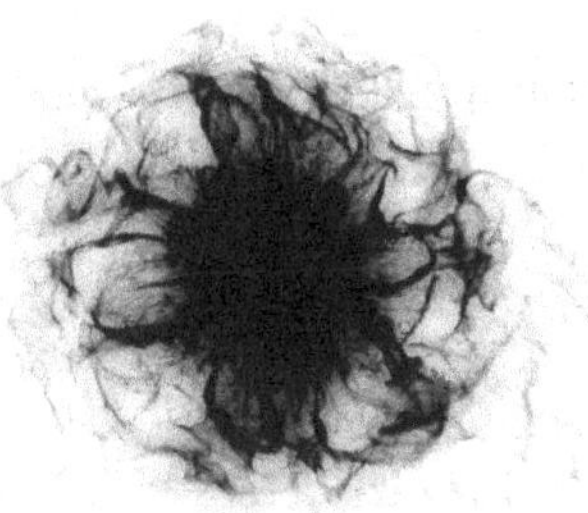

After breakfast, which consists of the typical stew—hot but thin and tasteless—we climb aboard Wyvern for the next leg of the journey. With Mom's map in mind, I touch Wyvern's back, and they take off at top speed through the crabapple grove, angling mostly west and a little north. For some reason, when the remains of the village fall out of sight, I feel almost worse than I did when I left home. As if I'm saying goodbye to a place that might have meant a lot to me, and I'll never be coming back to find out what it might have meant.

Now that the village has turned out to be a dead end, all we've got left is the map. I bundle with Wyvern—something I've gotten good enough at doing that I don't need the wyrm to start the session—and ask them if they've ever been to the three rivers, but I'm not surprised when the answer is no. What that means is that we're heading into *terra incognita* without a guide, and without a clue. I wish I could explain this to Leah, but every time I catch her eye, she gives me the thumbs up, which must mean she has confidence in me.

Either that, or she's as lost as I am.

We stop for lunch in a part of the Ecosystem none of us has ever been in before. The trees are mostly mauls and breaches, red leaves and white bark. Leah tries to interest me in another sword-fighting lesson, but I'm so edgy

I'm afraid I'll stab myself with the blade. I walk off alone after nibbling a few bites of fruit and nuts, and try to stare through the candy-striped trees to locate the *one* tree I need to find.

"That's peculiar," a nasally voice says at my shoulder, and I jump when I realize Peter's snuck up on me again.

"Do you mind?" I ask.

He ignores me. "I'm reasonably certain that's a quetzalcoati."

"A what?"

"Quetzalcoati," he repeats the tongue-twister, then makes it even worse. "*Nasua narica quetzalcoatlus.* Order Carnivora, family Procyonidae, genus Nasua. A feathered arboreal marsupial most common in deciduous forests, though they've been known to inhabit mangrave and leprous swamps. Insectivorous, mostly nocturnal. They're also believed to be extinct, which makes it more than a little striking that that's the third one I've definitively identified in the past two days."

I follow where he's looking, and see a tapered snout and large brown eyes peeking through bright red maul leaves. It's the same kind of animal I saw in Sarah's crabapple grove, and I guess I should be surprised, these things being extinct and all. Mostly I can't get over Peter's speech, which consists of by far the largest number of words I've heard him say, to me or anyone. As if that's not enough, he keeps talking, in that voice that sounds like he's reading from a script.

"I noticed the first one in the forest just outside the City of the Queens," he says. "I didn't think much of it at the time, because I reasoned that I must be mistaken in the identification. I told myself it had to be another member of the Procyonidae family, like a wreckoon, or even of the Ailuridae family, like a red pandalion, *Ailurus fulgens leo*, which are relatively common in the great forest. But then I saw the second one earlier today among the crabapples, which is entirely logical, since the rotting fruit would attract insects for it to feed on. I've never heard of one inhabiting a maul tree, however. There's not much for it to eat there, and the syrup would kill it."

I seem to have lost the ability to speak in direct proportion to him gaining it, because all I can do is stand there with my mouth hanging open.

"This could be an important scientific discovery," he says. "Not the mere fact that the species is still extant, but that they've seemingly developed an affinity for maul leaves. That could help promote the recovery of a breeding population if we're smart about forest management."

Those last words give me my voice back.

"You do know what's happening to the Queen, don't you?" I ask. "My mom explained why we're on this little expedition?"

He shrugs, his eyes fixed on the quetzal thingy. "It never hurts to plan for the future."

I feel like screaming at him. Why did Mom let this stuck-up jerk come with us, anyway? So he could take notes on the future of a forest no one will survive to manage? So he could spout big words like some kind of dictionary while people back home die one by one, their bodies burning up the way the firestarters used to burn up the turf outside the village when Dad was a thresher?

"I don't care about your stupid *forest management*," I say to him. "Or your stupid quetzal-whatever-y."

I pick up a stone from the ground and fling it at the creature that hangs from the tree fifty feet away. My arm must have gotten stronger from all the sword practice, because the rock misses its target by only a few feet. The dumb thing doesn't move, which might explain how it went extinct in the first place. It just stays where it is, feathered front limbs clutching the bark of the tree, dark eyes blinking at me as if it's asking a question.

I stare back, enraged at its boldness. I'm bending for another stone when Peter holds out a hand. Not touching me, but close enough. "You shouldn't—"

"Get away from me," I say, and he steps back, looking at the ground as if he's ashamed.

"Hadassah," he says, which is the first time he's ever called me by my name. "I'm sorry," he adds, which is the first time he's ever said that to anyone. "But don't you think we should investigate this further before we—"

He doesn't get to finish. An arrow whizzes past us, embedding itself with a sharp *thunk* in the maul tree where the creature is hanging. Another arrow follows a moment later, but it misses its mark and sails off into the forest. The animal doesn't move a muscle, not even to hide itself behind the trunk. I turn to see Simon loading another arrow onto his bow. He sights, aims, and lets fly again. He misses, but not by much.

The quetzal blinks at us.

"What are you doing?" Peter says to Simon, who's preparing another arrow. Catherine has come up behind her partner and is unstrapping her bow from her back.

"Getting sick of veggie stew," Simon answers, one eye

closed as he sights along the shaft of his arrow. "Seems like this little creep wants to be tonight's main ingredient."

Peter and I both yell "Stop!" as Simon's fingers release the arrow.

A black shape erupts from the ground, hitting Simon's arm just hard enough that his shot goes wide. He yelps, then drops his bow and yanks his sword free of its scabbard. Before I have a chance to warn him, the guard is wrapped so tightly in Wyvern's coils he can't gather air to shout or scream. His face turns purple, but when Catherine jumps to his aid, Wyvern flicks her away with their tail as if she's nothing more than a grossquito. The wyrm's teeth are extended, and I'm afraid of what they might do.

"Wyvern!" I say out loud, forgetting that they can't hear me. When I touch their snout, the teeth retreat.

Let him go, I say. *He doesn't understand.*

You-Hadassah are unharmed?

I'm fine.

Then we-Wyvern will do as you-Hadassah wish. But please ask-tell two-legs-armor-wearer never to draw sharp-point-thing at you-Hadassah again.

I will, I assure them.

The wyrm's coils fall from the guard like slack ropes. Simon collapses to the ground and lies choking for breath. Catherine leans over her partner, then looks up at me and Peter with a murderous expression on her pretty face. Leah must have been taking a bathroom break, because she comes running up now, hastily buckling her jerkin and glaring at her guards.

"What's the meaning of this?" she demands. Catherine's starting to tell the story—her side of it—when I cut her off.

"Peter saw something in the tree," I say, and point to where the creature hangs. Even with all the commotion, it hasn't budged an inch. "A quetzal… quetzaltotal—"

"Quetzalcoati," Peter corrects me.

"Whatever," I say. "He saw it this morning, and yesterday, too. They're supposed to be extinct. Maybe they *are* extinct. Which means the one he saw—"

"Three," he jumps in again.

"*One*," I say. "It's the same one. It's following us, don't you see? Or it wants *us* to follow it. Who has the power to bring extinct animals back to life?"

"The queens of old could create new species," Leah says. "Like Celestina's silverbloom bushes. I assume they could use the same process to recreate something that was gone. Not a specific individual, but—"

"A hybrid," Peter says, his nasal voice rising with excitement. "That's what Celestina informed me her silverbloom flowers are. She explained that not even a queen can create something out of nothing, but they *can* recombine genes to generate something new." He looks at me for the first time, and his pale eyes shine. "That's why I had trouble identifying the quetzal, and why it's not affected by maul tree venom. It's not a true member of the species, but a hybrid created by splicing quetzal genes with those of other species. The admixture was chosen carefully, too, because quick as traditional quetzalcoatis were, they could never have kept up with wyrm-riders. Which means she—"

"Wait a minute," Leah says. "Who's *she*?"

"Who else could *she* be?" I ask. "There's only one queen who'd want us to follow her trail." I smile at Peter, who actually smiles back. "And that's Sarah."

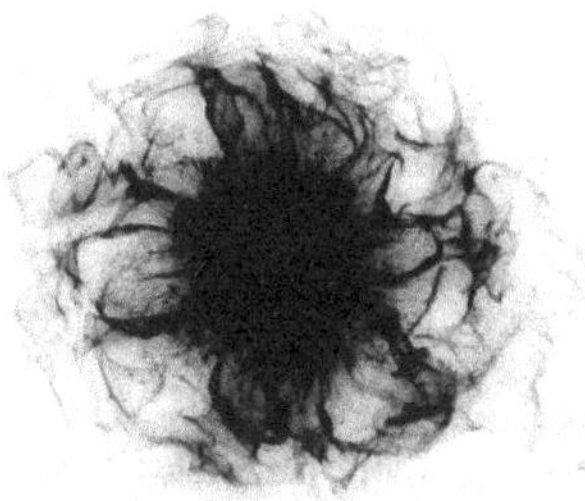

Wyvern is impressed by me and Peter's detective work. So is Leah. Not to brag, but so am I.

The guards, on the other hand, are angry about missing their meal and about Wyvern's attack on Simon. They rummage around in the bushes to retrieve their lost arrows, grumbling under their breath and taking far more time than they need to. I wonder if Wyvern was right, and if Simon actually was planning to go after me with his sword.

We douse our fire, pack our supplies, and grab still-steaming bowls of stew while we clamber aboard Wyvern's back. The quetzal stays glued to the tree, watching us patiently. I have to remind myself that there's still no proof Sarah's alive; maybe the creature will only lead us to the place where she died. But when I look at Leah, I see in her face the same hope I'm sure is in mine.

Peter takes the seat behind me, while Leah sits one space closer to her guards, eyeing them with suspicion. I touch Wyvern's snout and feel our minds merge.

You know what to do, I say to the wyrm. Then, to everyone else, "We're following that quetzal-copy."

"Quetzal*coati*," Peter says in his weirdly mechanical voice, then has to grab onto his bridle as Wyvern plunges into the forest.

We speed through the trees with the quetzal skittering from branch to branch just ahead. If I thought Wyvern was fast before, I realize that they were holding back, probably because they weren't sure where they were going. I give up on trying to sip from my bowl, since the broth only ends up in my eyes. My hunger, though, has vanished, replaced by urgency and excitement. I feel Wyvern humming with energy, and when I bundle with them, electric tingles raise every hair on my head.

Wyvern, I say. *Did you know her?*

Did we-Wyvern know her-who?

Don't be coy, I say. *Her.*

The wyrm seems abashed, but answers.

We-Wyvern know her in the bundle, they say. *We-Wyvern are brood of the queen-wyrm, mother-father of many. She-he-they knew the earth-walker, seed-bringer. And as such, so do we-Wyvern.*

You mean your… mother-father was Sarah's wyrm? The one that defended the city with her during the War of the Queens?

Wyvern replies in the affirmative. *We-they are bundled with our mother-father then, now, and forever. We-Wyvern were born of their flesh, and know their mind. The earth-walker is part of their bundle, and then-now-always will be.*

I blink into the stinging wind. For a minute, I wish I were a wyrm, so I could know what it means to hold onto someone forever. Not just in memory, the way Rebecca talked about Sarah during the funeral. For them to be a part of me, and me a part of them, now and for all time.

Pick up the pace, I say to Wyvern, trying for a lighthearted tone. *Are you going to let a little quetzal-cozy outrun you?*

I eat my words—literally—when Wyvern puts on a fresh burst of speed that leaves me gasping for breath.

In minutes, we exit the maul-and-breach tree grove into a stretch of open turf where half-grown aches are spread widely across rolling plains. My heart leaps at the thought that we might have entered the blank space on Sarah's map, but I remind myself that that's impossible; we haven't even reached the three rivers, and the blank is only on the map anyway, not in real life. The quetzal scampers ahead of us, covering ground faster than something its size has any right to. Every so often, it launches itself at one of the trees, and when it does, its brown-and-tan feathers flash in the sunlight. Behind me, Peter is mumbling under his breath.

"What?" I scream over my shoulder, the word whipped from my mouth into the slipstream.

"It's actually *flying*," he shouts back, right in my ear. "True flight, not gliding the way an unmixed quetzal achieves locomotion."

I squint at the thing. "How can you tell?"

"Note how the front arms move when it leaves the ground," he says. "They're flapping, which indicates that it's using its pectoral muscles to generate thrust. And the primary feathers extend beyond the claws when it's in flight, which means that the feathers aren't simply buoying the body on air currents or thermals, but that they're designed to sustain lift."

I look as closely as I can the next time the quetzal takes off, but it's moving too fast for me to pick up any of the details Peter's talking about.

"This is incredible!" he shouts.

I decide not to tell him he just spat in my ear. "What is?"

"She actually mixed quetzal genes with *bird* genes," he says. "In the case of true quetzals, the feathers are only mutated hair follicles. The rest of their anatomy is pure mammalian. But Queen Sarah must have manipulated the genes from birds to fashion the structural adaptations necessary to render a creature capable of flight. My best postulate is that she used raptors, but in theory it could have been one of the larger passerines."

I glance over my shoulder and see that he's leaning forward, which would explain the spitting in my ear. Despite how much he's blabbing away, I get the feeling that he's not really talking to *me*; he's totally focused on the quetzalbird, as if he really is taking notes for a book. His voice stops and starts the way the gigantic gear in the Queen's tunnel did when Wyvern first started to move it, which makes it sound like he's testing the words out loud then pausing while some other part of his brain writes them down.

"How do you know so much?" I ask.

He startles as if he forgot I was there. Then he blinks and looks away.

"I had to study extensively to prepare for admittance to the Sensor corps," he says. "I spent months in the library before I was ready to take the preliminary tests. None of it comes naturally to me."

"It sure seems like it does."

He shakes his head. "I wasn't born with the right genes."

"Oh." I try to think what Mom would say to that. "Anyone can join the order, if they're motivated enough."

He sniffs. "You've memorized the slogan."

"It's true," I say. "My mom doesn't discriminate against

people based on their genetic history. She only looks for talent and commitment."

"I'm sure that's easy for you to say," he replies. "Your mom and dad both have incredibly high concentrations of *A. impunita* genes, which means you're naturally talented beyond anyone else in class."

"What are you talking about?" I ask. "Sensing is hard for me, too!"

"Maybe," he says with a scowl. "But I'd kill to have your gift."

I try a laugh to defuse the tension. "You've seen the way my mom criticizes me. Not much of a gift."

"That's only because you don't try," he says, his face taking on the superior smirk I've seen so many times before. "I'm nothing but a technician out in the field, forced to calculate everything by measurement and formula. You were ushered into the Queen's Corps by default, not due to effort."

"So what, now I'm spoiled *and* lazy?" I demand, glaring at him so hard I forget to look where the quetzal is going.

He doesn't answer, but his lips curl into a nasty sneer.

"You think this is easy for me, Peter?" I say. "You think I'm having a great time out here chasing after something that might only be a fairy tale? Thanks to the stupid tree, my dad is sick, maybe dying. How's *your* dad doing?"

"My dad died when I was ten years old," he says. "So you can stop congratulating yourself on having the world's worst sob story."

He looks away, and after a moment, I do, too.

I relocate the quetzal, but my mind keeps drifting to the boy who's stewing right behind me. I guess I understand now why he's always seemed so obnoxious, why he acts like he enjoys watching me mess up in class so much. I feel bad that he lost his dad, and that he thinks of himself as a stranger surrounded by people with gifts he'll never have. I feel sorry for him, I really do.

But if I'm being honest, I have to admit I feel even sorrier for myself.

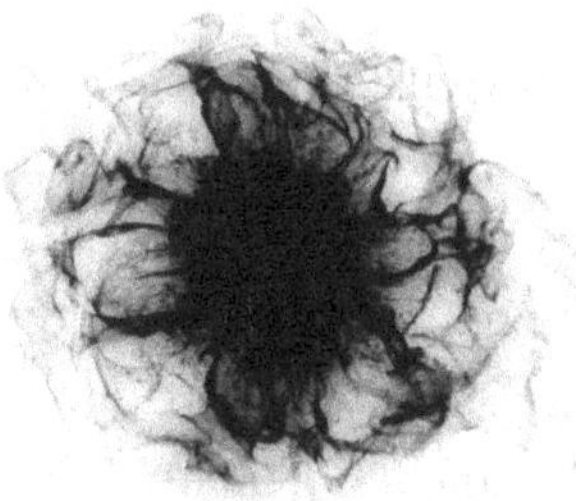

Five whole days pass in virtual silence.

Five days of flying over flat, open plains alternating with dense patches of forest, the trees growing taller and darker and weirder with each league we travel north and west. Five days of barely pausing for meals or bathroom breaks as we follow the quetzal, hoping it's truly leading us where we want to go. Other than my thought-talks with Wyvern, the only sound I hear that whole time is the wind whistling in my ears. Even Wyvern is less talkative—or thinkative—than usual, as if they're focusing as hard on reaching our destination as I am. It would help if Peter showed some of the excitement he did on the first day, but he's clammed up entirely, and though he takes his spot behind me each morning, he might as well not be there at all.

We stop at night, because unlike wyrms, quetzals—even hybrid ones—can't go without sleep. I spend the few minutes between supper and bedtime practicing sword-fighting with Leah, even though it gets to the point where my arm feels like it's about to fall off. The guards don't say a word to me, but they glare at me darkly as we sit around our campfire. Especially Catherine, who I'm starting to think is more than just Simon's partner. Peter pays no attention to any of us, preferring to wander off and study the landscape. He scribbles away with a graphite stick in a little notebook, but I never try to come close enough to read his words.

Instead, I wrap myself in my blanket and turn my back on him, telling myself I don't care what amazing wildlife management theory he's working on anyway.

On the fifth night, we bed down in a forest where the trees have gray bark and sweet-smelling white stuff drifting down from the branches. When I bundle with Wyvern, I Sense that the trees are called rotten trees, and that the white stuff will make you sick if you eat it. I tell Leah, who passes the information along to everyone else—a good thing, since Simon is staring at it hungrily like he wishes he could add it to tonight's meal. Peter wanders through the trees and scribbles down notes furiously, so I guess we've finally reached a place where he doesn't know everything about everything.

I lie in bed trying to sleep, annoyed by the bits of rotten tree fluff that keep tickling my nostrils. I'm exhausted from today's ride and anxious that we haven't reached the three rivers yet, but every time I close my eyes, they pop open as if they expect to see something that wasn't there two seconds ago. To spite them, I squeeze them shut and count to a thousand. The night is quiet except for the hooting of a bird I can't identify. I wonder if Peter can.

Then I hear a whisper at my ear. "Hadassah. Wake up."

I open my eyes, not realizing I fell asleep. There's a dark figure crouching by my side, but it's not Leah.

It's Sarah.

I jump up in bed, flinging my arms around her. She pulls me close, and I smell her scent, rich and earthy as always. I can't believe she's here, but when I look over her shoulder, I see the quetzal roosting in one of the rotten trees, and I realize it must have led us right to her. Maybe,

I think, it led us to *the* tree as well. As soon as I think that, I feel guilty. Finding Sarah after all this time should be enough, shouldn't it?

"How did you get here?" I ask her in a whisper.

"I've been waiting here all along," she says. "I was wondering when you'd find me."

"I didn't think we ever would," I admit. "Sarah—do you know what's happening in the city?"

She nods.

"And can you help? Do you know how to heal the Queen?"

She shakes her head. It's a sudden, definite motion, like a hatchet chopping through a piece of firewood.

"What can we do?" I ask.

"I'm impressed you made it this far," she says. "The rest is going to be even harder."

"But—"

She doesn't wait to hear what I was going to say, not that I knew what I was going to say. She stands, smiles, and touches my cheek, her fingers strangely cold. Then she whistles, and the quetzal flies from the branch to her shoulder, perching there like a stone gryphon. Sarah turns and, not looking back once, walks slowly into the shower of rotten tree fluff. It's as thick as a blizzard, so thick I can barely see her.

"Sarah!" I call out, forgetting to keep quiet. "Wait!"

She doesn't listen. She fades into the whiteness, and now it's a real snowfall, freezing cold on my hair and cheeks, piling up all around me. I try to stand, but the drifts are as high as they must be in the mountains northeast of the city, where Sarah had to search for Celestina during the

War of the Queens. I shiver in the cold, and realize that our campfire is drifted under too, along with Leah and the others. I try to dig through the snow for them, but my hands are stiff and frozen. The hooting of the unfamiliar bird turns into a howl, and I see yellow terror wolf eyes all around me. I scream as the first snow-white shape leaps at me out of the night…

My eyes open. I'm trembling, but not from cold. The ground is littered with piles of rotten tree fluff, not snow. The campfire has died down from when I fell asleep, but there's still enough heat to warm me. It takes me a minute to realize it was all a dream.

I stand, shaking. The reason the fire's dying is that both of the guards have fallen asleep beside it. I poke around in the ashes with a stick to try to revive it, and it flares enough that I see Peter's profile sticking out from under his blanket, his mouth wide open in a snuffling snore. I permit myself a smile before I realize something's wrong.

Leah's not there.

Her blanket is on the ground where she laid it, but there's no sign of her. For a moment, my dream gets mixed up with what's really going on, and I almost convince myself it was Leah who talked to me, Leah who walked off with the quetzal on her shoulder. But the birdlike creature is still there, nesting in one of the low-hanging branches of the rotten trees. When I tamp down my panic enough to think clearly, I spy a dot of fire off in the trees, looking no bigger than a candle flame in all the darkness. Quietly, I take one of the branches that's still burning and use it to light my way toward the other light. The rotten tree fluff makes a whispering sound under my feet, but no one wakes up.

In less than a minute, I see Leah's short, solid shape, her armor glinting in the light of the torch she holds. I breathe a sigh of relief, but that's a mistake with someone as well trained as she is. She spins at the sound, and I jump back, expecting to see a drawn sword in her hand. Instead, she's cupping a small black and white bird in her palm—a shriek, one of the fastest creatures in the Ecosystem. A scrap of paper tied around its leg flutters in the torchlight as Leah lets it fly.

She comes toward me, holding her torch above her head. I can't see her face that well, but I'd swear she looks guilty.

"What are you doing up?" she asks.

"I… I couldn't sleep."

"Well, you'd better get back to bed. We have another long day ahead of us."

"Does that mean you… know where we are? Did the shriek tell you…"

"Did it tell me what?"

The tone of her voice takes me aback. "Nothing. I just thought…"

"Well, you thought wrong. There's nothing to tell."

She's close enough now that I can see her eyes. They're hard and angry, the way Mom's eyes get when I mess up at Sensor training. After my dream about Sarah, the thought that Leah's mad at me is more than I can take.

"Leah," I say. "Please…"

She glowers at me a moment longer before her face softens. She sighs, then puts on a smile that looks as false as her sword looks on me.

"Your mother's been sending me birds since we left the city," she says. "One shriek each night."

"What did that one say?"

"That she's discovered an experimental medical procedure written down in the Queen's private archives. Something Sarah must have learned about and communicated to Rebecca. It doesn't make much sense to me, but it involves switching the blood from one person to another, using tubes and needles or something like that. For the past week or so, your mother's been selecting the strongest people from among the common folk to give their blood to the most critically ill, and it seems to be partially effective."

"My dad...?"

"Him too," Leah says. "He's not healed, but he hasn't gotten any worse."

That should make my heart lighten, but there's a note in her voice that betrays her. "Is something else wrong?"

She pauses before answering. Her face seems to change moment by moment in the flickering torchlight.

"Sorry," she says at last. "It's just that this is a lot to take at your age. I wasn't planning on telling you at all, as you probably figured out."

"I need to know," I say.

"You're just like my Huldah. But I suppose, if she were the one this was happening to, I'd tell her." Her eyes dart away for another moment before locking on my face. "The Queen's not doing well, Hadassah. She's not responding to the treatment, which your mom thinks is because the concentration of *Apis impunita* genes in her body is too high for common blood to have any effect on her."

"She's still in a coma?"

She nods. "Barely hanging on, from what your mom says. I'm not sure what Miriam's going to try next, but..."

"Will she send us another bird?"

"By tomorrow, we'll be too far away for it to reach us," she says. "Your mother knows that. It feels to me like she waited this long before filling me in so I wouldn't be able to question her if she decides to do something… drastic. Miriam fools a lot of people with the innocent act, but I know her. She can be incredibly frogbull-headed when she wants to be." She tries a smile. "Like a certain daughter of hers."

The thought of losing both Mom and Dad makes me tremble all over again. "Isn't there anything we can do?"

"We can find that blasted tree," Leah says in a harsh tone that's nothing like her normal voice. "I thought we were getting closer, but it's become obvious that the map isn't drawn anywhere close to scale, because we should have reached the three rivers long before now. I take it we're still not sure of the tree's exact location?"

I don't have to say anything for her to see the answer in my face. I've never admitted to her how lost we are, but Leah's too smart to be tricked.

"Then we'll just have to keep going," she says with her old resolve. "And, Hadassah…"

I freeze. What else could be wrong?

"Keep an eye out for Simon and Catherine," she says. "I've overheard a few things from them that go beyond soldiers' normal grumbling. Be smart, and stay as far away from them as you can."

"Why do they hate me so much?"

"It's me they hate," she says. "Both of them have wanted my position for a long time, and I suspect they see what's happening now as an opportunity to shake things up. They won't attempt an open coup with the wyrm watching, but I wouldn't put it past them to launch a sneak attack."

"Then why'd you choose them to come with us?"

She gives me a wry smile. "That's another thing I learned from Sarah. Keep the worst threat where you can see it."

She puts her arm around me and pulls me into a half-hug before we walk back to the campsite. The guards look anything but dangerous as they sprawl beside the dying fire, but I keep my distance anyway.

If sleep was hard before, it's impossible now. All I can think about is my mom, and what she might do to keep the Queen alive. I know this is crazy, but I can't help wondering if tonight's visit from Sarah was more than a dream—if she somehow knew about the danger we're in and sent a vision to warn us.

But even if she did, it didn't help. There are threats everywhere I look, but I can't see any of them.

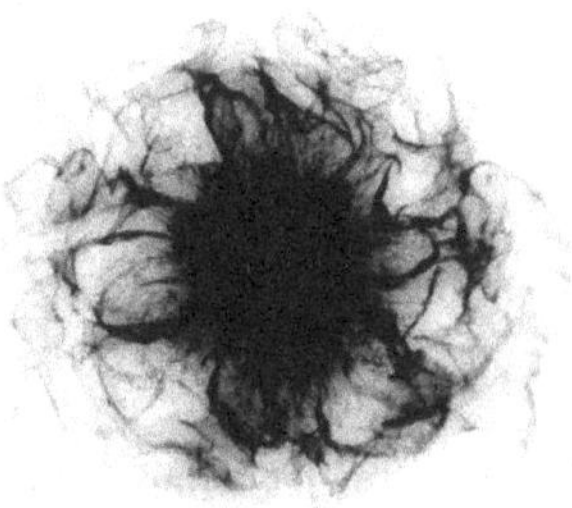

Late that morning, we exit the rotten tree forest into a place unlike anything I've ever seen.

We're on high ground, racing westward beside a deep gorge while the quetzalbird glide-flies a hundred feet ahead. The landscape is mostly bare, except for scrubby grasses and the stray prickly bush. The opposite side of the gorge is made of horizontal stripes of colorful stone or clay, red and brown and almost blue, like layers in an enormous birthday cake. When I risk a look over the edge, I glimpse a winding line way down below. It sparkles in the sunlight, blue as the cloudless sky.

I shout to Leah past Peter's averted face. "Is this it? Are we there?"

She's wrestling with the map, trying to keep it open while the wyrm's speed tries to rip it from her hands. "I think this is the northeastern branch!" she shouts back. "We must have intersected it when we left the forest!"

I bundle with Wyvern, telling them to slow down. When they do, Leah hops off their back and walks to the edge of the cliff, with me just behind.

"Careful," she says, holding out a hand.

My knees wobble as I look down. The sides of the gorge are even steeper than I realized, the river even farther away. From this distance, it looks as thin as the blue lines on the map, but I can hear a faint roaring sound, as if the water is shouting up at us.

"Rapids," Leah says. "We can't risk crossing here."

Holding her hand up to shield her eyes from the sun, she scouts down the length of the river until it disappears behind a bend in the gorge. Then she removes a bronze spyglass from among the endless tools and weapons on her belt. She adjusts the eyepiece to follow the river as far as she can see, but in the end, she lowers the glass and lets out a hard breath.

"Curse it," she says. "Rapids all the way, probably because of the depth of the canyon. Hopefully, it'll be less rough up ahead."

We climb aboard Wyvern, with Leah taking the seat behind me to give her a better view of the river. Wyvern creeps forward, but minutes pass without her reporting any change, not even when we round the bend in the gorge. If anything, the sound of thunder from below gets louder, more like a stampeding herd of wilderbeests than any noise I imagined water could make.

"Why isn't the canyon on the map?" I ask.

"Because Queen Sarah transmitted information for a planimetric rendering," a familiar nasally voice answers me. "It shows only basic geographic features, not declivities and elevations."

I turn to look at Peter, who's sitting behind Leah with his typical smug expression. I should have known that the first time he'd talk to me in six days would be to point out how stupid I am. "What if we can't get across?" I ask Leah.

"We'll get across," she says. "It just might take some doing."

She sticks the spyglass in her belt and crosses her arms. I wish I could believe she's as confident as she wants me to think she is, but the sick feeling I've carried since last night crowds out everything else.

Wyvern follows the course of the river westward as it winds through the gorge. With every foot of ground we cover, the roaring sound gets louder, until I realize that the land we're on is sloping steadily downward. That seems like a good thing if it really is the depth of the canyon that's making the water so rough, but then I glance ahead and see that the land falls away completely, as if there's a break in the canyon wall. Wyvern coasts cautiously to the very edge, and I discover that the gap marks a spot where two more rivers connect with the first, one carving a trail northwest, the other southeast. The three blue lines meet at an almost triangular point hundreds of feet below, which means we can't go any further without crossing one of the rivers.

Leah slides from Wyvern's back and studies the map. "This is the spot, all right," she says. "Three rivers, more or less oriented the way Sarah described. It's no wonder few people have dared to pass over into the wild lands."

"But Sarah did," I say.

"We have to assume so. And it seems her friend wants us to follow her."

I look where she's pointing and find the quetzal crouched at the edge of the gorge. It spreads its front legs and jumps, but instead of falling to its death, its feathers catch the breeze, and it circles effortlessly over the sheer drop. I watch as its powerful wingbeats carry it across the gorge until it's nothing but a tiny speck against the bright sky. A minute later, it wheels and comes back toward us, then brakes in midair and lands safely on our side. Peter turns to me with a smirk, but I've become an expert at ignoring him.

"Too bad we can't do that," Leah mutters. "Can wyrms swim, I wonder?"

I touch Wyvern's snout. The answer comes immediately, and I shake my head to let Leah know. When it rains hard, urthwyrms have to escape to the surface to avoid drowning in their own tunnels. Wyvern is trembling deep in their body at the mere thought of getting close to so much water, and they're not the only one. I can't swim; most people in the City of the Queens can't. There's no real reason to learn. I've been out with my dad in rowboats on the city's artificial lake—wearing life jackets each time—but that's all.

"What about tunneling underneath?" Leah asks.

"The ground is too rocky," I say as I translate Wyvern's bundling into words. "We'd have to go very deep to get beneath the riverbed, and there's a risk of suffocation or cave-in. We could try it, but the wyrm thinks it's a bad idea."

"Then I guess we're stuck," Catherine says. I wish I could smack the smile off her pretty face, but I'm fairly sure she'd kill me.

"No, we're not," Peter says. "Look!"

He points at the triangular piece of land. At first, I have no idea what he's so worked up about, but when I squint against the bright blue, I realize there's something in the water right where the three rivers come together. Leah lifts the spyglass and studies the spot, then hands the glass to me.

"Peter's right," she says. "There's a way across."

With the spyglass to my eye, the thing she's talking

about jumps out at me. It's a bunch of huge logs, as big as trees almost, that have gathered where the three rivers meet, as if they've been pressed against the banks by the force of the rapids. Enough water flows past them to keep everything running smoothly, but the way the logs are wedged together, people might be able to walk across them to reach the northern side. Still, when I bundle with Wyvern, I feel a trembling even stronger than before.

Wyvern? I ask. *Is something wrong?*

We-Wyvern do not know if something is wrong, they answer. *But we think that fast-water-place is...*

Is what?

Dangerous, is all they'll say.

"I'm not sure it's safe," I tell the others.

"Do you see something?" Leah asks.

"No," I admit. "But the wyrm seems worried. Maybe because the logs are wet, or because they might come loose if we walk on them."

"Why don't you *Sense* if they will?" Peter sneers.

I glare at him, but say nothing. He knows full well that even the Queen can't Sense things that aren't alive, and the driftwood logs are no exception.

Leah studies the logs a minute longer before stashing the spyglass in her belt. "I don't think we have a choice," she says. "We'll have to be careful, and we'll have to use rope. But we can't spend half the day trying to find a better place to cross."

I know she's right, so I don't say anything else. I lay a hand on Wyvern's nose to try to calm them, but for the first time since we formally met, they seem to shrink from me.

We have to go down there, I say. *You understand, don't you?*

Wyvern shakes their head in agitation, but answers me. *We-Wyvern would bear you-Hadassah wherever you-Hadassah wish to go. But we-Wyvern cannot bear you-Hadassah across the fast-water. We-Wyvern are…*

Scared. It's okay. So am I.

Wyvern purrs for my sake, but there's a tremble in the vibrations that's never been there before.

We climb into our bucket-seats, and with my hand on Wyvern's snout, the wyrm noses up to the edge of the gorge. Up, and over; for a second, their front end is hanging in midair, and since I'm in the first seat, I'm the one who's looking straight down. There's no trail; there's nothing but the nearly vertical cliff side, striped with multicolored stone. I hear the wyrm's voice in my mind, stronger and more determined than a moment ago.

Hold tight, you-Hadassah, they say. *This will not be pleasant for your kind.*

"Hold on!" I shout to the others, just as Wyvern drops over the edge.

We plunge straight down, my stomach flying to my mouth. I close my eyes as the floor of the gorge rushes toward me, and the last thing I think before we hit bottom is that Wyvern's fear of the water is so great they've decided to smash us on the rocks. But then, with a lurch that nearly makes me lose both my breakfast and my death-grip on the bridle, we land on something solid without breaking every bone in our bodies. I open my eyes to find that Wyvern has attached themselves to the wall of the gorge, sticking there, I can only think, with the slime that covers their skin. When I try to move into a more comfortable position, I find that the same sticky stuff holds me in place, and when

I look down at my legs, I see that they're sunk deeply into the wyrm's flesh. Wyvern has either softened the outer layer of their skin or expanded their mucus lining to make sure we don't fall off as they wind their way down the wall of the canyon. I pat their flank, my hand sticking just like my legs.

You told us to hold tight, I say. *You didn't tell us you'd be holding tight to us.*

The wyrm chuckles, and I find myself smiling despite everything.

Traveling at wyrm-speed, it's less than a minute before we reach the bottom of the gorge. My body releases from Wyvern's grip, and I'm able to slide off their back onto quivering legs. The sound of the rapids battering the logs fills my ears.

Wyvern, I say. *Can we borrow some of your… wyrm-slime? It'll help us hold onto the rope.*

We-Wyvern do not know what 'wyrm-slime' is, they answer. *But you-Hadassah may borrow whatever you-Hadassah wish.*

Thank you, I say, though I can't help making a face as I plunge my fingers into Wyvern's skin and slather the black gunk on my hands and arms up to the elbows. The others stare at me blankly until Leah gets the idea and joins in, then shows Peter where to apply the slime. The guards look disgusted, but a glance from their captain makes them decide they'd better not argue. When I'm done with my upper body, I lean down and spread a sticky coating on the soles of my boots for good measure.

Wyvern, I ask when everyone's slimed up, *how are you going to get across?*

We-Wyvern will tunnel deep, they answer. *We-Wyvern*

are sorry that we cannot bear you-Hadassah across the fast-water. We-Wyvern are sorry that we-Wyvern are… scared.

Everyone gets scared, I say. *That's one of the things that makes us human.*

But we-Wyvern are most decidedly not human.

Maybe you are. At least, a little more than you thought.

I wrap my arms most of the way around the wyrm, feel the deep vibrations that carry their anxiety and regret. I consider giving them a kiss, but the others are watching and the wyrm-slime *is* kind of gross.

Wyvern hangs back while the rest of us approach the river. Standing at the edge of the rocky bank, the crossing looks even rougher than it did with the spyglass: the water foams angrily over the logs as if trying to shove them out of its way, and every so often, a chunk of driftwood on the outer edge of the dam breaks free to spin down the north-western fork. Still, the whole time I'm watching, I don't see anything budge in the central mass of logs, which crisscross in a pattern almost like a knitted garment. Maybe, however many years ago she came here, this is how Sarah got across.

Leah gazes out over the river, then unwinds a length of rope from her pack. Her lips move as she measures out the distance.

"I'll go first," she says. "Followed by Hadassah and then Peter. Catherine, you'll go next, and I'll need Simon as our anchor."

Simon scowls, and the thought jumps into my head that Leah's just given him the chance he was waiting for. But she doesn't even look at him before knotting the rope around her waist, then around mine and Peter's. When Simon slips the loop over his head and tightens it at his belt, I see why Leah chose him for the job: with his feet planted firmly on the bank, he's strong enough to hold the rest of us even if we fall into the water. Leah winks at me, and I understand her other reason. She knows that Simon's too much of a coward to try anything against someone who's not afraid of him.

"Here we go," Leah says as she takes her first step onto the pile. "*Slowly.*"

I inch onto the log a few steps behind her, the stickiness of my hands helping me cling to the line between us. The log is slippery underfoot even with the wyrm-slime on my boots, but the dam feels much sturdier than it looked. When I think about it, there must be tons of water crashing against it every second; if that's not enough to loosen the pile, a few hundred extra pounds won't. I look behind me to check on how the others are doing, and see that Peter's eyes are fixed straight down at his feet as he edges forward like a baby taking its first steps. Catherine is much more agile, plus she chose not to tie the rope around her waist, so she has more freedom to move as she advances hand over hand. Simon might as well be another river rock for all he's changed position. I'm worried when I don't see Wyvern, but then I notice dirt and small rocks flying into the air behind Simon, the wyrm's tail waving a goodbye as they dive into the stony soil.

It's not far to the other side, a few hundred yards at most. Leah moves forward at a cautious, stop-and-go pace, making sure everyone has caught up before she takes the next step. The roar of the river deafens me, and the chilly spray makes it hard for me to see where I'm going, so I keep my focus on her. Even though it doesn't feel like a hard walk, I'm out of breath by the time we reach the middle of the dam, where the logs are piled three or four levels high. Leah pauses for a minute to give us a break before we have to climb over. My legs appreciate the rest, but I'm anxious to finish this journey and stand on solid ground again.

"Leah," I shout, even though she's right in front of me. "Can we—"

She holds up a hand to shush me. I lean carefully to the side to look around her at the far bank.

Something dark bursts from the rocks on the shoreline, too far away for me to make it out through the wet hair that hangs in my eyes. I realize it must be Wyvern, who's managed to tunnel through the soil, dive hundreds of feet down, and find their way to the other side of the river in half the time it's taking us humans. The wyrm arches high above the ground before coming back down, then repeats the motion, as if they're trying to signal us. I risk letting go of the rope with one hand so I can wipe the water from my eyes, and what I see makes my heart go cold.

It's Wyvern, but the wyrm isn't alone. Something else rises out of the shallow water near the bank, a being that's as big as a ghastly bear and glistening darkly as if covered with oil. The huge shape isn't distinct through the spray, but part of it seems to have Wyvern by the tail, which explains the wyrm's motions. Whatever the other creature is, it's trying to drag Wyvern toward the river, and Wyvern isn't signaling to us at all.

They're struggling to escape.

I feel a jerk on the rope behind me, and I spin to look at the southern bank, now farther away than the one where Wyvern's fighting. There's nothing to see except empty shoreline, and it takes me a moment to realize what that means.

"Where's Simon?" I shout at Leah.

Her mouth opens to answer, but an even more violent tug on the rope pulls us from the log pile, and my body crashes into icy water.

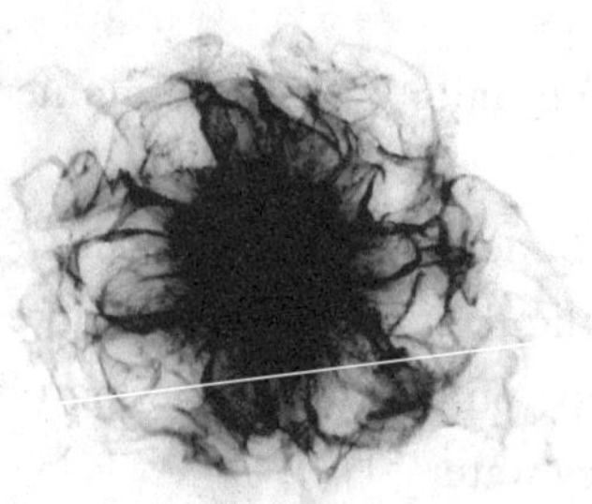

I BREAK SURFACE with a gasp.

My hands beat at frigid water to keep myself afloat. There's something heavy clinging to my waist, which I realize is the rope with Peter still attached to it. I can't see him—he must be underwater—but his weight is like an anchor dragging me beneath the surface. The water is about to close over me when the force of the river shoves me against the log we were standing on, and my gummed-up hands stick to the rough bark. But with Peter weighing me down, I can't pull myself onto the log.

Peter's head bursts from the river beside me, followed by Catherine's. The two of them flail at the water until, like me, they're pushed against the dam and cling there. I can't see Leah, who must have fallen over the other side of the log, and there's no sign of Simon. When Catherine gathers the strength to drag herself out of the water, I see that she's holding onto the frayed end of our rope. The other end—the end her partner was anchored to—is gone.

A freezing wave spills over me as Leah emerges from behind the log and pulls herself into a crouching position. From there, she's able to lean down and grip my hands, while Catherine does the same to Peter. Together, they haul us onto the log. Peter flops facedown beside me, coughing out water, so Leah rolls him on his side. Then she cuts the ropes that bind us and stands to gaze out over the river.

I turn my head to find what she's looking at. At first, all I can see are waves and white froth. But when I raise myself on weak arms and stare intently at the water, I spot a huge v-shaped ripple moving straight toward us. At the point of the *v*, something big and dark pushes the water aside as it picks up speed.

"Hold on!" Leah shouts, just as the thing collides with the log.

I sprawl beside her, my chin striking the wood so hard I taste blood. The log rises out of the water at an angle, as if something is pushing it from underneath. I try desperately to dig my fingernails into the bark, but the log tilts further and further until it's pointed almost straight at the sky, and I lose my grip, skidding down the incline toward the water. Leah clutches my wrist, stopping my slide for an instant, before we both splash into the river. Her hand lets go, and I'm on my own again, the water rushing over my head with a sound like some huge beast roaring in delight.

Panic takes over as I struggle to reach the surface. But my arms are too tired to keep me afloat, and I feel myself sinking deeper, bright sunlight fading into the river's gloom. I know that if I take a breath I'll die, but the burning in my chest is unbearable, and I don't think I can hold out for more than another few seconds. I kick as hard as I can and strike something solid, but it's not enough to propel me toward the dancing light above my head. The thing closes around my legs with a grip like iron, and I know that I really am going to die.

The next instant, I explode from the river's darkness into the light. My lungs gulp oxygen greedily, even though I take in almost as much water as air. Leah and Peter and

Catherine are nowhere to be seen, but I can still feel the thing wrapped around me. When I look to see what has me in its grip, I can't believe my eyes.

It's Wyvern.

The wyrm has slithered out onto the mass of logs and caught me in their mouth, teeth retracted so as not to slice me to ribbons. Despite their fear of water, they've rescued me, fishing me from the river before I went down. My foggy mind is trying to think of a way to thank them when the wyrm's voice cuts through my confusion.

You-Hadassah. We must flee this place at once.

What is it? What attacked us?

Bereavers, they answer. *A mating pair that built this dam. We-Wyvern did not recognize their presence in the bundle, perhaps because being scared of the fast-water deceived us. We-Wyvern have killed the one that ventured from the fast-water, but the other—*

Their words end abruptly as a shadow rises from behind the log pile. Wyvern can't make any noise, but if I had enough breath, I'd scream.

The creature that looms above me is ten feet tall at least, and that's only the half I can see. It consists of a furry torso thickly matted with oil that makes the water run off it in streams, stubby arms ending in almost human hands, and a face with a whiskered snout and yellow fangs as sharp as skewers. A huge tail shaped like a boat paddle rises from the water behind it, and when it slams down, an enormous wave hammers me against the log. It's only thanks to Wyvern, who takes the brunt of the pounding, that I'm able to hold on at all. The bereaver grabs the wyrm's tail in one of its clawed hands, and my protector is whipped into the air as if they're nothing more than a regular earthworm in a cruel child's clutches.

The monster slams Wyvern against the log pile, and black fluid spurts from the wyrm's body. Wyvern manages to wrap themselves around the creature's arm, their retractable teeth sinking into its fur. But the bereaver's teeth are just as sharp, and they clamp onto the flesh right behind the wyrm's snout, black blood smearing the beast's yellow fangs and coating its muzzle. Wyvern twists and strains until I'm sure their body is going to divide in two, but the grip of the bereaver's teeth is too strong to break. I try to stand, to do something, only to feel myself slipping into the water again. When the bereaver bashes Wyvern's coiled body against the log, I lose my balance and fall.

But I don't go under. I land against something hard that makes a clinking sound like metal.

Leah rises from the river with me clutched against her chain-link shirt. She's lost her jerkin sometime during the attack, but her sword flashes in the sun, flinging water in a rainbow arc before connecting with the bereaver. One of the monster's claws flies free, trailing drops of blood as red as my own. Leah swings again, and a gash appears in the creature's stomach. Its bellows are deafening as it whips its paddle-like tail sideways to sweep us from the log. Leah blocks the blow, but her blade is impaled in the leathery flesh and gets torn from her hand. The tail rises high in the air, and Leah tenses against me as its shadow hangs over us.

"Jump!"

I do, with her arm around me. The tail smashes into the log where we were standing, and wood splinters as we hit the water again. Leah holds me above the surface while she kicks for another log, but we've no sooner reached it than the entire dam collapses, tree trunks rolling toward us with enough force to squash us if they hit. Though she's halfway in the water herself, Leah boosts me over our log and throws me to the other side, where I'm protected from the logs that pummel ours. She's climbing over the barrier to join me when one of the loose logs swings around and strikes her head-on. Her face is only inches from mine, and I watch her eyes roll back before she slumps into the water and disappears.

"Leah!"

I try to scramble over the log to look for her, but I find myself rushing down the river on my log, leaving the tiny whirlpool where Leah vanished far behind. Peter and Catherine are gone. In seconds, I'm so far downriver the huge shapes of the battling monsters look like Tovah's stuffed toys. Then I'm whipped around a bend and lose sight of them entirely.

My log spins like a giant twirligig pod as other parts of the shattered dam bump against it. I can't tell which direction I'm going or where I'm going to stop, if I'm going to stop. For a second, I think I see the form of the quetzal-bird floating high above me in the bright blue sky, but then it's gone, too.

River water blinds me as I race downstream alone, into the wild.

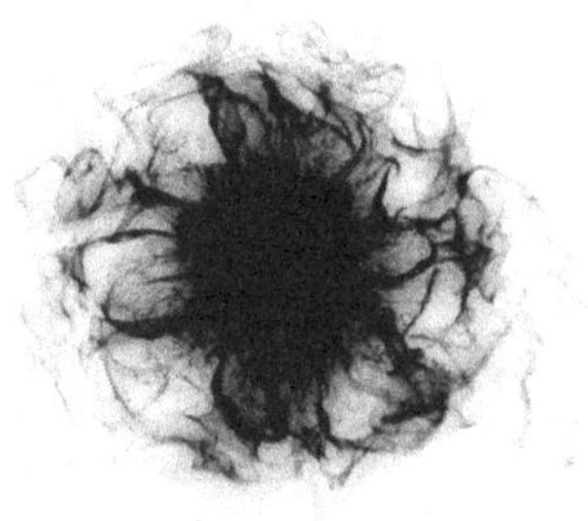

BOOK THREE:

WARNED

For formerly the tribes of men on earth lived remote from ills, without harsh toil and the grievous sicknesses that are deadly to men.

—Hesiod,
Works and Days (c. 700 BCE)

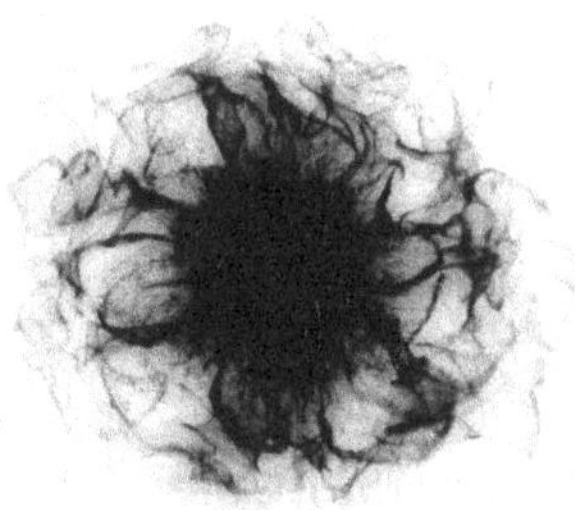

Evening has fallen by the time my log bumps against a sandbank and I'm able to drag myself ashore. I'm bruised and battered by floating logs and submerged rocks, exhausted from trying to keep my head above water while my log pitched and rolled. Even worse, I'm frozen from spending hours in the chilly river; my skin is no longer smooth and brown but puckered and purple. I shudder violently, waves passing through my body as if I've got the rapids inside of me. Hypothermia isn't much of a worry in the City of the Queens, but Dad has told me about the symptoms. If I don't get warm, I won't last the night.

There's no one within leagues, so I strip off my torn clothes—which isn't easy, because my hands shake uncontrollably and the drenched fabric clings to me like a second skin. I crawl across the bank and pull myself beneath a clump of plants with long, flat leaves. They don't do much to warm me, but at least I'll be out of the night wind. Hugging myself and curling into as tight a ball as my numb muscles will allow, I rock and shake and pray for my heart to keep pumping blood through my body.

I wake to find sunlight shining on the spot where I'm huddled. I can't remember falling asleep; the last thing I remember is trying to stop my chattering teeth from biting my tongue in two. But my bed must have been toastier than I thought, because my hands are back to their normal color and my fingers wiggle the way they're supposed to. I roll out from beneath the bushes and test my legs, finding them strong enough to hold me. My shins are covered with unsightly purple bruises, but nothing seems to be broken. Last night, I couldn't feel my body well enough to tell.

I step onto sun-warmed sand, which is when I realize I'm barefoot. The only thing I'm wearing is the token Mom gave me, its rawhide cord twisted so tight I'm lucky it didn't choke me to death. I cover myself with my hands and scoot to where my clothes are heaped on the bank, then spread them out in the sunlight. They've been reduced to rags, hardly enough to call clothes anymore. But there's no way I'm going to stand here in broad daylight with nothing on, so I wring out my tattered shirt and slip it over my head, dance into what's left of my shorts. Then I lie down in the sunshine for things to dry.

With nothing else to do while I'm waiting, I look around to try to figure out where I am. I quickly give up, because this place is almost as blank as Sarah's map, with sandy riverbanks and leafy hedges and not much else. The position of the sun and my memory of the rivers' flow makes me pretty sure I went down the northwestern branch, but that doesn't help me much to orient myself. Add to that the fact that I have no food, no drinking flask, no way to make fire to cook anything or scare off the creatures of the wild. I can't remember when I lost my boots and sword, but the belt and scabbard must have been stripped away by the river, and the boots must have filled with water and sunk to the bottom. Which is probably a good thing, because otherwise, they might have dragged me down, too.

Maybe it would have been better if they had.

You've got no time to feel sorry for yourself, a voice speaks in my mind. I know it's my own voice, but I can't help wishing it was Wyvern's. *You're the last one left, the only one who can find the tree and heal the Queen.*

But I'm lost, I argue with myself. *I can't do this all on my own.*

The others did their job, the answer comes back immediately. *Leah taught you how to fight, Wyvern helped wake up your Sense, and Sarah sent the quetzal to get you this far. Now it's your responsibility to finish what they started.*

What if I can't? I object.

Then everyone's lost, I answer. *The Queen, and Mom and Dad, and Chaim and Tovah, and everyone.*

I nod, take a deep breath. Though I'm less than thrilled at the thought of exposing my half-nude body to whatever might be watching, I stand, lift my head, and stretch out my arms. I close my eyes, partly so I don't have to see myself, partly because that's the best way to Sense. I remember the day Mom first showed me this stance, her hands gently moving my five-year-old limbs into the right position. Once I've made my body copy the image in my mind, I try to do everything else just the way she told me to: silence my thoughts, slow my heart, open my pores wide to the world. Forget my worries, my doubts, my fears. That's the hardest part. To make myself merge with the life that streams around me, when all I really want to do is hide.

A tingle like the lightest of breezes plays across the hairs of my arms. It's not the wind; it's my Sense coming alive, attuning itself to the wild the way insects pick up signals with their antennae. When I feel it, a combination of relief and sorrow washes over me—relief that I can do it on my own, sorrow that Wyvern's not here to experience it with me. They would have been so proud to feel me making contact, becoming part of the bundle.

So would Sarah. So would Mom.

I push those thoughts from my mind and reach out to the Ecosystem again. It's not as easy as it was with Wyvern. My Sense is definitely alive—it's even starting to hum with energy—but everything it comes into contact with feels foreign: mosses and ferns I've never seen, bramble bushes with sharp thorns, stumpy trees with fronds like one of Celestina's fancy hairdos. Maybe because I'm thinking about Wyvern, I decide to try something new, letting my Sense sink through the soles of my bare feet and burrow into the ground like the wyrm did when they carried me that first night in the Queen's tunnel. I'm taken by surprise when the trick works, my consciousness spreading through the ground far faster than it's ever gone through the air. Could this be why Wyvern said bundling is better than Sensing—because it connects you physically to the earth? Hoping that's true, I squeeze my eyes shut and focus on the ground I'm standing on, the ground that must lead to the tree, if the tree's there at all.

My mind spreads outward, slowly at first but picking up speed with each passing second. I weave my way through the roots of actual trees, slip underneath the canyon on my side of the river, then connect with another river that's narrower and less turbulent than the one I came down. The land grows swampy on this new river's banks; I can feel life multiplying there, strange trees and plants I can't name but can see as golden outlines glowing in my mind. No animals, though, which strikes me as weird. I don't know whether

I'm getting closer to the blank space on Sarah's map, but my Sense keeps tugging me that way, so I let it take over.

The moment I stop trying to control it, it leaps forward, as if I'm the one who's been holding it back. Before I know it, I'm moving at warhog-speed, then wyrm-speed, then an impossible speed where I cover leagues and leagues at a single blink, a single breath. I'm racing along a river that teems with plant life, then plunging through a dense stretch of forest, breaking through a wall of rainbow mist, and then…

I'm there.

The tree shines before me, filling my eyes with its silver glow and singing a song like a giant wind chime made of bronze and glass. I still can't see anything around it, no ground that it's standing on or sky that it's shining against, but unlike the times I saw it with Sarah and the Queen and Wyvern, it feels like it's anchored to a real place, a place I could actually reach. Not close, but closer than it's ever been. *I can get there,* I think. *I can find it, and find Sarah, and cure the Queen and everyone else.* I reach for it, see a globe of fruit glistening in its branches, close my hand around it…

There's a crackle of energy, a flash like a lightning bolt. The tree recoils, its glow flickering, its song failing. I Sense fear, confusion, anger—all the things the Ecosystem isn't supposed to feel from a Sensor anymore. It's the way Mom told me it used to be in the village, when the Sensorship was at war with the Ecosystem, and the Ecosystem hated all people with their blades and fire and cutting tools. The feelings boil up from the earth, building higher and higher until they take the form of a scream of rage. Everything goes dark and silent and still, the tree blinking out in my mind as if I've been severed from the earth itself.

I feel a rumbling deep in the ground, but it's not Wyvern. Something else is coming for me, moving as fast as thought. Something much bigger and deadlier than anything I've encountered before.

Without taking the time to look, I turn and run.

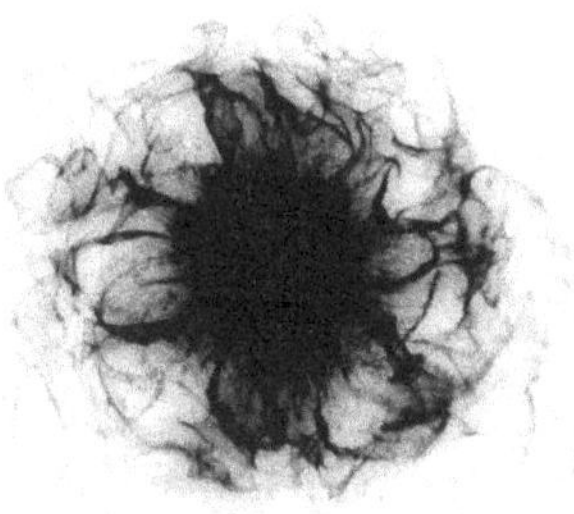

Instinct shouts at me to seek cover. I race away from the bank and plunge into the foliage that lines the canyon wall, swatting and kicking at branches to force my way deeper into the brush. The sharp edges of fern leaves slice my soles, while thorns prick my arms and cling to my hair. I'm breaking every rule in Mom's book: calling attention to myself, letting my heart rate and breathing spiral out of control. Showing fear. But I can't help it. The only thought in my mind is to get away from the thing that's after me.

I break through the bushes to find myself faced with the massive cliff that borders the river. There's no way I can climb it, so I turn left and run beside it, over a strip of spiky grass that cuts my feet like millions of tiny blades. Tears stream into my eyes, blurring what's up ahead. The only thing that keeps me running is the certainty that my pursuer is just behind me, gaining on me.

Hunting me.

I'm going too fast to see the ground drop off at my feet, and the next thing I know, I'm tumbling headfirst down a hill.

I land with a jolt on a stretch of rocky ground. The fall stuns me, and for a second I'm unable to remember where I am or what I'm doing. My body remembers faster than my brain, because it's up and running again, ignoring a new pain in my right ankle and an even worse pain in my side.

Hazily, I Sense that I've pulled ahead of the thing that's chasing me, as if it had even more trouble with the hill than I did. If I can only stay ahead a little longer, if I can only find a place to hide…

A sparkle up ahead warns me of a bend in the river. I'm limping badly, and it feels like knives are stabbing my lung with each breath, but I push myself harder, trying to stretch the distance between me and the thing behind me. When I reach the water's edge, I come to a sudden, painful stop, a breath escaping me that's nothing short of a scream.

The river curves sharply to the right, then cuts straight through the cliff, into a tunnel of rock with no clearance overhead. I know this is the way I need to go to reach the second river and the tree, but even if the pain in my chest didn't prevent me from taking a deep breath, there's no way I can swim underwater to get there. My adrenaline rush is wearing off now that I've stopped, leaving my muscles as limp and heavy as wet sand. I turn clumsily to look behind me, but my foot slips on the rocks of the shoreline, and I land with an impact that feels like my lost sword's been shoved straight through my side.

Weakly, I raise my head a few inches from the ground. The strip of land I just ran over is empty, nothing but pebbly soil stretching away into the distance. I hold my breath, unwilling to make a sound or to risk the stabbing agony of filling my lungs. For a dizzy moment, I tell myself I outran the thing, that I'm safe.

Then I see it.

Fifty yards away, stones quiver as if something is tunneling beneath them. As the thing comes closer, I see that it's shoving the stones aside one by one, revealing the sand that lies deeper down. The sandy trail inches toward me, one rock at a time, before it splits, carving twin paths toward the river with me caught in between. When it's only a few feet away, I see tiny dimples forming in the exposed sand like the first drops of a rainstorm, though the sky is perfectly clear. The holes multiply until there are hundreds of them, maybe thousands, each one the size of a thumbprint. I crab-crawl into the water, the pain in my side so intense my vision goes red. It's only when I'm sitting waist-deep in the icy stream that I realize there's something behind me as well.

Plants are growing from the shoreline and shallow water, shiny green tubes as big around as my pinkie finger. No sooner do they rise clear of the ground than they thicken, until they're the width of fence posts. They grow with impossible speed, adding inches every second as if someone is feeding them upward, hand over hand, from underground. In less than a minute, they've formed a cage around me, twice my height and growing taller with each shaky breath I take. It seems as if, given enough time, they might reach the height of the sun.

I know what this thing is called. My Sense whispers its name.

Baneboo.

The stalks sway, rattling against each other with a hollow sound. At first I think they're blowing in the wind, but then I realize that a shape is forming across them, green bulges and wrinkles emerging from the closely packed stems. I watch as the shape becomes familiar: forehead, nose, cheeks, mouth. When it's done, I see that it's a woman's face, as green as the baneboo, with long hair made of segmented strands that wave like snakes. She stares at me with sightless eyes, and I recognize whose face it is.

Catherine's.

Her mouth opens in a silent scream. I cover my ears as if to block out her wail of torment, even though there's nothing to hear. Green hands reach from the baneboo to pull mine away, and the face leans close, but it can't free itself. The lips open and close without making a sound, the face twisting as if it's pleading with me. I wrap my arms around my middle, trying to hold in the pain and sickness. I know that the baneboo grove will never let me go, and in a few days, after I've starved or died of exposure, the plant will devour me the way it did Catherine, mimicking my body while my bones wash down the river into the sea.

"Hadassah!"

The sound of my name is so unexpected, I look up thinking it's Catherine's dead green lips that have shouted. The call comes again, and I crane my neck to the top of the baneboo thicket twenty feet over my head. The face in the baneboo tilts toward the sound as well, searching the sky with sightless eyes. Those eyes don't even blink as a shadow from above blocks the sun.

An unseen creature lands on the riverbank outside the baneboo screen. A second later, a smaller shape swoops through the opening at the top of the cage, and claws grip my arms. With a lurch that makes my injured side scream, I'm torn from the water and lifted into the air. The stalks of baneboo put on an extra growth spurt to try to catch me, their tips wiggling like slender fingers as long as tentacles. I leave them far behind as the thing that's carrying me aims for the sky.

I make the mistake of looking down. I'm hundreds of feet above the water, so high I can barely see the human figure that stands on the riverbank in front of the baneboo forest. A bright shape flashes in its hand, and my heart jumps at the thought that it must be Leah, fighting the plant with her sword. Somehow, she survived, and as soon as she defeats the baneboo, she'll join me so I don't have to do this alone.

The baneboo wiggles like a forest of snakes. I realize that no matter how many stalks Leah lops off, there are always more to lash out at her, as if there are as many strands as hairs on Catherine's head. They force her into the water where another wall of baneboo waits to pull her under. I try to gather my breath to shout a warning, but the pain in my side stops the words from coming.

A second later, I find myself tumbling toward the plateau at the top of the cliff. Even though it's a short drop, my injured side explodes when I land. I don't have the strength to crawl to the edge and look below, but I see a flurry of bright feathers as the thing that brought me here swoops out of sight.

A rush of wingbeats tells me it's returned. I look up into a blinding sun, and all I see is a dark shape standing above me.

Leah. She won. I'm safe. I wish I could get up so I could feel her arms wrap around me, but I'm too weak to move.

"Hadassah?" my rescuer says. "What happened to your clothes?"

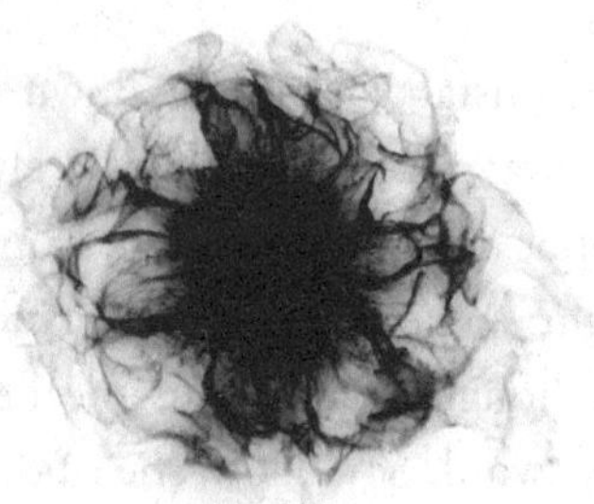

I SQUINT INTO the sun, and see that it's not Leah standing before me.

It's Peter.

A sword hangs in a scabbard at his side, and his arms are coated in what looks like green blood. His shirt and shorts are in somewhat better shape than mine, plus he's got a green bandana wrapped around his head.

"Don't look!" I scream, my hands flying to cover every part of me at once. The movement is so painful, I feel like I'm going to pass out. Peter's mouth falls open before he turns away.

"I'm sorry." He rummages in a pouch at his belt that might be the remains of his backpack. "I've got something that will help."

"What is it?"

"Leaves that appear to possess medicinal properties," he says. "I got knocked out at the river when that… that thing attacked us. The quetzalbird brought me to a grove of trees, and I discovered that the leaves cured the symptoms I was experiencing: headache, double vision, the classic signs of concussion. Within a few hours, I was back to normal. I think the medicine might have the same effect on your injuries, if you'll just let me tend to them—"

"No, thank you," I say, then grit my teeth against the pain my words cause. "I can do it myself."

"You can barely move," he says. "And if your ribs are broken, you're risking pneumonia or a punctured lung or worse. I promise I won't look. I'll… I'll close my eyes. I'll even wear a blindfold if that would help."

I swallow a laugh that would probably tear me in two if I let it out. "How are you going to wrap my chest blindfolded?"

"By touch…"

I've heard enough of that. "Get over here," I say.

He takes a step closer. His face is the color of an over-ripe gnooseberry, even though his eyes are focused on a point above my shoulder.

"You can wrap my chest," I say. "But don't touch me any more than you have to. You'd better wrap my ankle, too," I add. "I think it's broken."

He kneels beside me. His eyes shy away as he reaches into his bag and unrolls a long strip of green, the same stuff he's wearing around his head. He wraps the ankle first, his fingers carefully avoiding contact with my skin. The moment the dressing is on, the hot throbbing gives way to a pleasantly cool sensation.

"I don't think it's broken," Peter says. "It appears to be simply a bad sprain. Based on my own rate of recovery, you should be able to bear weight in an hour or two."

"Wonderful," I say. "Now the ribs."

He unwinds an even longer strip of green and holds it out as if to measure my chest, which is pretty much impossible for him to do when he won't look at me. I grab his hand, but he flinches away and mumbles something I can't hear.

"Peter," I say. "I'm not *completely* naked."

That doesn't do much to help the mumbling.

"Look in my eyes instead," I say. "Then you won't have to..."

He lifts his eyes to mine. This close, they're even paler blue than I noticed before, like reflections of themselves in a glass. I feel something flutter strangely in my stomach before his eyes flick away.

"I won't look," he says. "And I'll be careful, I promise."

I lift my arms over my head while he holds the bandage out. My shirt's in decent enough condition that it covers the part of my chest that matters, but I can't help turning my head away when the dressing touches my skin. He works from top to bottom, underarms to just above my belly button. His hands tremble, but they don't touch me once.

When he's done, he mutters a few more words and turns away. I study the green wrapping and see that I look as stupid as I expected, like a piece of brown fruit wrapped in a lettuce leaf. But the soothing sensation is so incredible, I don't care. I can breathe again without wincing, and while Peter is busy wrapping up what's left of his bandages, I push myself from the ground and stand.

"I wouldn't do that if I were you," he says. "You need to give the ankle sufficient time to heal."

"I'll take my chances. We have a long way to go."

He glances up at me, pale eyes washed out by the sunlight. "Do you know where we're going?"

"I think so. I'm not sure how far it is, though."

"Which direction?"

"It would help if I knew exactly where we are."

"You were washed down the river that flows northwest," he says. "You probably traveled fifteen miles from the crossing. Once the river went through the cliff, it turned more or less directly north."

"Then that's the way we're heading," I say. "We need to connect with another river not far from here, then follow it to the end. But without the wyrm, it's going to take us forever to get there."

He holds my gaze for a second longer, then walks to the edge of the plateau and puts two fingers to his mouth to let out a high-pitched whistle. There's a rustle of wings, and the quetzalbird rises over the edge of the canyon. It stares at Peter with bright eyes, its leg-wings flapping hard as it hovers before him. He turns to me and flashes a smile like a little kid who's about to share a secret.

"Stay here," he says. "I'll be right back."

With a beating of wings, the quetzal catches his shoulders in its back feet and lifts him from the ground. He gives me another look that's a mix between pride and shyness before the bird whisks him away toward the canyon floor, and I lose sight of them in the shadows.

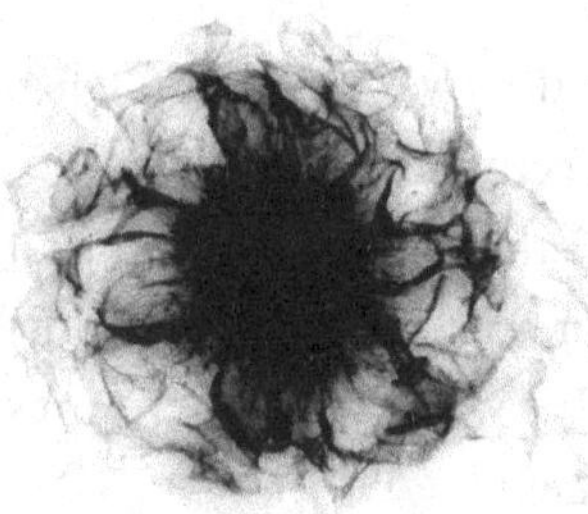

Peter's gone for hours. I lie down on the edge to watch what he's doing, but all I can see is the flash of his sword by the bank of the river where the baneboo grows. My chest starts to hurt from holding that position, so I roll onto my back, close my eyes, and urge the medicine to work faster.

The sound of wings makes me look up. Peter lands beside me, his face red and sweaty, his arms loaded with pieces of baneboo cut into four-foot lengths. The wind on the ridgetop blows through the stems with an eerie moan.

"How are you feeling?" he asks.

I sit up, take a deep breath. "Better."

"Good. You can help me with this stuff."

"Baneboo."

"Right. Baneboo."

He lays the stems on the ground, his lips moving soundlessly as if he's committing the name to memory. The quetzalbird lands beside the pile and preens its feathers. How an animal not much bigger than a fell-cat could carry all that weight is beyond me, especially when it must have hollow bones for flying. I glance at Peter, who seems to read my mind.

"It's an amazing creature," he says. "It could probably transport us both at the same time if it had an extra pair of legs, but it can't hold anything in its front claws while it's in flight. I could spend months just studying the structural adaptations Queen Sarah built into it to give it such strength and endurance."

"And you trust it?"

He stares. "What are you talking about?"

"Nothing," I say. "Just if it's as strong as all that, it could have saved everyone at the river crossing. Not just the two of us."

He shakes his head. "It didn't have to save anyone."

"It also didn't have to make us cross the river right where that monster's dam was," I remind him. "So it's not exactly like it doesn't have blood on its… claws."

The quetzalbird tilts its head as if it knows that I'm talking about it, then goes back to licking feathers with its long tongue. Peter reaches down to stroke its fur, and it nuzzles against the back of his hand.

"Look," he says. "I'm sorry about what happened to Lieutenant Leah. But the dam was the only place we could have crossed. It was either take a chance there or give up any hope of completing our mission."

"And you're absolutely sure of that."

"My conclusion is based on observation and analysis," he says. "So yes, I'm sure."

I simmer, but let that go. It's not like anything I say gets through to him anyway. "Did you see how the others died?"

Peter stops playing with his pet, but he doesn't look at me. "I told you, I got knocked out. It's evident that Simon was killed by the water-monster before it attacked the rest of us. Catherine's body must have been washed ashore, where it was consumed by the baneboo. That's the only explanation I can offer for how her face and limbs could have appeared in its xylem. Leah and the wyrm, I don't know. They might have drowned or been slain by the monster. But with the baneboo colonizing the area all along the shoreline, I doubt they would have made it across in any event."

"Hm," I say. "Interesting."

"What?"

"Oh, nothing. Just gathering more data for you to analyze."

He frowns, then stoops beside the pile of baneboo and arranges the stalks so they're parallel to each other. He pulls his sword out of its scabbard and hacks at the stalks to even them out.

"Where'd you get my sword?" I ask.

He glances at me. "What?"

"That's my sword," I say. "The one Leah taught me how to use. It's my belt, too, come to think of it. Did the quetzal find those things, too?"

He stands, wiping his hands on his shorts. "Listen," he says. "I'm not going to keep trying to defend myself. I already said I'm sorry about Leah."

"I heard. Do you have something to be sorry *for*?"

"Nothing except the fact that I have to spend the rest of this journey with you," he says. "If you want to know about the sword, I found it by the riverbank. And if you think this is some kind of elaborate ruse to lead you into danger, did it ever occur to you that I could have left you for the baneboo to finish off? Then I could have flown away with my feathered co-conspirator, burned the tree to the ground, and let the Queen die, thereby ensuring the doom of the Ecosystem and everyone in it, myself included. Except there's one small problem with my nefarious scheme."

"And what might that be?"

"I don't know where the stupid tree *is*," he says. "Which is why I'm forced to take this trip with you, even though it's the last thing I want to do. And we'd already be on our way if you'd help out instead of trying to make me look like the bad guy."

His face is flushed even worse than before, not with embarrassment but with anger. And when I think about it, I have to admit I'm being a bit of a jackalass. He did save me from the baneboo and help heal my injuries. His little hybrid pal did get us to the other side of the canyon, where we needed to be to set off toward *edinnu*. I wish Leah and Wyvern weren't gone, but it's not fair to blame him for things I only wish were different.

"All right," I say, picking up an armload of baneboo as a big green peace offering. "What do you need me to do?"

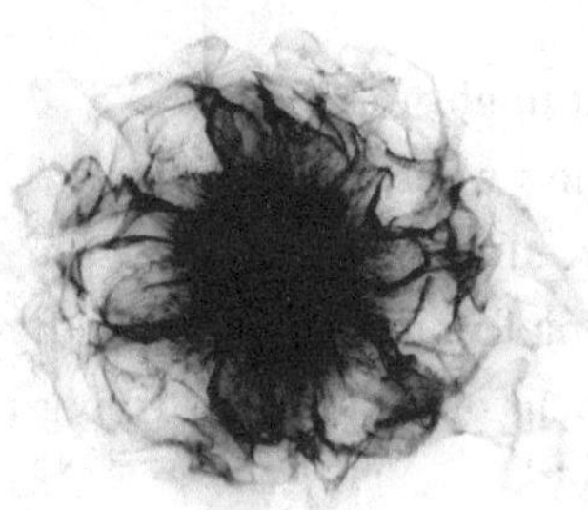

It takes forever to build the raft. I blame both of us for that: Peter's instructions are really complicated, and he gets impatient when I don't follow them to the letter. We waste a lot of time with him complaining and me trying to rein my temper in. Eventually, my ribs feel healed enough to unwrap the bandage from my chest, which is a good thing, because we need it to tie the stalks together. While we work, the quetzal makes extra trips to the river to get more baneboo. It never tires or issues the slightest squawk of complaint, which is more than I can say for myself.

When we're done, though, I have to admit our raft looks good. It's square and even, lashed tightly, and more than big enough for both of us. As Peter stands there with his hands on his hips, nodding in satisfaction, it strikes me that he would have made a great builder like Master Gideon, and I wonder why he decided to join the Queen's Corps instead.

"How are we going to get it to the river?" I ask.

He looks at me. "What?"

"We built it up here," I say. "How are we going to get it down there?"

I expect him to look aghast at the flaw in his brilliant plan, but he smiles smugly.

"That won't present a problem," he says.

Before I can answer, the quetzalbird grabs me by the

shoulders and takes a stomach-emptying dive toward the river that stretches to the north. It drops me none too gently on the bank, then heads back to the cliff and returns with Peter. He shoots me another smile as it flies off again, and I'm amazed when, a few minutes later, it comes back lugging the raft in its rear talons. The raft must weigh two hundred pounds at least, but other than a little up-and-down motion in its flying, the quetzal doesn't seem bothered at all.

"I calculated that we'd save time by building our craft on the ridge rather than having the quetzal spend multiple trips transporting the materials down here," Peter says. "Based on observation and analysis of its previous flights, I was confident it could manage the extra weight."

"There's more to life than observation and analysis, you know," I say.

"I'm sure there is. Notwithstanding, I pity the person who has to build a sea-worthy craft without them."

I stick my tongue out at him, but he's too busy tucking in loose fronds to notice.

The sky has turned a deep shade of purple when we push off from the riverbank. I'd be uneasy about traveling at night if not for the fact that there's a full moon out, lighting the river with a trail of silver sparkles. The quetzalbird flies ahead, its bronze feathers outlined by the glow. While Peter was putting the finishing touches on his masterpiece, I had the idea to make paddles out of spare stalks wrapped with our last remaining fronds, and those help us to steer, with me on one side of the raft and him on the other. The current goes in our direction, though, so mostly we just sit there, not talking, staring straight ahead as the empty land slips by on either side. If I could only forget that the boat we're riding on ate one of our companions and stole her face, I might almost be able to relax.

It's only an hour or so before the river forks, the main branch flowing westward while a smaller branch heads due north. We steer toward this new stream and slip into its more gentle current. It's much narrower than the main river, and just as I Sensed from the other side of the canyon, the land around it is marshy, full of pools and streams that form silver webs in the dark. Here and there, lone trees stand out against the moonlight. Though I didn't Sense any animals earlier today, now I see white birds with long legs and curved necks stalking along the shoreline, erupting into flight when we come near. Watching them soar over the marshland with moonlight shining on their backs is both beautiful and sad, as if they're courier birds sent by missing friends.

The river is clean enough to drink from, but after another hour, I can't hide how famished I am. Peter looks pretty peaked, too. We try to nibble the fronds, but they're too tough to swallow, and they have a funny flavor I don't trust. Once in a while, an island pops out of the darkness, and each time, we bring our craft to a gentle landing against the soggy banks, then hop off in hopes of finding something to eat. We're always disappointed, though. The islands are filled with weeds and prickly hedges, not anything that might bear fruit. We push off again and continue downstream, our arms moving mechanically and the rumbling of our stomachs almost drowning out the soft plashes from our paddles.

When the moon sets, we pull up to the next island, lash our raft in place, and find a grassy spot to sleep. It feels uncomfortable to lie beside Peter, even though he faces the other way with the quetzal curled against his stomach. I consider asking him for my sword, but decide I've insulted him enough. I close my eyes, finger the token around my neck, and try not to dream either of home or of the place we're going.

I wake to sunlight and strange chirping sounds. Before I'm fully aware of where I am, I find Peter crouched beside me, excitement in his face.

"You're not going to believe this," he says.

I sit up and look around, and he's right.

The island isn't more than ten yards across, and I'm sure it was empty last night except for us and the quetzal. Now it's covered with birds flitting from place to place—birds that look vaguely familiar but not exactly the same as the ones back home. There are birds shaped like blurjays, except their bodies stay solid blue instead of changing color in the dizzying way blurjays do. There are little brown-and-white birds I'd swear are scarrows if their claws weren't tiny and harmless, unlike the large hooked feet that make it necessary to handle those birds with extreme care. There are others as well, but with each one, there's something off, something not right. Even if it's only a matter of their calls—which are almost musical, unlike the croaks and squawks I've heard all my life—it's obvious these birds aren't native to the area surrounding the City of the Queens. I send my Sense toward them, but it seems to pass right through their bodies without telling me so much as their names.

"Where did they come from?" I ask Peter.

"I've been trying to ascertain that very thing," he says. "It could be that they're strictly diurnal, and that they all arrived at the same time this morning. That seems statistically improbable, though. My best speculation is that we disturbed them when we approached last night, but they came back once they became accustomed to us. It should be simple to test my theory…"

He stands up, waving his arms. The birds shriek—sounding much more like the bloodbirds and scarrows I used to hear outside my bedroom window each morning—and scatter in a hundred different directions. The quetzal lifts off as if to chase them, but they're gone so fast it sinks back to the island in defeat.

"That's weird," I say.

"Not at all," Peter says. "If, as I hypothesized, these birds were unsettled by us last night, they'd have acclimated to our presence when we were essentially motionless during sleep, and therefore—"

"That's not what I meant," I say. "It's weird that they were bothered by us at all. Birds in the Ecosystem aren't afraid of human beings. Some of them are hostile, and most are friendly, but none of them gets spooked like that."

He rubs his chin in thought. "True enough. Which would appear to indicate…"

I'm sure he's about to confuse me with some other complicated theory, but then his voice falters and his eyes grow wide. A sound that's less than a word escapes him, and I follow his pointing finger.

My mouth falls open at the sight.

The land on either side of the river is full of animals I've never seen before, way too many of them for me to have missed Sensing them yesterday. They're big, too, much bigger than the animals back home: spotted cats seven feet long from whiskers to tail, deer-shaped creatures as tall as me not counting their curved antlers, gray-skinned behemoths with sharp horns on their noses. Big as they are, I can't help feeling that they appeared as quickly as the birds disappeared, as if they all strolled out from behind the trees at the exact same time or were camouflaged against the ground and became visible only when they stood up. I try to send my Sense toward them, but it's the same as it was with the birds: for all I can tell, they might as well not be there at all.

I'm trying my hardest to focus my unsteady Sense when an animal that towers above all the others appears from behind a clump of trees and lopes to the river's edge, where it spreads its impossibly long, gangly legs and bends its ten-foot neck to drink. A smaller version of the same creature follows, moving with the slow, awkward grace of the grown-up. It looks at me before leaning over to drink, and I see that its huge brown eyes are ringed by thick lashes, its mouth shaped into something like a shy smile.

I turn to Peter. His dazed expression hasn't changed.

"What are those things?" I ask.

"They're… giraffes," he says. "Genus *Giraffa*, family *Giraffidae*. I'm not entirely certain which subspecies these two are, but based on their spot patterns and coloration, I believe they should be classified as *G. reticulata*. The old world's tallest land mammal, which pre-Darwinian evolutionary theorist Jean Baptiste Lamarck famously but erroneously speculated—"

"Wait a second," I say. "The *old* world?"

He frowns at the interruption. "Native to the continent previously known as Africa, they reproduce slowly and thus were particularly vulnerable to habitat loss and other deleterious effects of human population pressures. *Contra* Lamarck, they seem to have evolved from—"

"Peter," I cut him off again. "I don't need a natural history lesson. I just need to know one thing."

"Which is what?"

"If they're from the *old* world," I say, "what are they doing here?"

He opens his mouth to answer, but no sound comes out. I'm tempted to giggle, because he looks so much like a little boy dazzled by a birthday party magic show. Except I feel like I'm at the same party, and I just discovered that the magic trick is real.

"When we entered this river…" he says slowly.

"We passed into a different world," I finish. "A world that hasn't existed since before the Ecosystem began."

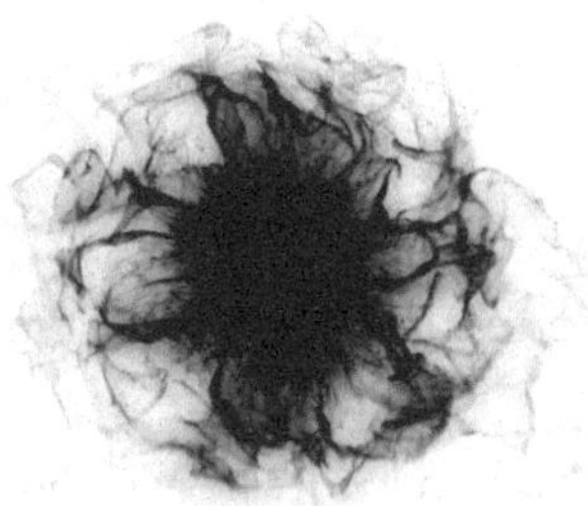

We drift down the river, surrounded by animals that were supposed to have gone extinct two hundred years ago. I can't Sense them no matter how hard I try, but Peter names every last one.

"Muskrat. Okapi. Komodo dragon. Kangaroo. Ostrich. Wolverine. And, holy cowl, those are sandhill cranes…"

I look overhead, where birds with five-foot wingspans soar against the cloudless sky. The quetzal joins them, darting playfully among the lanky shapes.

Peter watches for a minute, then shouts, "This is incredible!"

"I know," I say. "It's—"

He shakes his head. "I don't think you understand. It's not only that these creatures shouldn't still exist. It's that they *never* existed in the same place. Some were from temperate climates, some arid, some sub-Arctic. Some were from different continents. Some were nocturnal, others diurnal. There's no way they should all be here at once."

I stare at him in wonder, then say the first thing that comes to mind. "You're like an encyclopedia!"

He frowns, and I wish I'd kept my mouth shut.

"My dad used to say my brain works differently than other people's," he says. "He told me it's what makes me special. But in my experience, it only makes everyone else think I'm showing off."

"Hey," I say. "Some people feel the same about natural Sensors."

"I wouldn't be surprised," he says. "The only difference is, *your* kind receives the red carpet treatment, while people like me are—"

"Peter," I stop him before he gets too worked up. "Not everything needs to be a competition between us. Can't we both just be good at our own thing?"

He thinks about that for a moment, nods stiffly. Then he goes back to naming the creatures that shouldn't be there.

"Cheetah. Wombat. Golden eagle. Pangolin. Koala. Echidna. Blue-footed booby…"

He looks at me so strangely when he says that last name, I have to laugh. For once, he doesn't seem to mind.

A few hours into the morning's journey, we come across an island filled with something even more amazing than Peter's animals: berry bushes. Like everything else, the berries are a kind I've never seen, bright red and shaped like hearts, with little dimples all over them. Peter calls them strawberries, and for the first time since yesterday morning, my Sense works well enough to tell me they're safe to eat. We stuff ourselves with the sweet-tasting berries, staining our lips and fingers red. People should have called them bloodberries instead.

We're sleepy from the meal, but I'm afraid to waste time, so we put as many berries as we can in Peter's empty pack and push off from the island, the quetzal flying ahead. The river gets wider and deeper as we sail farther north, which gives Peter a chance to rattle off the names of the swimming creatures he sees alongside us: mackerels, leatherback turtles, reef sharks, sunfish, manta rays, marine iguanas. I can tell he's trying to figure out how so many different species could have ended up in the same place; he lost his notebook during the river crossing, but his eyes are turned inward as if he's taking mental notes. I wait for a pause in his stream of words before jumping in.

"Peter," I say, "can I ask you a question?"

Irritation creeps into his face, but he nods. "Certainly."

"You learned about all of these things in the library, right?"

"It's where I did my primary research," he says. "In a few cases, I was able to supplement my reading by working backwards from existing species. Bloodbirds, for example, are clearly descended from old world thrushes, and prowler monkeys are anatomically identical—with the exception of their larger, more resonant vocal chambers—to their predecessors among the New World monkeys of South and Central America. The term *New World*, of course, referring in this context to pre-Ecosystem geographic classification systems, and not to be confused with the post-Ecosystem period."

"Okay," I say. "Can I ask *why*?"

His face scrunches up. "Why what?"

"Why spend all that time studying things that don't exist?" I ask. "Or *didn't* exist, so far as you knew. Isn't it our job as Sensors to adapt to the Ecosystem the way it is, not to learn about the way it was?"

His expression darkens, and for a moment, I think he's going to forget our truce and lay into me. But then he relaxes, and his eyes meet mine before glancing away.

"I told you I think about things differently," he says. "I had an idea when I was five years old, and my dad encouraged me to pursue it. He even took me to see your mom, who thought the idea had merit, which is why she accepted me as an apprentice Sensor even though I had nowhere near the genetic endowment I needed to Sense in the traditional manner."

That clears up one mystery. "What was your idea?"

"Something very simple," he says. "But like most ideas that go against the mainstream, it was one that no one else had dared to explore. I asked myself if the Sensors might be cutting off their own legs by ignoring the evolutionary history that brought us to this juncture. If even the Queen was limiting herself in the same fashion. Yes, we have to live in the world as it's currently given to us, but couldn't we learn a lot about the existing world by discovering what it was like before? If we understood lost ecosystems—individual ecosystems, before they became knitted together into the single entity we call the Ecosystem—wouldn't we be in a better position to understand present-day ecosystemic relationships *logically*, not just intuitively?"

I make a face, which fortunately he doesn't see. "I guess so..."

"That was my idea, in any event," he goes on as if I didn't say a word. "So I dedicated myself to learning everything I could about the past: the names of extinct species, the conditions of prior habitats, the ways in which human beings interacted with other living things. I learned, for example, about large-scale agriculture, the system whereby people called farmers used to plant huge fields of staple crops and irrigate them with massive amounts of water, rather than cultivating small gardens like we do now. I researched people's diets and eating habits, how they hunted and traded various animals and parts of animals, how they synthesized compounds in the laboratory from biologically-derived elements, how they conducted experiments on non-human creatures in the name of advancing human health and industry. To tell the truth, some of it was pretty ugly, and lots of it was full of holes because so many records have been lost. But taken together, it gave me a… a *feeling*, something I couldn't put my finger on. Not, that is, until now."

He looks at me, his eyes shining. It strikes me that most of the time I've known him, he hasn't been talking to himself, not really. He's been talking the way he used to talk to his dad.

"What have you figured out?" I ask.

"That we *need* the old world," he says. "That the Ecosystem is… *layered*, I guess you'd call it, with the world we live in only the topmost layer, and everything else that's ever happened on earth layered underneath. On this side of the canyon and especially on this river, we've penetrated to a deeper layer, a layer that holds up all the layers above. Which means that, to learn the truth, we have to dig down to the very deepest layer, and that layer is—"

"The tree."

He nods. "I suspect so. And your mom must have agreed with me, or I wouldn't be on this expedition at all."

Another mystery solved. "You're sure the tree will heal Rebecca? Her, and… and everyone?"

"I'm not sure about that," he says. "All I'm sure about is that without it, we won't be able to heal *anyone*."

His face is solemn, and he's not looking away.

"Peter," I ask, "how did your dad die?"

"Oh," he says. "Well, he got sick."

"From what?"

He shrugs. "The Queen said it was cancer. Of the pancreas. A kind that grew really fast, and by the time he started showing symptoms, it was too late for her to heal him."

"I'm so sorry," I say.

"I used to be mad at the Queen," he says. "This was five years ago, when she was only a teenager, and I thought… well, I thought if she'd been a grown-up, she might have been able to make him better. I was mad at her for pretending to be a queen before she was ready. But now I know that it wouldn't have mattered. It was his time, and there was nothing anyone could have done to save him."

Tears are on his cheeks to match mine, but he doesn't turn away. My fingers itch to reach out and touch his hand, something to show him I know how he feels. The Queen is powerful, but my mom has told me a hundred times that everything in the Ecosystem happens for a reason, that we're its creatures, not its masters, and we can't stop death any more than we can stop the world from turning. No matter how hard Peter and I try, no matter if we find the tree or not, my dad might die. The Queen might die. And if she does, everything on our side of the river will die too, and only these lost creatures will be left.

Peter is untying the belt from his waist. My eyes widen for a second until he holds the sword and scabbard out to me.

"This is yours," he says. "I'm sorry I kept it so long."

"It's okay," I say. "Thank you for… for saving me."

He shrugs, ducks his head.

"And I'm sorry I doubted you," I add. "I was just…"

"I know," he says.

I take the sword from him. My hand touches his, and he jerks back, then smiles bashfully. I tie the belt around my waist. The weight of the sword in its scabbard feels familiar, like a piece of my life I've been missing for a long time.

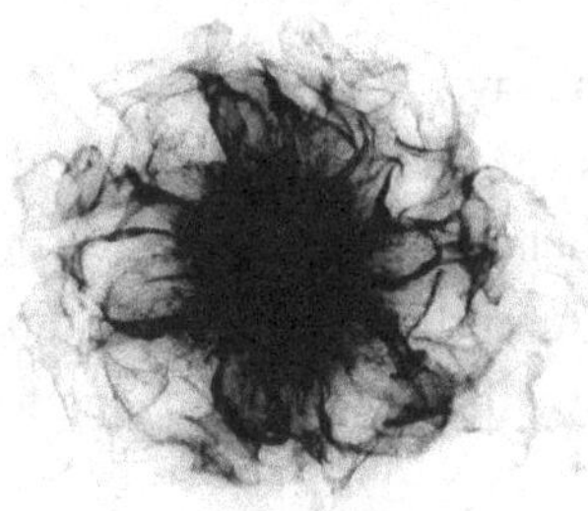

I WAKE THE next morning with a scream.

Dinosaurs stalk the shoreline. Real dinosaurs, not the wooden toys Master Gideon made for Chaim when he was a baby. I've seen drawings of dinosaurs in books, and it turns out the artists came pretty close to the real thing: huge, colorful reptiles with long snouts and lizard eyes, some with feathers instead of scales, some running fleetly across the swampy ground, some wheeling overhead. I shrink down and try to make myself invisible, but Peter stands there shouting out strange names like he doesn't have a care in the Ecosystem.

"Struthiomimus. Ornitholestes. Protoceratops. Euoplocephalus. Pachycephalosaurus. Parasaurolophus. Quetzalcoatlus..."

"Wait. You mean like our quetzal?"

"They're related," he says. "It seems that genetic material from extinct pterosaurs of the family *Azhdarchidae* was recombined with coatimundi genes during foraging activities by female *Apis impunita* workers, resulting in..."

I half-listen while he babbles on. It's hard to believe that the flying terror above our heads, its thirty-foot wings almost see-through in the rays of the sun, could be related to the harmless animal that glides underneath it.

"Woah," Peter says. "That's a new one."

I lower my eyes from the quetzal-monster to see an

even more terrifying creature lumbering toward the riverbank: a gigantic two-legged beast that looks something like a Tyrannosaurus, except it has a wickedly long snout and a sail-like fin on its back. My fingers tighten on Leah's sword, but Peter waves a hand dismissively as the monster leans down to drink.

"I wouldn't worry about it attacking," he says. "I've noticed that these animals are entirely oblivious to us—they don't demonstrate a natural fear response, but neither do they display any tendency toward aggression, the so-called 'fight or flight' dyad. The only creatures that have paid attention to us at all are the egrets we saw the first night and the birds on the island the following morning. I've been trying to understand the discrepancy, but my data set's too limited to draw any definite conclusions."

"Okay," I say, but my eyes never leave the colossal snout that's guzzling water just ahead of our raft. "What is that thing, anyway?"

"*Spinosaurus aegyptiacus.*" He pronounces the tongue-twister as if it's as easy to say as his own name. "Considered to be the largest theropod of them all, even larger than Giganotosaurus. A little too large for your sword to handle, in any event," he says with a grin.

"Peter," I say, "did you just tell a joke?"

He looks surprised, then turns away. But he keeps on talking, probably to cover up his embarrassment.

"Actually, the lack of interest these animals have shown us isn't their only peculiarity," he says. "I've been taking notes since yesterday, and I've identified quite a few anomalies."

"Like what?"

"Well, for one thing, we've witnessed no predation," he

says. "There are both herbivores and carnivores, but they ignore each other every bit as much as they ignore us—the herbivores go about their business despite the presence of predators, and the carnivores exhibit no hunting or tracking behavior. It's the same with social groupings: there are wildebeests and springboks and other quadrupeds you'd expect to see congregating in herds, but each member of the species seems to keep aloof from the others. Ditto with adults and their offspring: I haven't observed anything in the way of nurturing, socialization, even basic care. Then there's the apparent absence of scavengers—hyenas and buzzards and that sort of thing—and, as I'm sure you've noticed, there are no insects at all."

I hadn't noticed, but I say, "Uh-huh."

"Which is highly irregular, all the more so in light of the dinosaurs," he goes on, ignoring my response as usual. "If we've traveled back in time to a Jurassic or Mesozoic ecosystem, we should be seeing dragonflies the size of our quetzalbird and cockroaches as big as fell-cats. But there's nothing. It's as if this landscape is…"

"Is what?"

"Unfinished," he says. "As if someone put the most obvious aspects of a functioning ecosystem in place, but forgot to consider the details, the subtle interrelationships that make a true ecosystem come to life."

"Some*one*?"

"That was merely a figure of speech," he says. "It could be that these regions are… *embryonic*, as it were. In an early stage of development. Or it could be that this ecosystem obeys laws fundamentally dissimilar to those of the

Ecosystem we know. Laws that are generated by some other power we've never encountered."

"The tree?" I guess.

"It always seems to come back to that, doesn't it? I suppose we won't know for sure until we get there."

He presses his lips together and gazes off into the distance. There are a million things I want to ask him, especially now that we're past the spinysaurus and I'm not holding my breath anymore. Like why my Sense can't detect these giants right in front of my face. Or how creatures that have been extinct for millions of years could have come back now. But I've learned enough about Peter to know when he's in a *no more questions* mood, so I keep my thoughts to myself.

Some other power, I repeat as we steer around a small island covered with plants that look like poisonrose bushes, except their blossoms don't have teeth. It would make sense if this other power came from the tree—if it's the one that's been blocking me all this time, the one that woke up the baneboo and sent it after me. It seems obvious that the tree doesn't want me to find it, and that it'll do anything to stop me. Though if that's true, why doesn't it simply send a swarm of velociraptors to leap onto our raft?

Nighttime falls with those questions still in my mind. I ask Peter if he's ready for bed, but he tells me he'd like to stay up a little longer. Nervous as I am about falling asleep with monsters all around us, the heaviness of my eyelids makes the decision for me. The last thing I see is Peter standing at the head of the boat, his blond hair outlined by moonlight, his eyes fixed on the quetzal as it soars ahead into the night.

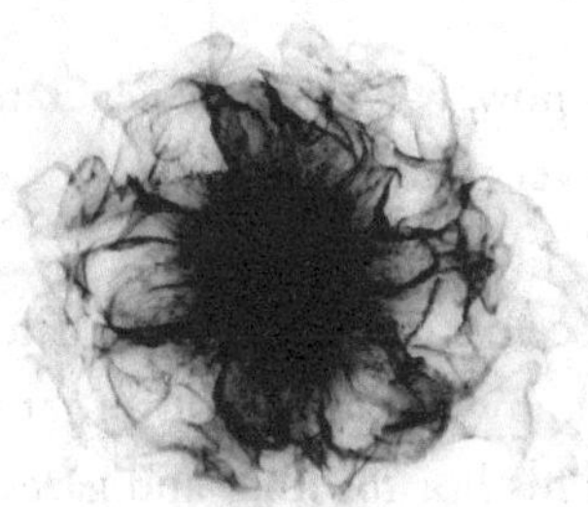

RAINDROPS TEASE MY eyes open. I find Peter spread-eviled on his back, snoring away. There are no more dinosaurs, so maybe he waited to make sure they were all gone before he fell asleep.

I nudge him with a toe until he yawns, stretches, and sits up, looking stiff and bleary-eyed. We're floating down a part of the river that's wider and faster-moving than before, and the marshlands have given way to dense forest, with trees shaped enough like aches and mauls and pains that I assume they're distant cousins. The sky is filled with the first rainclouds we've had on this whole trip, but the rain is warm and gentle enough to be refreshing instead of annoying. I don't see any animals, not in the water or woods or sky, and I don't hear any birds either. Even our quetzal is gone. That should make me uneasy, but the patter of raindrops against the river has a lulling effect after a night filled with dreams of dinosaur growls.

"Someone used to live here," Peter says.

I follow his finger until I find what he's talking about: a rust-colored shape hidden among the trees, so covered with branches and vines it blends into the forest. Squinting through beads of rain, I realize it's a building, long and boxy like the guardhouse in the City of the Queens. It's followed by another, and another, and another, all of them made of the same reddish brick, all of them swallowed by the woods.

Though the color and style aren't the same as the buildings back home, they're close enough that for once, I beat Peter at his observation-and-analysis game.

"This used to be a university," I say. "Before the forest destroyed it."

He nods, rubbing his chin thoughtfully. "Built along the banks of a river. The way ancient civilizations used to build their cities thousands of years ago. For irrigation of their fields and commerce with other cities."

I frown. I should have known he'd have to get the last word in.

The rain eases up as we continue down the stream, and the sun emerges to show me that this campus was even bigger than the one where I grew up. There are whole rows of the red-brick dormitories, plus a collection of buildings with large—and mostly broken—windows that might have had classrooms behind them. There's a big, oddly shaped building made of corroded metal that I guess was a dining hall or student center, followed by a clump of buildings made of gray cement block with the dangling letters *F E   A R S* on the central one. "Fine Arts," Peter says. "For painters and musicians and things." The largest building of all has ornately carved pillars standing like tree trunks amid the actual trees; the greedy way Peter eyes it makes me sure it must have been the library. Standing slightly separate from the rest of the campus is a stone structure with a soaring clock tower, though the clock itself has been torn loose by climbing vines. I wonder if this used to be their council house, where their queen would hold her meetings and ceremonies. But if there ever was a queen here, it's pretty clear she lost her struggle against the wild years ago and faded into the trees along with the city she once ruled.

A low sound interrupts my train of thought. I look up to see that we've cleared a bend in the river, leaving the buildings behind. But that's not what catches my attention. As soon as I see what lies ahead, I grab Peter's arm.

"We need to steer for shore," I say.

He shakes loose from my grip, turns from staring at the last of the campus buildings. "Why?"

"Because of that," I answer.

The rumbling sound has grown louder, and we can both see where it's coming from: rapids have formed up ahead, the water rushing toward a point where white mist hangs in the air. Peter looks at me in alarm.

"Waterfall!"

"No kidding," I say. "Come on, let's paddle to shore."

He doesn't wait for another invitation. The two of us plunge our paddles into the water and pull with all our strength. The tall trees that stand along the shoreline get closer, and for a minute, I think we're going to make it.

But it's too late. Before we're close enough to jump into shallow water, the rapids catch us and pull us back to the center of the stream. From there, they drag us toward the drop-off that booms two hundred yards ahead.

"We're going to fall!" Peter cries.

"I know!"

Urgently, I scan the river for a way out—an overhanging branch we can grab onto, a rock jutting out of the water where we can abandon ship—but there's nothing. If there was any chance we could swim against the current, I'd grab Peter and leap from the raft. But the river is boiling like a pot of soup on the fireplace, and the moment we enter the rapids, we'll be swept downstream and over the falls.

I see a small shape break through the mist, and I yell at Peter over the roar. "Hold on to me!"

"What?"

"Don't argue! Just do it!"

He makes a face, but wraps his arms around my stomach and locks his hands together. I reach up just as the spray from the waterfall hits me and our raft tips over the edge.

The quetzal catches my hands in its back claws and lifts us free of the raft. In an instant, we're soaring over the falls, with rainbow-colored spray in our faces and the sound of the water thundering in our ears. I risk a look down, but I can't see anything through the mist. The bird's flight isn't as smooth as it was when it was carrying just me—it dips up and down, wings pumping furiously to stay airborne—but Peter's hunch was right: it *is* strong enough to carry us both, at least for a short distance. The wind and the mist swirl around me so wildly I can't catch my breath, but I mouth my thoughts silently and hope that the one who sent our savior can hear.

Thank you, Sarah. For everything. I promise, if you're there, I'll find you.

The bird lets us drop onto the rocky ground below the falls. With Peter hugging me, it's a rough landing, but my ribs must be completely healed, because they don't hurt on impact. Peter gets the worst of it, letting out a pained grunt as my weight comes down on top of him. I try to free myself, but his hands remain as tightly tied around my middle as the bandage used to be.

"Peter," I say. "You can let go now."

"Where are we?" he moans with a gurgling sound that makes me think he must have water in his lungs.

"I don't know. Are you okay?"

He coughs, spits water. Then he moans again, which I take as a yes.

Shakily, we climb to our feet. I'm relieved to find that I still have Leah's scabbard and sword, along with the token that's never left my throat since Mom gave it to me. My shirt and shorts have disintegrated to the point where they only cover the bare minimum, while Peter's pack is gone and his chest is practically naked. I get the same butterfly feeling I did when he put on the bandage, and I try to force the image of his arms wrapped around me out of my mind.

We make our way down slippery rocks to level ground. With the mist from the falls no longer blinding me, I see that we're standing on the shore of a broad lake circled by wooded hills. Wisps of smoke rise from the water along the shoreline, where the reflections of trees are broken by ripples from the falls. Farther out in the sunlight, the water is perfectly calm and such a breathtaking blue-green it's as if the sky and trees have dripped down to gather in its shining depths. The lake is too big for me to see to the other side, but I spot an island standing far out from shore. It seems much larger than any of the islands we passed on the river, though it's covered in a thick blanket of mist that shows only the tops of trees. The mist swirls and pulls aside for a moment, and something dazzlingly bright peeks through. The second my eyes fall on it, I know.

Peter is standing beside me, shading his vision with a hand. When I touch his arm, he jumps.

"That's it," I tell him. "We're here."

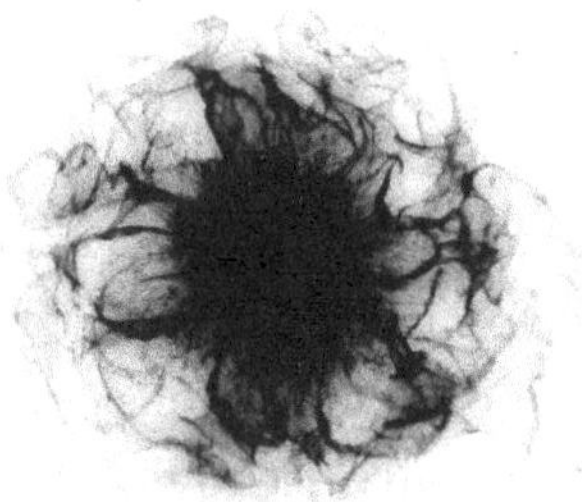

Peter stares at me. "Are you sure?"

"Absolutely," I say. "It's on that island. The tree, the answers, everything. Now all we have to do is get there."

"Okay," he says. "How?"

"The quetzal?" I look around, but can't find it anywhere. I worry it exhausted itself carrying us both.

"If only we hadn't lost…" Peter kicks a stone into the water with a soft *plop*. "The raft!"

He runs down the shoreline toward a swampy cove where tall reeds that look like cat o' nine tails stand in the shallows. Caught by the reeds, what's left of our raft bobs on the water.

I plunge into the muck to help drag the raft to shore. It's only half as big as it used to be, and that half is held together by a few threadbare fronds. But it floats, and there's enough room for both of us if we sit close together. I stand in the shallow water, tearing reeds from the lake's soft bottom for Peter to lash around the raft and tie tight. For oars, I slice the stems of large leafy pads that float on the surface of the lake, then tie them around fallen sticks that Peter gathers at the forest's edge. When we're done, his face is red with exertion and I'm streaming with sweat under the midmorning sun. We don't wait before climbing aboard, leaning over the side of the raft to take a long drink of cool lake water, then pushing off for the island that floats in the blue distance.

We don't talk. Peter's eyes are glued to our goal, while I reach out with my Sense to try to detect the presence of the tree. It's there, I know it's there, but it must know that *I'm* here too, because it's invisible to my inner sight. I can feel the power that protects it laying a final trap for us, and I wish I could read its mind well enough to know what form that trap will take. I glance at my partner out of the corner of my eye, and I know I have to say something to him. He turns to face me, and my lips feel too dry to speak.

"Peter," I whisper. "I—"

"Don't even think it," he says. "I wouldn't miss this for the world."

He smiles, and I smile back. When he returns to paddling, I join him with new strength. My arms are tired, but my heart feels much lighter.

The roar of the waterfall fades as we creep ever closer, and then there's silence except for our paddles dipping into the water. No birdcalls emerge from the woods, no fish splash from below to catch insects—which could be because, this time, I notice that there are no insects to catch. The water grows deep, but it's such a clear and brilliant blue I can see reeds reaching up from the bottom. We're close enough that the island's misty mantle reveals glimpses of sandy beach, a grove of trees with bushy needles. Then we're inside the mist, cool droplets forming on our sun-warmed skin. A few strokes later, we break through into clear water again, and the thing I couldn't see distinctly from the other shore shines out at last.

It's a building shaped like a globe, made entirely of glass

that mirrors the perfect blue of the lake and sky. It rises above the treetops on tall silver struts as if it's an enormous beetle. Unlike the campus buildings, this one is untouched by trees or vines, its curved sides as spotless as they must have been on the day the structure was built. It throws back the light of the sunny day as if warning us not to come any closer.

"Look," Peter says.

He points at markings in shining silver just below the building's curved top. They might be letters or words, but I can't read the language. Peter's lips move as if he's trying to figure out what the words mean, but if he succeeds, he doesn't let me in on it.

Our boat scrapes against the shoreline. I step into shallow water to help Peter drag the raft onto dry land.

"The sword," he says. "You better…"

"Right."

I pull Leah's blade from my belt and hold it in front of me in the *Plow* position. Nodding to Peter, I lead the way up the bank toward the trees, the glass dome shining above us like a moon.

The trees make no move to stop us as we pass through. On the other side, there's a grassy slope, with rectangular white stones forming a path to the building. The footpath ends where stairs of shining metal climb to a silver rectangle midway up the globe that looks like it could be a door.

"Do you see…?" Peter asks.

"What am I, blind?"

A fence of ten-foot baneboo stalks—brown instead of green—grows all the way around the building's struts. To get to the stairs and the door, we're going to have to walk straight through them.

"This could pose a complication," Peter says.

"Why's it brown?"

"Age?" he guesses. "If this plant is related to old-world bamboo, I seem to have read that the stalks live no longer than—"

"Tell me later," I say. "We've got company."

The baneboo rustles, though there's no wind. A shape forms in the brown, each stalk adding a new part to the whole. I watch legs develop, arms, body. When it's finished, a human figure steps out of the fence and stands on the slope above us. Its limbs are slender stalks of baneboo; its long hair is made of jointed baneboo links, rattling as its head moves. In its right hand, it holds a curved stalk with a sharp cutting edge, and in its left, it grips a shield made of baneboo shoots. Its empty brown eyes are clouded with yellow spots.

It's not Catherine this time. I don't recognize the face, but it must be one of the people who lived or worked at the university before the baneboo consumed them.

I switch my sword to the *Tox* position as the baneboo warrior takes a step toward us. It seems a little unsteady on its feet, which makes me think Peter is right about it being old. I rush up the hill, shifting to the *Roof* position as I run, then swing at the creature with all my strength.

It lifts its sword stiffly to block mine. The blades hit without the ringing sound I'm used to, but with a thready feeling like a hammer striking rotten wood. The warrior backs away a step, so I jab at it. This time, when our blades make contact, my opponent's fingers splinter and its sword spins to the ground. I sweep my blade sideways, the baneboo warrior clumsily parrying with its shield. When I lift

Leah's sword again, the warrior's shield rises too slowly to stop me from bringing the blade down on its head.

The warrior falls to its knees. It tries to stand, but I slash at it again, and there's a tearing sound as the head bursts open. The warrior pitches face forward onto the grass, the hole in the top of its head spilling twenty or more small brown ovals the size of teeth.

"Oh," I say. "That's not good."

The ovals have started moving, standing on end before tunneling into the ground. Peter and I back away as the first delicate shoot of newborn baneboo pokes from the turf, looking like a small green guarder snake as it waves back and forth. It grows fast, lengthening and thickening until it's a solid stalk as tall as a man. New shoots fork from its top, becoming arms and head. With a tug, it pulls itself from the ground, the single stalk splitting to form legs. Its right hand opens, and a curved blade grows from it; its other arm shrugs, and a shield folds outward to cover its body. I think it's done, but then I see additional limbs growing from its hips and shoulders, until it looks more like a giant green tyrantula than a human being. Its face forms a toothy smile all the more terrible for the blankness of its eyes.

To either side of the leader, other baneboo warriors are forming the same way. Most of them have more than two arms and legs; a few have more than one head. All of them hold baneboo shields and some kind of weapon: swords, spears, sticks linked by what looks like a length of green chain. There are as many warriors as there were seeds, a solid wall of them in front of us. Their leader waves its sword and they advance downhill, marching in formation like a moving forest.

"Get back to the raft!" I tell Peter. "I'll try to hold them off."

"You can't fight all of them!"

The first warrior swings its sword, and I parry the blow. But it must be much fresher than the one I killed, because contact sends pain through my arm like slivers of glass. When I return the stroke, it brushes my sword aside with two of its extra arms, throwing me off balance and making me lose my footing. I try to remember Leah's lessons, try to think of the right position to use against something with this many limbs, but my mind is a blank. All I can do is watch as the warrior switches its sword back and forth between its many hands so fast it's nothing but a blur. I can't tell when the blade finally stops moving or which hand is holding it when the warrior raises it for another strike.

For once in his life, Peter was wrong. I can't fight *any* of them.

The sword is coming down when Peter throws himself at the warrior's four legs, ruining its aim and making the blade embed itself in the ground. While it strains to pull the weapon free, I hack at it, slicing through its sword hand at the wrist. Disarmed, it hurls its shield at me, but Peter jumps between us and takes the blow with his body. He cries out in pain and sprawls at the warrior's feet, its shield clattering on top of him. For an instant the warrior pauses, taking a step backward as if it's changed its mind. Before it has a chance to change it back, I swipe at its neck and watch its severed head tumble to the ground.

The head rolls down the slope, landing face-up. From every hole, eyes and mouth and nostrils and ears, slim green shoots begin growing. They plant themselves in the ground, and new warriors emerge all over the hillside.

I grab Peter's arm and yank him to his feet. The first army of warriors has almost reached us when I take off through the trees, pulling Peter behind me.

"Wait!" he cries. "I think I—"

"Save it!" I shout back. "We've got to get out of here!"

"But—"

I don't listen to him as I race through the trees. I can hear the warriors gaining on us, their many-limbed bodies rattling as if they're wearing suits of armor.

We burst through the trees and run for the raft, which rests on the sandy shoreline. The warriors are right behind us, too close for me to risk a backward glance. I don't know how we're going to get to the raft and launch it before they catch us, but I can't think about that now. I just hope Peter doesn't have some ridiculous theory that will slow us down even more.

We're halfway across the beach when I see other bright green warriors rising from the shallows, forming a barrier of bodies and swords and shields our raft will never be able to get through.

My legs weaken, and I would fall if Peter didn't put on an extra burst of speed and drag me toward the raft. I'm about to tell him it's pointless when he slides across the sand, pulling me down with him. I land facing back toward the globe, but all I can see are hundreds of hands reaching out for us like a thicket of deadly green.

"Help me with this!" Peter says.

He's got his shoulders under the heavy raft and is trying to tilt it upward. My mind is too fuzzy either to object or to obey, but my body reacts to the urgency in his voice.

Together, we lift the raft from the sand and cower beneath it like twin turples under a single baneboo shell.

The beach falls silent. I can't hear the rattling of the warriors' bodies, can't see them through our shield. I wait for the attack I'm sure is coming, but when it doesn't, I peek around the edge of the raft.

The warriors have frozen in place with their many arms held rigidly at their sides and their vacant eyes staring over our heads. The wind on the shoreline blows through their hollow bones with a moaning sound. I stare at Peter, whose smile is as smug as ever.

"It was only a hunch," he says. "Based on something I observed. You saw what happened when the other one dropped its shield on me?"

"Um... maybe?"

"It didn't attack," he says. "At first I thought it might be a coincidence, but then I reasoned that the baneboo shielded me from its eyes, or its senses, or whatever it uses to detect foreign bodies. The simplest way to put this is that the baneboo doesn't recognize anything composed of its own material as potential prey. Which would make sense for a predatory plant that grows so profusely in such close quarters, because otherwise it might attack a member of its own species."

"You're a genius," I say, and I would hug his nearly shirtless body if I weren't holding a sword and didn't need my other arm to brace the raft. "So, um, we're going to keep this thing in front of us until they go away?"

"They're not going to go away. They've lost sight of their quarry for now, but they're going to stand here forever until it returns."

"That might make it a little hard for us," I say. "You know, with the *forever* thing."

"You don't need to worry about that," he says with another smile. "We're going to march right up to the front door while they're standing here, and they're not going to lay a finger on us. Just stay close and do what I do."

Carefully, making sure to match movements, we stand. Now that our half-raft is completely out of the water, it weighs a ton, so the steps we take are less of a march than a slow, painful shuffle. But as usual, Peter's right. Not only do the warriors on the beach leave us alone, but the solid forest of them covering the slope makes space to let us pass. Even the aging brown fence that the first warrior grew from creaks open just wide enough for us to wrestle the raft through. When we reach the bottom of the stairs, I turn to Peter, who nods.

"The second we let go of the raft, they're going to swarm," he says. "With any luck, we'll have enough of a head start that we can get inside."

"*With any luck?* What happened to logic?"

"I think I've used up my quota for the day."

We share a look, then heave the raft behind us and run up the stairs toward the silver rectangle at the top. Instantly, I hear the rattle of the warriors as they spring into action, and I can only pray the raft slows them long enough for us to reach the door.

My prayer is only partly answered. We do get to the silver rectangle first.

But it's not a door.

I search frantically, but it has no knob, no handle, nothing we can use to open it. The stairs echo with the metallic sound of stamping feet, and the sky-blue glass turns green as the warriors appear. I throw myself in front of Peter, knowing I can't save him, only hoping they'll kill me first so I don't have to watch his blood splatter the glass.

Peter slams his hand against the rectangle as if he's trying to break it down. There's a hissing noise, and the rectangle splits in the center, opening just wide enough for two bodies to squeeze through. Before the warriors can reach us, Peter pulls me into the building and the door seals shut behind us.

I spin, expecting the windows to shatter as the warriors rush through. I can see them through the glass, but they've frozen in place the way they did on the beach. I look to Peter, and as always, he has a theory.

"The one-way mirror must prevent the baneboo from sensing intruders, just as our raft did," he says. "That's why this building is completely untouched by the island's vegetation. I assume the glass was specially designed for that very reason."

"Then we're safe?"

"We're inside. Whether we're safe remains to be seen."

I sheathe my sword and turn to look at the interior of the building.

It's dark, the only illumination coming from a weakly glowing circle high up at the top of the dome. The circular room has an open space in the center, with the shadowy shape of a tall staircase rising to a disk-like platform. Around the edges of the room, my eyes catch glints from glass cases. I'm about to join Peter at the nearest case when a voice booms all around us, making me jump and the glass ring.

"Welcome, visitors," the voice says. "Welcome to *edinnu.*"

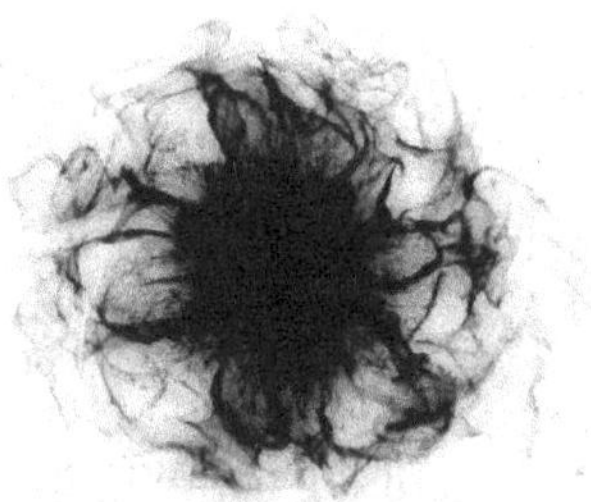

AT THE SOUND of the magic word, the circle overhead flares brightly, casting a beam of white light on the platform.

In its glow, I see two people standing side by side. Where they came from I can't tell, but there must be a door up there. They take each other's hands and descend the stairs, the light following them. As they come closer, I see that they're a man and a woman, dressed in the old-fashioned clothes my mom showed me in photographs from library books: a dark suit and tie for the man, a gray jacket and skirt for the woman. She looks like an older version of Rebecca, very pretty with brown skin and long curly hair. The man, on the other hand, has pale skin and short blond hair like Peter. Both of them are wearing eyeglasses, which Dad told me were common in the old world before the *Apis impunita* genome made people's eyesight better. They're both smiling, their extremely white teeth glowing in the light that bathes them from above.

"Welcome to *edinnu*," the woman says in the same voice I heard before, deep and rich but a little warbly from the echoes off the glass. "I am Dr. Meredith Cowley-Dawson, and this is my colleague and life partner, Dr. Reginald Dawson. We're so glad you could join us here."

I shake my head in disbelief. I don't want to be rude, but I can't help asking.

"Are you the parents of Dominique Dawson, the first ruler of the City of the Queens? I thought you were…"

I can't finish, because the word that comes next is *dead.* Killed two hundred years ago, victims of the Ecosystem that grew from their own research, their own daughter's genes.

The Dawsons regard me with kindly smiles, but when the woman answers, she only confuses me more.

"We are the founders of the *edinnu* project," she says. "From an ancient Akkadian word meaning 'fruitful' or 'well-watered plain,' which is believed to be the root of the Judeo-Christian *Eden.* We welcome you to the site of our work, but we regret that we cannot satisfy your inquiry concerning *Dominique Dawson* or *City of the Queens.* Those terms are not found within our databanks."

I'm trying to think of a better way to ask about their own daughter when Peter interrupts.

"They can't understand what you're asking," he says. "Look."

He points at the circle in the ceiling, and I see that the light that shines on the Dawsons isn't pure white. Instead, it's made of three different colors, pink and yellow and blue, flickering so fast they seem to blend together. I follow the beam back down to the Dawsons and notice that there's a faint, shimmering outline of the same three colors around their bodies. I shiver and look at Peter.

"Are they ghosts?"

"There's no such thing as ghosts," he says. "It's probably best to think of them as… memories. Or recordings. Sort of like photographs."

"Photographs can't move."

"These are holograms," he says. "Projected recordings,

stored here using a technology that existed a long, long time ago. These recordings must have been made before the birth of Dominique, before the rise of the Ecosystem, before the City of the Queens came into being. The events that are in our distant past couldn't have been recorded when these holograms were made, because those events were still in their future."

I turn back to the Dawsons, who stand there faintly glowing, helpfully smiling. Now that I study them closely, I realize that their eyes behind the eyeglasses aren't focused straight at us, but seem to look through us, as if *we're* the ones who aren't completely solid.

"If they're not here," I whisper to Peter, then feel stupid for whispering in the presence of imaginary people, "how can they talk to us at all?"

Peter's about to answer when Meredith Cowley-Dawson responds.

"We are interpreters for the *edinnu* project, programmed to conduct tours of this facility and to answer a range of questions about its history and operations," she says. "Our interactivity is limited, but our databanks contain a wealth of information for your enlightenment."

I throw Peter an *explain that, Smart Guy* look, but he doesn't hesitate.

"They're artificial intelligences," he says. "Capable of voice recognition and response, though on a pretty basic level, it sounds like. Similar to computerized call centers from the past." When I look at him blankly, he says, "Oh, come on, Hadassah. You must know what computers are."

"I know what they are. They're boxes full of wires and things, not human beings walking around."

"I'll admit these simulacra are more advanced than your run-of-the-mill desktop, but they're still computerized data storage and retrieval units. Watch." He turns to the Dawsons. "Can you tell me how long Queen Leonida ruled?"

Meredith Cowley-Dawson smiles. "We regret that we cannot satisfy your inquiry concerning *Queen Leonida.* That term is not found within our databanks."

"But you can tell us about the founding of the *edinnu* project, can't you?" Peter asks.

This time, it's Reginald Dawson who answers. "The *edinnu* project was founded in the year 2039 CE in response to accelerating rates of extinction among terrestrial and aquatic life, vegetable as well as animal, as a direct result of the burgeoning of the human population and its associated destructive activities. As geneticists whose research involved the mapping of the planetary genome, my life partner and I concluded that it was necessary to take immediate steps to preserve the biome against further incursion—"

"See?" Peter says, smiling.

"I see. Now shut up so I can listen to someone else for a change."

He looks crestfallen, but clams up.

"—our principal recording efforts were completed within five years of that start date," Reginald Dawson continues. "Compiling a comprehensive genetic map of the planetary biome had long been considered a pipe dream, but working around the clock with the aid of revolutionary gene-mapping technologies patented by ourselves, my life partner and I succeeded in gathering the genetic data for all known species."

"That's incredible," Peter says. "So you effectively had the genes for every living thing on the planet?"

"That is correct," Reginald Dawson says with a satisfied nod. "Excepting, of course, the genetic material of *Homo sapiens*, which it was never our intention to perpetuate."

Peter looks at me, shaking his head. "That's incredible," he says again.

"It's great," I say. "But what does it have to do with the tree?"

As if in response to my question, Meredith Cowley-Dawson speaks up. "With this genetic map in hand," she says, "we established our research facility right here on the lake bordering the beautiful campus of *data corrupted fatal exception error abort reboot system...*"

When she says those strange words, her voice screeches unnaturally and her face slants sideways in a truly alarming way. I look at Peter, who shrugs.

"Glitchy program," he says, whatever that means.

"...our purpose," Meredith Cowley-Dawson picks up, smiling as if she never missed a beat, "was to store the planetary code as a resource in case the latest major extinction event should prove insuperable. In a perhaps whimsical tribute to the supposed Tree of Life or 'world-tree' spoken of in a range of ancient mythologies—including the Old Norse Yggdrasil, the sacred fig or *Ficus religiosa* so central to Buddhism, and the Tree of Knowledge of Good and Evil described in the Judeo-Christian Book of Genesis, Chapters Two and Three—we housed the planetary genetic code within a tree of our own design and planted it here, in this garden, where we might watch over it and care for its preservation—"

"That's it!" Peter bursts out. "The tree!"

"I got that part," I say. Then, to the Dawsons: "Could you describe the tree in more detail, please?"

Not at all bothered by the interruption, Meredith Cowley-Dawson smiles and continues. "As we said, the world-tree contains the genetic code for the complete planetary ecosystem, excepting that of our own species. With this resource, any nonhuman species threatened with extinction can be 'reanimated,' as it were, via the material stored in the tree. This includes not only extant flora and fauna but, where available, species no longer extant, including—"

"Dinosaurs?" Peter jumps in.

The Dawsons smile.

"Why, yes," Meredith Cowley-Dawson answers. "Though the genetic registry of extinct species is by definition incomplete, the world-tree does contain sufficient material from several thousand known prehistoric species to make possible the return, in a limited fashion, of the Age of Reptiles."

"That explains the dinosaurs," Peter whispers to me.

"Gee, you think?"

"Recognizing the importance of preserving the genetic code for future study and in case of accidental damage or sabotage to this facility," Reginald Dawson picks up the story, "we made arrangements for the tree's material to be deposited in cold-storage vaults at numerous research facilities and institutions of higher education throughout the continental United States and abroad. Thus, though the world-tree itself is one of a kind, its 'seeds,' as it were, lie dormant in a variety of locations, ready for future 'planting.'"

"As fate would have it," Meredith Cowley-Dawson continues for her husband, "we were ourselves called upon to 'crack open the code,' so to speak, when in the years immediately following our creation of the world-tree, the crisis of worldwide colony collapse disorder reached epidemic proportions."

My ears perk up at these words. I know about colony collapse disorder; everyone in the City of the Queens does. It was because of the extinction of bees that the Dawsons created the *Apis impunita* strain, the hybrid bees that were supposed to re-pollinate the world. Instead, they spread the genes that gave rise to the Ecosystem.

"To our considerable regret, we were forced to relocate from our beloved garden to a neighboring academic institution in order to address this more immediate and urgent crisis," Meredith Cowley-Dawson goes on. "It was in the days just prior to our departure that we recorded our own holographic images in hopes that our research station might become much more than a museum—that it might serve, instead, as a living laboratory or wilderness preserve where the fruits of our labors could be showcased, where ongoing research could flourish, and where future generations could be educated about the *edinnu* project until we ourselves might return to resume our work, here on the island that had become not only our laboratory but our home."

She pauses, and for the first time, it seems that her eyes and her husband's grow sad behind their eyeglasses, as if it was hard for them to record themselves talking about leaving *edinnu.* Though they're not really real, I decide not to tell them that they never did return—that the Ecosystem took over, that they were killed inside the university where they created the *Apis impunita* colony, and that the university became the City of the Queens, with their own daughter the first to sit on its throne. The first, as their many-times-great-granddaughter Rebecca might be the last.

Peter, though, has lots of questions. I can see in his face how hard it was for him to keep quiet this long.

"You said this place is a wilderness preserve," he bursts out as soon as Meredith Cowley-Dawson stops talking. "Does that mean all the species along the river are real? Or are they like you?"

"The plant species within the estuarine system that feeds this lake are genuine, unadulterated life forms, bred from the world-tree," Reginald Dawson says with a proud smile. "However, the terrestrial and aquatic animals are no more than sophisticated holographic recordings such as ourselves, placed there for visitors' enlightenment and entertainment. Before our work was interrupted, we did manage to program several species with basic routines making possible limited interactivity with visitors, but none, unfortunately, is anything but a simulation."

"That explains why the ecosystem seemed so incomplete out there," Peter whispers to me.

"And why I couldn't Sense any of the animals," I whisper back, but he's already moved on to his next question for the Dawsons.

"What about the baneboo?" he asks. "Was that bred from the world-tree, too?"

"The term *baneboo* is not found within our databanks," Meredith Cowley-Dawson answers. "However, we did tap the world-tree to breed considerable groves of *bamboo*, a perennial evergreen plant in the subfamily *Bambusoideae* of the grass family *Poaceae*, which serves both cosmetic and functional purposes on this island. As one of the world's fastest-growing plant species due to its rhizomatic root structures, bamboo acts as a 'living machine' that plays a key role in purifying our atmosphere, recycling wastewater, and generating the biomass energy necessary to power this station without human activity or intervention."

"They don't know about the baneboo," I say. "It's a mutation, something that happened to this rizo-automatic stuff after they left."

"Obviously," Peter says. "But then how do you account for its hostility to human beings?"

"You're the genius," I say. "You figure it out."

"I would," he says, "if you'd give me a moment to think."

The Dawsons stand there hand in hand, smiling the way grownups do when somebody else's kids quarrel. Based on what they've said, it's plain to me that the Ecosystem didn't truly start on the campus where I've lived my whole life, and it didn't start with the *Apis impunita* colony either. It started *here,* on this island, with the tree that was meant to save the world. Maybe putting all the genes from all the plants and animals together in one place made it easier for the Ecosystem to grow? But if that's true, I don't see how the world-tree can hold the cure to the Queen's sickness.

Still, there's one more question I need to ask the Dawsons, and it has nothing to do with their tree.

"A friend of mine came here," I say. "Or at least, I think she did. A woman named Sarah. Do you know where she is?"

The two of them trade a look, and for the first time, I

wonder if they're hiding something. *Can* recorded people hide something?

"No member of our species by the name of *Sarah* is found within our databanks," Meredith Cowley-Dawson says. "However, it is not uncommon to christen plant species with human names, such as the *Kalmia latifolia* or mountain laurel, nicknamed 'Sarah' by playful botanists, or the so-called Chinese evergreen of the genus *Aglaonema*, puckishly termed 'Sparkling Sarah' due to its colorful foliage and preference for dappled shade. There is also the example of the—"

"That's very interesting," Peter says. "But can you take us to see the tree, please?"

"Of course," the Dawsons say in unison, and smile broadly. "Right this way, lucky visitors."

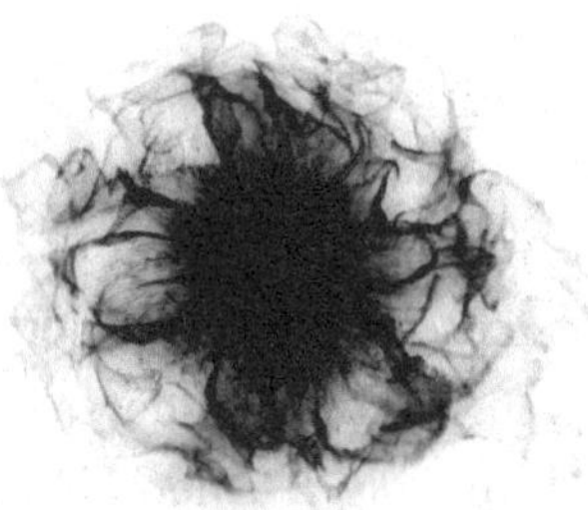

The Dawsons cross the room hand in hand, the overhead light matching their movements. Peter charges after them, but I hang back, touching his arm until he slows to face me.

"What's wrong?" he says.

"How did you know what to ask them?"

He grins. "We speak the same language."

"Yeah, well, don't get too chummy with them too quick."

"Why not?"

"I don't know," I admit. "I just have a feeling, okay?"

"They're projections, Hadassah," he says. "Photons and sound waves, with a computerized algorithm for responding to queries. They can't hurt us."

"I'm only asking you to be careful. That's not too much to ask, is it?"

Doubt shows in his eyes, but he nods before heading toward where the Dawsons are waiting for us.

They've stopped at the back of the room, next to one of the glass cases. I scan the objects inside: seeds, vials, old books, each on a little shelf with a card full of words only Peter could understand. Meredith Cowley-Dawson reaches out a shimmering finger toward the glass wall, and with the same hissing noise as the front door, the glass splits to reveal a closet-size room with metal walls and nothing inside. The Dawsons enter, their forms flickering out for a split-second before another beam from the small room's ceiling makes them reappear. With a glance at me, Peter steps into the room after them. I touch the sword at my belt, wondering how well it will work against photons and sound waves. Then I take a deep breath and join Peter and our guides.

As soon as I'm inside, the doors close and the room starts downward, moving as smoothly as the lift Wyvern operated beneath Rebecca's cottage. Now that the Dawsons are squeezed in here with us, I can tell that they're definitely nothing but images: their bodies glow but don't give off heat, and though their chests rise and fall, I can't hear or feel their breath. My mom's lesson about spells comes back to me, and I wish I had some way of knowing what desire lies deep in the earth that's closing in around us.

The ride lasts less than a minute before the room comes to a smooth stop and the doors open. Peter and I step out onto a white walkway that seems to float in the middle of a dark vault, with a single light so high above it looks like a distant star. I can't see the walls or the ceiling or, for that matter, where the light is coming from; everything is as dark as night except for the walkway. The Dawsons join us, blinking out for a second then reappearing in the weak beam of light from above. They seem fainter than before, almost see-through, but they smile and gesture ahead where the walkway curves into darkness.

"The world-tree lies at the end of this bridge," Meredith Cowley-Dawson says. "There, it is protected from trespass, preserved for all time. Coming into its presence is a unique privilege. You will never see anything as beautiful again, I promise you."

"I'm sure," I say. "And you're showing it to us because…?"

"Because you requested this privilege of us," she says.

"Because it is our purpose to show the tree to all who wish to see it, that they may understand the great worth of what we have achieved."

I purse my lips and look at her. Both she and her husband are smiling cheerfully, seeming proud and hopeful. I'm about to ask them another question—I don't even know what it is at this point—when Peter nudges me with his shoulder.

"Come on," he says. "This is what we came for, right? Everyone's counting on us to see it through."

He's practically bouncing the way Chaim does the morning of his birthday. I feel like I owe him for all the times he's helped me, all the times he's saved me. He's so much smarter than I am about so many things, how could he be foolish enough to walk us into a trap? And he's right—without the tree, our whole journey will be for nothing. We *have* to go on, no matter what.

"All right," I say. "Just stay close to me, okay?"

I hold out a hand, and after a moment's pause, he takes it. The Dawsons grip each other's hands too—I don't know how, since there's nothing to grip—and start down the walkway. I slide a foot forward, not trusting the ground to hold us, but Peter pulls me along as if we're the Dawsons' shadows.

We haven't gone far when a pale glow softens the darkness. Not from above, where the beam blinks on and off as the Dawsons move. The new light comes from up ahead, a silver radiance that shimmers like a star-filled sky. My heart races, and my hand feels sweaty in Peter's. I seem to be walking on air, as if I'm made of nothing more solid than our guides. We round a bend on the bridge, and my eyes grow wide as they're flooded with light.

The world-tree shines before me.

It's not so much a tree as a ball of perfect silver light nested inside a nimbus of gold. I can't see roots or branches or leaves, only a pulsing, streaming globe that floats in the darkness just above the level of the bridge. It's as if the tree that contains all life on earth *is* the earth, hanging in space with nothing to hold it up. Tears spring to my eyes, and I realize that all of the times I thought I was seeing the tree were nothing but pale reflections of the reality. The Dawsons weren't lying about this: I've never encountered anything that makes my heart sing and ache so powerfully, and I can't believe I ever will.

"Behold the tree," the Dawsons chant. "Behold all life that was, and is, and will be forevermore."

I nod, tears blinding me. I can't feel Peter's hand in mine, but I can tell he's as awed as I am. I can tell, because he's not saying anything, which must mean that for the first time in his life, he doesn't have anything to say. I wish I could tease him, make some joke like *fell-cat got your tongue?* But I can't say anything either, and so I simply stand beside him and stare.

Peter takes a step forward, his face glowing. His hand leaves his side, rising shakily toward the tree. It looks like he's waving to it, but then I realize he's reaching for something, a bright red spot that's appeared at the tree's heart like fire burning inside a crystal. The spot grows brighter, becomes round and solid in a way the light-shining tree can't, and when it settles into its final shape, I see what it is.

I know why Peter wants to touch it, because I do, too.

It's a fruit, bright as blood and glistening like sugar. It hangs in the air as if it's suspended from an invisible branch, and I think how easy it would be to pick it. I imagine its taste, its sweetness on my lips, its juice on my tongue. I want to sink my teeth into it, bite through crunchy skin into soft, delicious pulp. I want it more than I've ever wanted anything in my life, and when Peter's hand is about to close on it, I swat him away.

"Hey," he says.

"Back off," I warn, and I'm shocked by the low growl that's become of my voice.

The Dawsons lean forward, white teeth gleaming. Meredith Cowley-Dawson bends down until she's right beside my ear, and when she speaks, I could swear I feel her breath stir my hair.

"The tree is life," she whispers. "Taste of it, and be reborn."

I reach for the fruit, but Peter knocks my hand away. I spin toward him, pulling the sword from its scabbard and holding it in the *Tox* position. He faces my blade without fear, and in his eyes, I see twin reflections of the fruit, turning their natural blue the color of blood. He feints as if he's going to attack me, but when I jump back, he leaps into the air and takes the fruit in both hands.

I cry out in anger as Peter raises it to his lips. If I rush him with my sword, I can still stop him—can pierce the fruit with my blade before he takes a bite, even if that means stabbing him too. But the instant that thought enters my mind, my anger leaves me, the sword dropping from my hand. The tree pulses with power, and I see what swims beneath the skin of the fruit.

"Peter—don't!"

Too late.

His teeth chomp down, and his face freezes as if he really has been stabbed through the heart. He crumples like a doll, the fruit rolling from his hand. A black thing like a tiny worm slithers from the bloody spot where Peter took a bite, moving so fast I lose it in the light of the tree.

"Peter!" I cry, falling to my knees beside him.

He lies motionless, his eyes closed, his skin ashen. The only color is on his lips, which are smeared red from the fruit. I touch his forehead, but my hand leaps back when I feel the heat pouring from him like a coal on the hearth. I glance up to find the Dawsons leaning over me, their eyeglasses solid silver in the tree's blinding light. Meredith Cowley-Dawson lays a hand on my shoulder, but it passes through me like vapor.

"The tree is life," she says. "It must be preserved at all costs."

"What have you done to him?" I scream.

"He has done it to himself," she answers. "By your own acts, those of your kind have sealed your doom."

She touches my face with the tips of her fingers, but I can't feel a thing. With her husband's hand in her own, she steps toward the empty space where the tree floats. I expect the two of them to plunge into the darkness, but instead, their bodies flicker and fade, until I can see straight through them to the void behind. A second later, what's left of them breaks into millions of tiny pink and yellow and blue particles that join the silver light streaming from the tree.

"The hex take you!" I swear at them. "The hex take you, you cursed vermice!"

I grab my sword from the floor and swipe at their afterimage, but something—maybe a branch of the tree—catches the blade in a grip much stronger than mine and flings it into the pit. As it falls, the Dawsons' answer comes back to me.

"We regret that the expressions you use cannot be found within our databanks," they say, and then they're gone.

I lean over Peter, wrapping my arms around him. His bare flesh is almost too hot to touch, but I hold him close and rock him. Tears slide down my cheeks to sizzle against his skin. I try to lift him, but he's too heavy. And even if I could pick him up, where would I go? What could I do to save him, to save anyone?

"I'm sorry, Peter," I whisper. "I wish I'd never brought you here. I wish I'd never come here at all."

"Wishes are cheap, girl."

The voice startles me. At first I think it's the Dawsons returning to torment me, but this voice speaks in a way completely unlike their smooth tones: it's low and ugly, more a growl than a voice. I squint against the light of the tree until I become aware of a dark figure standing on the far side of the bridge, human-shaped but covered with thick fur. It's too far away for me to make out its face, but I can hear its heavy breathing, and even from this distance, my nose wrinkles at its animal stink. It takes a step toward me, and there's a scraping sound like claws on stone. I see that it's holding a spear in one furred hand, the point facing downward so the blade scratches against the floor. I clutch Peter, but there's not a thing I can do to protect him if this half-animal decides to attack.

It limps closer, leaning on its spear. When it's near

enough that the light of the tree shines fully on it, I see that its furs are covered in what looks like dried blood. Its hair is so long and tangled I can't find a face underneath, even when it stands right in front of me. It reaches for me with the hand not holding the spear, and I catch a glimpse of brown skin soiled almost black, yellow nails as long and sharp as a pandalion's. I try to turn my head away, but it grips my chin with such strength I'm afraid it's going to break my neck.

Dark eyes glint beneath matted hair. Its carrion breath is hot and rotten in my face. It leans as close as Meredith Cowley-Dawson did and sniffs me like a predator inspecting its prey. Then it speaks softly in my ear.

"How does it feel," it says, "to know you'll never see home again?"

When I hear that voice, my heart shrivels like a leaf in the fire.

"Sense preserve us," I say. "Sarah."

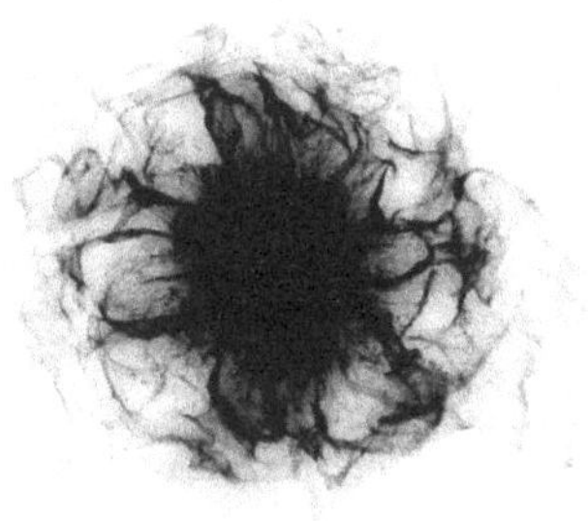

BOOK FOUR

WILD

There can be no prescription, no set of rules, for living within Gaia. For each of our different actions there are only consequences.

—James Lovelock,
Gaia (1979)

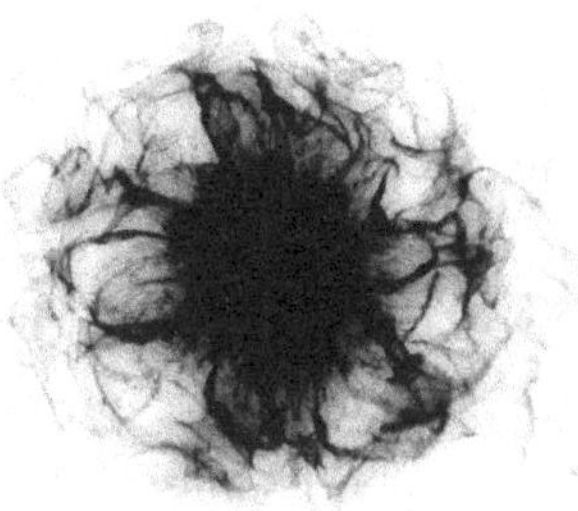

SHE SITS CROSS-LEGGED on the bridge ten feet from me, her spear across her lap. I can't take my eyes off the wicked tip, a piece of black stone carved into rough facets. She rubs it between her thumb and forefinger as if she's remembering the days when Sensors armed themselves to battle the Ecosystem. Except the only blood that flows is hers, the serrated edge slicing flesh that's already covered with old scars.

Her smell is overpowering. I can tell she hasn't washed or—the thought nauseates me—used the bathroom properly in weeks. She scratches beneath the bulky furs as if the filth of her own skin maddens her, clears her throat loudly and spits something I can't look at on the ground. Even worse, she mutters words too soft for me to hear, but I know from the angry tone that they're curses.

Every time I gather the courage to look at her face, I find her watching me darkly, warily, like an animal about to pounce. I wonder if she remembers who I am, or if that part of her is gone, too.

"Sarah…" I say.

"Don't touch me!" she shrieks, though I haven't come close to her.

I back farther away, but keep an eye on Peter in case she tries to attack him. When I speak again, it's hard to control my voice.

"Sarah," I say. "It's me. It's… Hadassah. I came like you told me to. I came to… to find you."

Her eyes narrow on my face, while her lips move as if she's repeating my name. She throws back her head and laughs, a horrible cackle that dies out quickly in the hollowness of the world-tree's chamber.

"Little fool," she says. "I thought it might be you."

She sets the spear down and crawls on all fours toward me. I try to hold my place, but when her smell hits me, I can't help shrinking back. A bloody hand reaches out and touches my cheek in a way that might seem gentle if I couldn't feel her nails.

"It's too late, you know," she says in a hissing whisper. "Too late for you, too late for him," and she jerks her head toward Peter. "Too late for everyone. You'd be better off dying right now."

Her fingers slip from my cheek and snake around my throat. They tighten, and I can feel my pulse beating against her hand. I hold perfectly still, not even breathing as her claws sink into my flesh.

Then she lets go. Her body huddles into itself, her shoulders shaking with hysterical sounds: groans, whimpers, shrieks. It seems like her heart is breaking, and it breaks mine to listen to her.

"Lost!" she wails. "No light, no hope. Everything is lost!"

Not knowing what she'll do, whether she'll try to strangle me again, I lay my hands on her back, feel her shuddering as if she's frozen through and through. I think about all the times she visited me in my room, or all the times I thought she did—how she'd sit on my bed, talk to me softly, listen to my stories and gripes and dreams. Those were the times she made me feel safe, made me believe there was a place for me in the world. I don't know what's happened to her, but I can never forget what she did for me.

Cautiously, I stroke her matted hair, my fingers catching in the snarls. She stiffens, but doesn't push me away. Though her smell repulses me, I lean down and part her hair as best I can to kiss the crown of her head.

"I'm here, Sarah," I say. "I'm here, and I'll never leave you."

A long, deep moan of terrible pain bubbles up from inside of her. I keep smoothing out tangles, shushing her, whispering words that are nothing but sounds. I hear her say, "Don't touch me," but it's quiet and weak this time, more like a child's pout than a threat. She's so much bigger than me, it's hard to hold her in my arms, but I do anyway, rocking her back and forth, humming a melody Mom always uses to settle Tovah when she's fussy. Sarah draws a deep, tear-filled breath, and her body grows still. For a second, I think she's fallen asleep.

Then I find her looking at me, so close we could touch noses.

Her cheeks are covered with dried tears and dirt and snot, and her breath—oh, it's better not to say anything about that. Beneath all the grime, I can tell how wrinkled her face is, much more than Dad's, even though he's a couple of years older than her. I'm so accustomed to seeing the vision of Sarah that came to my room, it never occurred to me what a toll her years in the wild took on her actual body. Or maybe it's the time she spent trapped in the world-tree's chamber, remembering the Dawsons' mocking smiles and believing she would never be free again.

I gaze into her eyes. They squint at me as if the tree's light punishes them, and her wrath's-nest of hair keeps falling into them no matter how often I try to smooth it away. But they're no longer the eyes of a beast, the eyes of a madwoman. They're the eyes of my old friend, brown with a touch of blue, and they sparkle with tears that look like opals in the tree's glow.

"Hadassah," she sighs. "I knew you'd come for me."

She reaches up to lay a hand on my cheek. Her fingertips are dry and cracked, but their touch is soft. When she rests back and closes her eyes, a wave of exhaustion washes over me, and I have no choice but to give in. I lie down beside Sarah, reaching for her hand. It curls around mine, but I don't even feel the claws. She sighs again, softly, and I join her in healing sleep.

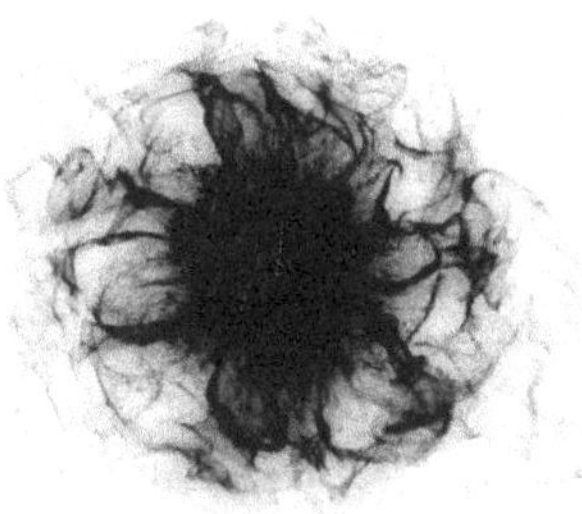

I WAKE TO find her gone.

I jump up, looking around the chamber in the chilly light of the tree. Peter's lying where he was, eyes closed, breath coming in ragged gasps. I touch his forehead and feel the fever slowly burning his life away. I walk to the place where I first saw Sarah, only to discover that the bridge comes to a sudden end with nothing but black emptiness beyond. If it weren't for the light of the tree, I would have fallen. Cold sweat breaks out on my face at the thought that that's what might have happened to her.

But when I return to Peter, I find her kneeling beside him with a hand on his forehead. She's holding the spear in her other hand, her head bowed so low I can't see her face. Then she shakes her head, using the spear to push herself to her feet. When she turns, she sees me watching.

"He was a friend of yours?" she says, sounding out of breath.

"His name is Peter."

"Well, I'm sorry. Whatever the tree did to him, it's beyond my power to heal."

She lowers herself to the ground, her movements slow and stiff. When she crosses her legs, she winces, then sets her spear aside so she can brace herself with her hands. I sit across from her and wait for her to find a comfortable position. After a few more grunts and lots of frowns, she gives up and looks at me.

"Hadassah," she says.

The light of the tree shows me every detail of her face. She seems to have wiped some of the grime away, which draws attention to the deep lines beside her nose and the ravener's-feet at the corners of her eyes. She's tried to do something with her hair, but the quick twist she put it in only highlights how filthy it is. I've either grown used to her smell or it's gotten better, because my nose doesn't wrinkle when it wafts my way. Still, I can't help thinking it's more of a brute's scent than a human's.

"The door's locked, by the way," she says. Her voice is the one thing that hasn't changed; it's the same as always, soft and deep. "What they used to call an elevator. I tried to force it open, but it wouldn't budge."

"I think only the Dawsons can open it."

"The who?"

"The… the people," I say. "The ones who guard this place."

I see the confusion in her eyes. They rove over my face as if she's forgotten who I am again, as if she's forgotten what a human face looks like. Her lips sound out a word, but I can't tell what it is. I'm afraid she's slipping back into the spell she was under, and I don't know if I'll be able to do anything about it this time.

Then, all at once, her expression clears, and she smiles. It softens her features, making her look more like the Sarah I've been seeing in my dreams.

"You'll have to forgive me," she says. "I've been away

for so long, it's going to take me a while before I'm fully… myself again."

I bite my lip and try to smile back. Her eyes fall on the token at my throat, and she reaches out to touch it. "Where did you get this?"

"From my mom. She told me it was yours."

She shakes her head as if she's trying to jog her memory. It doesn't seem to click for a while, but then her words come, soft and low, as if she's talking to herself.

"That was a long time ago," she says. "A lifetime."

"You can have it back," I say. "I know you wanted me to be a Sensor, but… I'm not very good at it."

She looks at me, her head cocked. Her fingers toy with the token for a moment, then she drops her hand into her lap.

"Keep it," she says. "If your mother gave it to you, it's yours."

She looks away from me, not toward the tree but into the darkness on the other side of the bridge. She's quiet for so long, I begin to feel uncomfortable in a way I never thought I could feel around her. "Sarah…"

She glances back sharply. "What is it?"

"Nothing," I say. "Just… what are we going to do?"

She laughs. It's an ugly sound, and it startles me.

"There's nothing we can do," she says. "The tree trapped us here, and there's no way out."

"Then why did you…" I start to say, but quail before her angry gaze.

"Why did I what?"

"Why did you… call for me?" I ask. "Why did you send the… the…"

Her eyes narrow. "What in the Ecosystem are you talking about?"

"The vision," I say. "You sent a vision of the tree to me, and I thought…"

She looks at me so intently, I want to shrink into myself. Her hand falls to the spear point again, three fingers running over it in a slow, almost loving motion, the way you'd stroke a pet. With an obvious effort, she stops herself and puts her hand into her lap, lacing it with the other so the yellow claws overlap her brown skin.

"I sent no vision," she says. "I couldn't, not from this hexed place. I've sent visions to your home for years to keep track of you, to hear your voice. But not this time. Whatever it was you thought you saw, it didn't come from me."

I try to say something, but my throat won't open to let the words out.

"The only way you could have received a vision of the world-tree," Sarah says, "is if it was sent by the tree itself."

"The tree—?"

"The tree," she confirms. Her eyes flick toward the pulsing ball of light, and for a second, I see another light inside the silver, orange and red like a wad of paper on the hearth. "The tree…"

She stands smoothly, picking up the spear without using it for support. At the edge of the bridge, she faces the ball of light, her dark, shaggy form outlined by silver fire. The arm that holds the spear draws back, then hurls the weapon into the light, where it disappears with a crackling sound and a burst of red fire. Sarah turns back to me, and though I can barely see her face with the light behind her, what I can see scares me to death.

"It tricked us," she says, her voice a low rasp. "Tell me about the vision. Tell me everything."

She sits beside me, and I tell her. About the different visions the Queen and I saw that first night, the funeral service two days later, with everyone in the city in attendance. She sniffs humorlessly when she hears about that. I describe my meeting with Rebecca in the garden, the night in her brood chamber, my dad's sickness the next morning. Sarah taps her long nails on the ground when I go into the journey to the village, so I cut out some of the less important parts. When I mention our meeting with the quetzal, her eyes fly open wide.

"You saw Archie?" she asks.

"Archie?"

"That's his name. Where is he?"

She looks at me eagerly, almost hungrily. I choose my words with care. "He guided me and Peter here. He saved us, more than once. But we… we lost track of him at the falls. I'm sorry, Sarah. I haven't seen him since."

Her hand tightens into a fist as if she wishes she still had her spear. I inch backward, but with an effort, she cleanses the scowl from her brow.

"Tell me the rest," she says. "Every word. And don't worry about Archie. He'll be all right," she adds quietly, as if she's talking to herself again. "He has a knack for showing up when he's least expected."

Slowly, trying not to say anything else that might upset her, I finish the story. I tell her about the birds my mom sent, the operation she's using to keep people alive, the crossing at the bereaver dam. I hesitate more than usual when I have to tell her about Leah, but her expression doesn't change a bit when she hears the news of her best friend's death. The doubt clears from her eyes the more I talk, and by the time I've told her about me and Peter's encounter with the Dawsons, she smiles in a way that looks more like a leer.

"So *that's* it," she says. "The tree must have known I was the Queen's agent, so it planted a vision in your mind to poison Rebecca from afar. Genius!"

The blue fire that lights her eyes scares me all over again. "Sarah?"

"The tree hates our kind, Hadassah," she says. "Killing the Queen is the surest way to remove us once and for all. Simple. Clean. Final."

"But *why* does it hate us so much?"

She laughs bitterly. "Look outside. See what we've done to its world. Wouldn't you hate someone for that?"

"But," I say, "*we* didn't do this. Ever since the War of the Queens, we've been trying to understand the ways of the Ecosystem, to reconcile ourselves to it. The Queen's Corps calls us to—"

"It's pointless to argue," she says. "Whatever you might think you're *called* to do, the tree has a different vision, and that's… that's…"

A look of astonishment spreads across her face. She swings to face the tree, staring into the light as if she's mesmerized by it. I touch her arm. "Sarah?"

She jumps as if I've given her an electric shock. Collecting herself, she shakes her head, mumbles something I can't hear, and turns to me. The silver light reflects off her eyes the way it did off her great-great-great-great grandparents' eyeglasses.

"The tree never wanted me to discover its domain, and it made me pay for my trespasses," she says. "It's different in your case, Hadassah. You're here because the tree called for you to come."

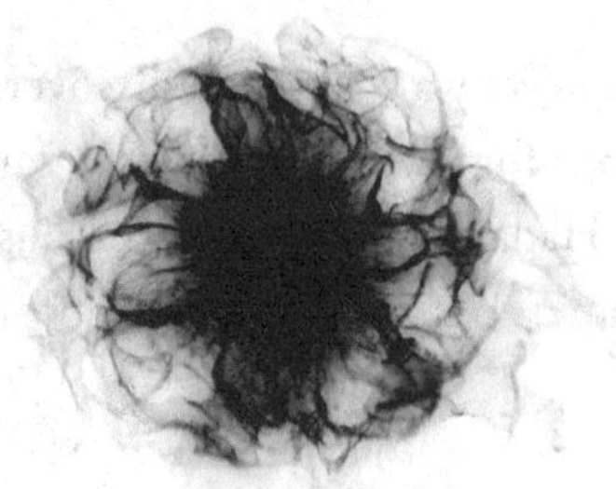

SARAH'S WORDS HANG in the air, pulsing in my ears the way the tree's light pulses before my eyes.

"Me? I ask. "It tried to kill me!"

"If it had truly desired your death, do you think it would have failed?" she asks. "Do you think it would have dispatched its blight to the Queen through you—one of only two people in the city who could *not* be felled by the disease?"

"But—"

She waves a hand. "It set the whole thing up, Hadassah. There's not a doubt in my mind. It wants something from you, something it can't get from anyone else. Otherwise, why not kill the Queen directly, without involving you at all?"

She looks at the tree again. The red light flashes at its heart, and I get the creepy feeling it understands every word we're saying. Sarah nods as if she's made up her mind, then turns back to me.

"It brought you here for a reason," she says. "And that reason is because it wants to strike a bargain."

I stare at her, thinking I must have heard wrong. Sarah looks at me for a long time, then throws back her head and laughs. Her teeth, I can't help thinking, are longer and sharper than they should be.

"It's not as crazy as it sounds," she says. "The first queen of the city, Dominica, was able to bargain with the Ecosystem because each of them had something the other needed: she the Ecosystem's power, it the Queen's protection. Your challenge is somewhat the same. You need the tree's power to remove the blight and restore the Queen to health. It needs assurance that the Queen and her people will leave it in peace. The question is, what do you have to offer that will convince it you'll uphold your end of the bargain?"

The way she says that makes my heart go cold. "What would it ask me to do?"

She doesn't answer right away. Her eyes grow distant, and the strange thought passes through my mind that she's not really here, that she never has been. That after all these years of sending her dream-self across the wild, her real, solid self is gone forever. Then she takes my hands in both of hers, and when I feel their warmth, I know it's really Sarah, the one I'd do anything for.

"Let's find out," she says, and pulls me to my feet.

We walk the few steps to where the tree hangs in the darkness. I watch the red flashes forming deep inside its silver heart, and I tremble at the thought of trying to bargain with something this ancient, this angry. I can't think of any words I could say that it would listen to, any offer I can make that it would accept.

"What am I supposed to do?" I ask Sarah nervously.

"Reach out to it," she answers. "Find its mind, the way a Sensor would. Then try to forge a connection."

"I already told you," I say. "I'm not a very good Sensor."

"You can't let doubts hamper you," she says. "The tree brought you here, so it must be waiting for you to make contact. But it doesn't know whether it can trust you yet, so what you have to do is…"

I wait for her next words, but they don't come. She's staring at the tree again, nodding slightly. "Yes?" I ask.

She snaps out of it and smiles at me.

"Earn its trust," she says.

She lets go of my hands and steps back. Though the tree's right in front of me, I close my eyes and reach out to it with my mind. Slowly, its image takes shape, fuzzy at first then growing as sharp and bright as the real thing. I see its silver glow, its steady pulse; I can even hear the tinkling sound it makes, though I know I'm not hearing the sound with my actual ears. A rush of sensations flows from the tree, some of them waves of warmth and joy and contentment, others burning throbs of fear and anger and pain as if the earth has been wounded to its core. Rage swells inside its heart the way it did when I made contact on the beach, and I can tell it wants to stamp me out for good, send something even more deadly than the baneboo to end my life. My legs grow weak as the tree's cry courses through me, and I open my eyes and look helplessly at Sarah. "It won't listen to me."

"You've been at it for five minutes," she says. "The tree's genetic code has existed for billions of years."

"Yeah, well, I don't have billions of years."

"Try, Hadassah," she says. "Don't be afraid. I'll be right here."

"Why can't you help me?"

"Because I'm not the one it wants," she says. "You are."

"It doesn't seem like it wants me either," I mutter, but I close my eyes and try again.

The image of the world-tree is there where I left it, as clear as ever. The pain is there, too. I bite my lip to draw some of the pain into myself, and when I do, the tree surges with light, nearly blinding my inner eyes. I breathe deeply and steady my heart, calm my mind. Then I call out to it, the same way I used to speak to Wyvern.

Are you there? I ask. *Are you listening?*

Dead silence.

My name is Hadassah, I say. *Can you… can you hear me?*

The tree says nothing. Talking to Wyvern was usually easy, though sometimes confusing. This is like throwing myself against a wall.

I wish I knew how it feels, I go on, for no better reason than that I can't stand the silence. *To be all alone here. It was probably easier when the scientists were alive, even though they weren't really your mother and father. Did they come to talk to you? They were so proud of you. Did you know that?*

There's a flicker of response, a burst of anger. If I'm understanding it right, the tree is annoyed that I'm speaking to it like it's a toddler.

I beg your pardon, I say. *I don't know how I should talk to you. If you'd only tell me what I'm doing wrong, I'll do my best to learn.*

More silence.

I'm willing to make a bargain, I say, deciding I might as well get straight to the point. *If you promise to let us go, I promise to protect you from the Ecosystem. The Queen is wise, and if she knows what you are, she'll understand why you have to be kept from harm. She'll order the Ecosystem to stay away, and you can go on living forever, without having to worry about anything. I promise you.*

Something stirs in the depths of the tree. I reach out to Sense what it is, only to be hit by a massive surge of energy so strong it knocks me backwards. Out of the whirlwind of its rage, the tree screams at me that mortals die, and other mortals take their place, and no one keeps their promises forever. It reminds me that I'll die too, so I can't know that the vow I make today will never be broken. It tells me I'm a fool to stand here, presuming to know what it knows. Strong as the energy is, I realize it's merely a fraction of the tree's power. If it chooses to, it can not only keep me here—it can kill me, despite anything Sarah says.

What do you want? I ask it in desperation. *Tell me what you want, and I'll give it to you.*

The image of the tree flickers out, leaving me in silence and darkness. I can't see it anymore, can't feel its energy. It's withdrawn from me completely, and I have a feeling it's not coming back. I was right: I have nothing to give it, nothing that can make up for what the Ecosystem has done to it. A tree that's lived for billions of years knows better than to waste its time bargaining with me.

I'm about to tell Sarah I've failed when the tree speaks, not in words but in images, and everything else vanishes as its life flows through my mind.

I see its planting. Its seed carried down deep into the soil, its bed lovingly prepared by the Dawsons, watered with their sweat and tears. I see it begin to grow, first a sprout, then a sapling, then a slim trunk laced with gold whose branches unfold like petals to give birth to its first weak ray of silver light. The light plays across the Dawsons' faces, their smiles growing broader each time they visit to see the tree become taller, brighter, more lucent and beautiful. When its first leaves open, the Dawsons are delighted to hear the music it makes, and they spend days by its side, forgetting to eat and drink, finding all their nourishment in its embrace. The tree shines brightest when they're near, and years pass without their missing a day beneath its sheltering branches.

But then a day arrives when they don't come to visit. The tree waits for them all that day, then the next and the next and the next, but they fail to return. Used to measuring life in eons, not days or even lifetimes, it waits and waits, confident that they'll be back. While they're gone, it sheds shining leaves, ceases its song; its silver glow fades, because there's no one to see it. It bides its time, holding all the world inside its branches, and waits for the moment when it can shower its blessings on its creators once more.

One day, it feels something stir outside its chamber, and it brightens at once, welcoming them back home.

But it's not who the tree thought it was. It's something else, something it's never heard of, not in all the endless years of its life. This thing buzzes with power, prowls the darkness aboveground with a nervous energy so unlike the Dawsons' calm and stately reverence. It hammers at the door of the tree's sanctuary, and when the tree reaches out to discover what this unknown thing could be, it finds that the creature has overwhelmed the forest along the river, devoured the buildings where the Dawsons used to work, boldly advanced across the lake to smother the island with a dark, swarming mass too dense for the tree to see through. When it looks more closely, training its vision on the darkness, the tree finds that this sprawling monster, so huge it covers the land in an unbroken blanket for leagues and leagues around the island, is made of trillions of tiny things, winged and furry and many-legged, with compound eyes and sharp stingers jutting from their bellies. They're something like one of the beings the tree holds inside itself, beings the tree loves perhaps more than any of its offspring, since these tiny hive-hunters make the world blooming and fruitful. But the things that have assaulted its home have no interest in life: they are carriers of death, with a gnawing hunger inside them that makes them voracious and murderous and cruel. The tree can't understand what this alien is, where it came from. It can't understand how anything could exist in the world without its knowledge, much less why such a thing should want to destroy the source of all life.

Then one of the invaders sneaks inside the building, flies down the shaft, enters the tree's chamber. It dives straight toward the tree, which kills it with a burst of light. It's the first thing the tree has killed, and it wonders why ending this hateful creature's life brings such awful sadness. It catches the falling insect in its branches, holds it up to the light. And when it cracks the thing open with filaments as fine as moonbeams, when it sees what has been inserted into the invader's sequence and reads the names that have been stamped on the monster's code for all time, it finally understands.

The tree's rage knows no bounds, and it breaks the walls of its cage, exploding upward into the deserted building above it. It finds the ones who made it—or not them, but their bodiless echoes, airy visions without sight or soul. It demands to know how they could have done such a thing, how they could have betrayed it so. They plead with it, these streaming particles of light, telling the tree that it pained their physical selves more than they can say to leave it here, that they longed to remain on this island forever, reveling in the tree's beauty till the end of their days. But they had no choice, they tell it: their world was dying for lack of things that grow and bloom, and they were forced to answer its call.

You saved your world, the tree tells them. The world of

your own kind. But in so doing, you doomed my world to invasion and decay. The only thing that bloomed from your labors was death.

And then it curses them, sending them flitting back to their cell like the ghosts of birds returning to their empty nests. And it does something else it has never done before: it reaches down deep into its own code, finds a plant that grows thickly along the river and marshes that lead to its island. It twists that plant, changes it, makes it stronger and faster and more cunning than it's ever been, every bit as much a monster as the hive-things that have invaded its home. It hates itself for doing this to its own offspring, but it hates its creators even more for forcing this sacrilege upon it. Once it fortifies the island with its baneboo army, it retreats into its underground lair, fearful of what lies beyond its borders. It knows that it can never leave this place, can never strike back against the invader directly, for the entire world beyond edinnu belongs to its enemy. But it vows that, at the first opportunity, it will take revenge against the ones who have orphaned and violated it—not only against its creators but against anyone who walks on two legs as they once did.

And so it waits, and broods in silence, and grows subtle and solitary and strong. And when chance comes its way, it strikes.

I feel like I'm about to fall, but somehow, I hold myself upright. The tree's power hums inside me, alive with grief and anger. Grief at being abandoned by the ones it loved, anger at the human genes the Dawsons took from their daughter to create the *Apis impunita* hive. I don't know why they did that, whether they thought the hybrid bees needed to be as smart and daring and sneaky as human beings in order to re-pollinate the globe in the short time they had left before all the food on earth was gone. I only know that the tree's grief and anger festered in its heart for nearly two centuries, and that those feelings spilled out the moment it had a living person in its clutches. It had sworn never to let another of our kind corrupt the elder code, and when it realized that it could use the visions in Sarah's mind to kill the source of the Ecosystem itself, it acted without mercy or hesitation.

Now do you see? it asks. *Now do you understand?*

I can't speak, but I nod my head.

Then see this as well, the tree says. *And once you have seen, tell me if you accept my terms.*

Something new streams into my mind. It's not words, not images—it's *code*, the primal code that existed before the Ecosystem stole it away. The shimmering sequence pours into every corner of my mind, every fiber of my being, folding me more completely in the world that was than in the world I've known all my life. I understand now why the fruit of the world-tree is so tempting, why it's practically impossible for anyone, even a queen, to resist. It offers a glimpse into a world that once existed, a world that's gone forever. Next to that, what does my own little life matter? What wouldn't I give to bring that billions-of-years-old world back, to save it for all time? For the seconds or hours or years that the code courses through me, I know what it is to be a world, and what it's like to lose one.

I come out of the vision with a jolt that feels as if I've been hurled across space. If I were to open my eyes, I know I'd find Sarah standing there as if frozen in time, having seen nothing except me closing my eyes one second and opening them the next. But for me, it's as if billions of years really have passed. Before I have to return to the world that's my own, I reach out one last time, giving the tree the answer it wants.

I understand, I say. *Truly, I do.*

And you accept the terms?

I bow my head. The world-tree's bargain is as bitter as its fruit, but how can I refuse? *I do,* I tell it.

Good, the tree says. *Then heal the boy, and be gone.*

I open my eyes to find the tree shining as never before, its silver light so strong it shows me the ceiling of rock far above my head, the cavern walls all around. I shield my eyes from the glare and see that my hands are glowing like the tree, twin silver halos surrounding my brown skin. Without a moment's thought, I fall to my knees beside Peter and lay my hands on his forehead. He stiffens and struggles, but I pull him close and don't let go. It hurts to hold him like this, as if I'm taking all his wounds into my own body, but the pain lasts only a few seconds before the fever in his skin subsides and the light in my hands flickers out. I lay him down on the bridge, then touch his forehead to check him one more time. His eyes remain closed, but his skin no longer burns like fire, and his breathing and color have returned to normal. A few more hours of sleep and he'll be back to annoying me as much as ever.

When I get back to my feet, I'm met again by the tree's full light. Yet something is different this time: I can see *through* the silver sun to the slim trunk, the delicate branches and heart-shaped leaves. A sound falls on my ears, and when I still my heart to listen, I make out the notes of a song, one I know I've heard before. It's vibrant but sad, the kind you'd sing at a friend's funeral. Every note thrills me, though I couldn't repeat them if I tried.

They're the notes of the world-tree singing.

My eyes travel down the trunk, and I discover that the tree doesn't hang in space after all, but is upheld by countless silver roots as thin as hairs, each root a strand of the elder code. The roots go down far past the point my eyes can see, but my mind traces them to where they grip the ground deep below. They vibrate like strings, speaking to me in a wordless language as old as time.

I understand, I say in reply. *And I promise, the terms will be kept.*

The tree approves, sealing the bargain for good. I break contact and look at Sarah, who's standing with her face turned away from the light.

"I did it," I say. My words sound strange after hearing the tree's voice for so long. "We're free to leave."

She squints at me. "How?"

"The roots," I say. "They'll take us where we need to go."

Her brow lowers in doubt, but she bends to lift Peter from the floor. I step to the edge of the bridge and speak to the tree in the language only we share.

Take us home, I say.

Roots rise from below to wrap around Sarah. She stiffens at the touch of something she can't see, but relaxes as they lower her and Peter. A single root curls around my waist, warmth flowing through me as I soak up its ageless strength. The memory of what I've promised to do might terrify me in time, but not now. With the notes of the world-tree's song echoing inside my soul, I descend into the darkness from which all things came.

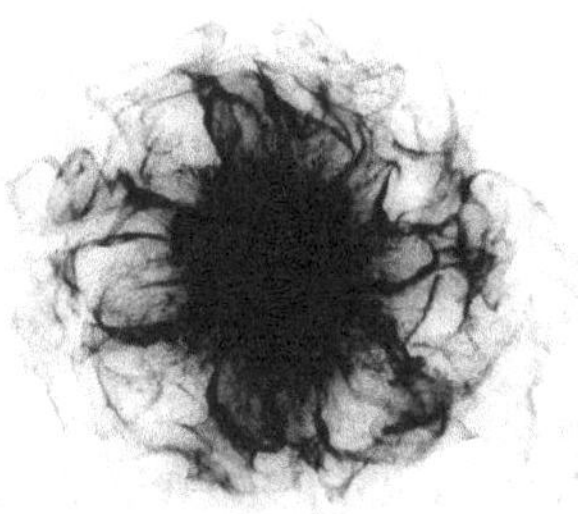

It's a long way to the bottom. The cavern is dark, with only the glowing bundle of roots streaming beside me like a silver waterfall. I can't remember if I fall asleep while I listen to the roots sing their song; maybe I don't need to sleep to feel like I'm inside a dream. All I know is that when we finally touch ground, the song ends abruptly, and there's nothing to hear but water dripping and my own feet scuffing against stone. Now that our bargain is sealed, I know I'll never hear the tree's voice again.

Peter is beginning to wake up, struggling in Sarah's arms. She sets him down as if she can't wait to get rid of him, then stalks away from the glowing roots and starts poking around in the semidarkness. A second later, Peter opens his eyes, gazing around woozily before his face takes on the look of intensity I know so well. Observation and analysis, I think with a slight smile. Some things never change.

"Where are we?" Peter asks.

"In a cavern beneath the world-tree's chamber," I say. "We're headed home."

"What happened up there?" he asks. "We were talking to the Dawsons, and then there was the tree, and then…"

"You got sick," I say simply. "But you're much better now."

His face tightens, looking lost in a way he almost never

does. "You said we're going home? How are we supposed to get there?"

I smile. "We have a guide."

Sarah steps into the light. As soon as Peter sees her, his mouth falls open and his eyes practically pop out of their sockets. She scowls back, but he remains frozen, staring at her like a drooling jackalass.

"Queen Sarah," he says at last. "It's… you."

"No kidding," I say. "Who do you think we've been looking for all this time?"

He shakes his head over and over, as if he thought we were chasing a legend, not a real person. "I didn't… I mean, there was the quetzal, but…"

"With an emphasis on *was*," Sarah says. "Hadassah told me the two of you lost Archie."

Peter gapes. "Archie?"

"My quetzalopteryx," she says. "Do we have to go over this again?"

Now Peter looks downright constipated. "A quetzal… quetzalopteryx? Does that mean he's…?"

"Of course," Sarah says. "Why else would I name him Archie?"

Peter stammers something unintelligible. I look back and forth between the two of them. "He's a *what*?"

"A hybrid," Peter says, then swallows, "of quetzalcoati and Archaeopteryx. A genus of bird-like dinosaurs considered by most authorities to be the link between ancient reptiles and old-world birds. There's been some dispute among paleontologists about whether they were capable of true flight, but…"

"But Archie puts that dispute to rest," Sarah says. "He's

one of the strongest fliers I've ever seen, and he's smart, too. He'll turn up," she adds under her breath. "He always turns up."

"But this is incredible!" Peter blurts out. "Archaeopteryges have been extinct for hundreds of millions of years. To create the hybrid, you'd have to splice their genes with those of a contemporary species using a scientific process that's been unknown for centuries—the same process, presumably, by which the original Ecosystem disseminated its genetic material. And that's assuming you had a ready supply of Archaeopteryx genetic material on hand, which seems almost impossible. How did you find it? *Where* did you find it?"

For a moment, Sarah looks abashed. Then her face clouds, and she pulls herself to her full height, her furs adding to her size and broad shoulders. I've seen so many different versions of her in the past day—my gentle friend, the raving beast that nearly attacked me in the tree's chamber, the woman who seems confused about who and where she is—I don't know which one to expect now.

But I certainly don't expect the one I get.

"I can see you're the type who always wants answers," she says icily to Peter. "You'd be better off if you kept your mouth shut and learned to seek wisdom instead."

She turns her back on him and stomps away from the light. I'm shocked and embarrassed that Sarah would be so rude, but I remind myself that I felt the same way about Peter's annoying little habits just days ago. Still, I can't understand why she's turned so surly now, right after I made the bargain with the tree. I step closer to Peter, speaking softly so only he can hear.

"She hasn't been around people since she left the city," I say. "Plus she's been trapped in the tree's chamber for weeks, maybe longer. I think that might have… changed her a little."

He looks at me, his face drooping like a very sad harpy dog's. "I never meant to offend her. She's been… well, ever since I learned about her and the War of the Queens, she's been…"

Your hero, I think. I squeeze his hand, and he gives me a small smile.

"Anyway, you were telling me I got sick up there," he says. "From the tree's fruit, I assume? How'd I get better?"

"You wouldn't believe me if I told you."

"Try me."

"You were…" I wonder how to tell him without saying too much. "You were healed by the tree's power."

"Really? By Queen Sarah?"

"Um, no. Actually, by me."

His eyes bug out of his face again. "So it's true what Leah said, that there's some unique connection between you and the tree?"

"*Leah* told you that?"

"Right before we crossed the river," he says. "She told me that no one else on the journey mattered as much as you, that we had to protect you at all costs. Even if that meant giving up our own lives in the process."

I lower my eyes so he can't see my face, knowing that Leah wouldn't have wanted him to tell me, wishing he hadn't. He doesn't seem to realize the significance of what he just said, because he's off to the races again.

"Now, this is most intriguing!" he says. "I would

imagine that, to wield the world-tree's power, you'd have to tap into its code or something analogous. Not unlike the way the queens manipulate the Ecosystem's genetic material—which is, of course, why Queen Rebecca's sickness poses such a threat. But how'd you gain access?"

I take a good look at the boy who's done so much for me, who obeyed Leah's final order and saved my life at the risk of his own. Even more than that, who became my friend. His eyes are wide, his face flushed with anticipation as he waits for me to tell him the secrets of the elder world. If things were different, I feel like I could spill my guts to him, let him in on doubts and fears I'd never have dreamed of telling him before.

But Peter's smart. If I start telling him about the tree, he won't be able to stop himself from asking questions, and before I know it, he'll have figured everything out. He's already guessed about the code—or not guessed, but analyzed and deduced. How long will it be before he asks about the bargain? Much as I hate to cut him off the way Sarah did, I don't have the strength for another argument.

"I'm too tired to go into it right now," I say. "Maybe later, okay?"

He frowns, opens his mouth to object, but for once, decides not to.

"Any time you feel like talking," he says, "I'm here."

I feel a rush of affection for him, and I wish I could say something to match his trust in me. But I can't, so I simply smile.

"This is all very sweet," Sarah's voice comes from nowhere. "But we might want to get a move on. The Queen won't last forever."

She reappears out of the darkness beyond the tree-roots' light. Her face is a mask, her eyes shadowed beneath her brow so I can't see the slightest flicker of blue in their depths. When she turns to Peter, there's a mocking edge to her voice.

"Unless, of course, you have any more pressing questions," she says.

He looks down, shakes his head. Sarah smirks. I take a deep breath and ask her something I hope doesn't get *me* on her bad side. "Which way do we go?"

"We have to head east and hunt for wyrm-trails," she says. "We'll never make it in time otherwise. So, if the two of you are ready…"

Peter and I nod in unison. Sarah looks us over for a moment, then hitches her furs up on her shoulders and sets off.

We follow. I can't see much, just wet stone that glistens in the light of the world-tree's roots. The air smells as wild as any place I've been, thick and musty like a living creature's breath. Sarah walks in front of us, setting her bare feet on slippery rock and using her arm strength to pull herself over uneven ground. Peter and I stumble after her as best we can, with him tripping and losing his feet even more than me. A few times, he opens his mouth as if he's about to ask me something, but then he glances nervously at Sarah's back and stays quiet.

The light from the tree grows weaker and weaker the farther we go. Right at the point where the silvery gleam fades for good, a grove of baneboo has rooted itself in the rock, as if it's guarding the tree even down here. I'm worried about trying to make our way through it in complete darkness, but Sarah produces a flint from one of the pockets in her furs, along with a branch coated in tarry stuff. She strikes the flint and the torch lights on the first try, casting stark shadows across her face.

"I learned that from Gideon," she says. "He was a fire-starter back in the Sensor village."

"I know," I whisper, but my voice comes back as a spooky echo, and I hush myself like a child afraid of the dark. Which, at the moment, is exactly what I am.

With the light of Sarah's torch turning her into a giant furry shadow, we creep through the baneboo grove. It rustles, but doesn't attack. The torch shows me human faces forming and disappearing in the stalks, the flickering fire making the faces seem to melt and flow like images in a nightmare. Peter reaches for my hand, and I don't object when he squeezes it tight.

In a minute or two, we're past the baneboo and back into an empty space where the only things to see are the rocks at our feet and the darkness all around. I reach out with my Sense and become aware of blind fish glowing in deep pools on either side of our path, but I can't tell if they were born from the tree or the Ecosystem. Other than that, the cavern seems empty of life, which is a real disappointment after my experience in the tree's chamber. I wish I could get the feeling back of Sensing a whole world all at once. I would reach out to try to hear the tree singing if I weren't so certain I'd hear nothing at all.

But then, when I least expect it, I *do* hear something. It's a low rumbling sound, and it seems to be coming from everywhere all at once, as if an earthquake is shaking the rock deep beneath us. Sarah must hear it too, because she pauses with the torch held high. I look at Peter, expecting to see his eyes as wide as saucers, but he doesn't seem to hear anything. I close my eyes and send a silent question toward the source of the sound.

The answer comes back so quickly I'm startled. I hold out a hand to touch Sarah's arm, but she's already frozen in place, her head cocked as if she's listening to the same voice that hums inside my head.

Hail, two-leg-walkers, the voice says. *We have been searching for you for many long days.*

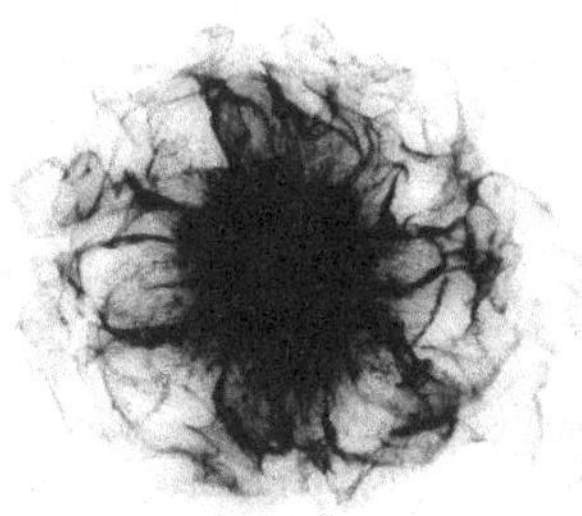

I DROP PETER's hand and hold my arms out just as the blunt head breaks through the rocks at our feet. The long black body slithers clear of the hole it's dug and curls up to my hand so I can stroke their nose.

"Wyvern!" I say out loud, too excited to remember they can't hear me that way. "I thought you were dead!"

Wyvern nuzzles me, but doesn't respond until I repeat the thoughts in my mind.

We-Wyvern were not returned to the soil we-Wyvern consume, they say, which I guess is a wyrm's way of talking about dying. *We-Wyvern destroyed the bereavers and left them for other wyrms to transform into the soil-they-consume. We-Wyvern are grateful that you-Hadassah have not been so transformed.*

My heart skips a beat, but I try to keep my thoughts to myself.

And yet, you-Hadassah, Wyvern says, sizing me up, *there is something about you that differs from your former presence in the bundle. Something we-Wyvern cannot…*

The wyrm's thought-stream pauses, and the head shakes in uncertainty. I pat their slimy nose and try to help out.

I've joined the tree-bundle, I say. *You don't need to find it anymore, because you've found me.*

Wyvern thinks that over. *And the earth-walker*

accompanies you-Hadassah. This is most good. It betokens a coming-together of that-which-is-meant-to-be.

What do you mean?

Your kind have been separated, Wyvern answers. *But it is not good that your kind should be so. Knowing this, we-Wyvern offer a return of one who was near joining the soil we-Wyvern consume. We offer this as a sign to you-Hadassah and she-earth-walker that there is a coming-together of all things in the bundle.*

Show me! I say impatiently, only to feel Wyvern grow strangely reluctant.

We-Wyvern will show the sign to you-Hadassah, they say. *But you-Hadassah must understand that the fiber-bundle can be sundered even in its strength. That-which-comes-together is not always that-which-once-was.*

Now I'm totally bewildered, but my confusion falls away when Wyvern unfurls their tail and I see what they're holding.

"Leah!"

I leap for her and crash into her arms. Maybe too hard; she wobbles and falls against Wyvern's side, as if she's still weak from the accident at the bereaver dam. Studying her face, I see that one of her eyes isn't focused on me, while her mouth droops unnaturally. I'm squeezing her as tight as I can, but her arms hang limply around my neck, with a tremor in the muscles that used to be so solid and strong.

What's wrong with her? I send an anxious thought to Wyvern.

She-warrior-woman was… The wyrm pauses as if they're trying to find a gentle way to say this in my language. *She-her-warrior-woman's head-fiber-bundle was-is…*

She has brain damage, I translate. *From almost drowning.*

Wyvern nods sorrowfully. *Our kind are fiber-bundle,* they say. *We-Wyvern have shared our head-fiber-bundle with her-warrior-woman, and she is mostly whole. But her head-fiber-bundle was grievously torn, and We-Wyvern could not make it fully whole again. We-Wyvern are sorry, you-Hadassah. We-Wyvern tried.*

It's okay, I say, resting my head on Leah's shoulder. *Thank you for saving her life.*

Wyvern says nothing, but I feel their misery at failing to heal the bundle.

"Sarah?"

It's Leah's voice, slow and hesitant, like someone just learning to talk. I pull back to see her staring at Sarah with her one good eye, her head wobbling. Sarah returns her gaze, though she doesn't lose the guarded look she's had since we left the world-tree's chamber. I step away from Leah, who slumps against Wyvern's tail but manages to hold trembling arms out to her friend. Sarah doesn't move, which leaves Leah awkwardly embracing the air as if she's reaching for a ghost.

"Leah," Sarah says, and that's all.

I look back and forth between them, at the tears creeping down Leah's cheeks while Sarah stands stony-faced. Even with what Leah told me about her and Sarah's fight, I never expected their reunion to be like this. I'm at the point of turning away when Sarah passes her torch to me, and in its glow, I see the single tear that's fallen from each of her eyes.

"Leah," she says, the warmth restored to her voice.

She steps into her friend's arms and squeezes delicately,

then buries her head in Leah's neck. Leah pats her back with quivering hands, makes inarticulate shushing noises in Sarah's ear. My eyes are streaming so badly I can hardly see through the sharp points of torchlight.

The chilly cavern fills with warmth. At first I think the torch must have flared, but the heat is much stronger than that, as if the underground world has turned to summertime for a single bright moment. Leah's hands have taken on a calm, relaxed rhythm as they stroke Sarah's hair. Her eyes fall on me—both of them at once—and I know what's happened.

Sarah healed her. Where Wyvern could only patch Leah's injuries, Sarah tapped into the urthwyrm's nervous system and used it to fix the damage. Her voice emerges from Leah's shoulder, sounding smaller than I've ever known it to be.

"I'm so sorry, Leah," she says. "This is all on account of me. I never… I never even said goodbye…"

"Hush," Leah answers. "You're here now."

"But I won't be for long," Sarah says. "I'll be gone again, just like you always said I would, and I don't know what I'll tell you then."

"You don't need to tell me anything," Leah says. "You never did."

She leans down to kiss Sarah's filthy hair and squeezes her in a tight embrace. Somehow, I know this isn't the first time she's held her friend this way.

"Did you find what you were looking for?" she asks softly.

Sarah's head jerks in a nod.

"Good," Leah says, and turns her eyes to me. "Did you?"

"I… I think so."

"Then it's time for us to go." She kisses Sarah one more time on the cheek, then holds her at arm's length like a mother inspecting her child on the first day of school. "We'll do something about the hair later."

Sarah smiles, and for a second, she looks young again, like the dream-self who's been visiting me all these years. Her voice, though, is like Leah's, brisk and full of authority.

"Onto the Queen's wyrm, both of you," she says to me and Peter. "We won't be stopping for food or rest until we reach the city."

Before I can ask her how we're going to last another week without eating anything, Wyvern flips me onto their back, Peter landing behind me. Leah and Sarah climb aboard in the rear, with enough space between us that I figure they want to spend time catching up. I lean forward and place my palm on the wyrm's snout as I picture the road back to the City of the Queens.

You-Hadassah are indeed one with the tree-bundle, Wyvern asserts when they feel my touch. *You-Hadassah will share this power with the two-leg-walker your kind call Queen, yes? You-Hadassah will make the bundle strong and lasting?*

I'll do my best, I say.

It seems to me that Wyvern pauses for a moment, as if they're about to ask another question. Then they're off, shooting down the tunnel at lightning speed while Leah shrieks with glee behind us.

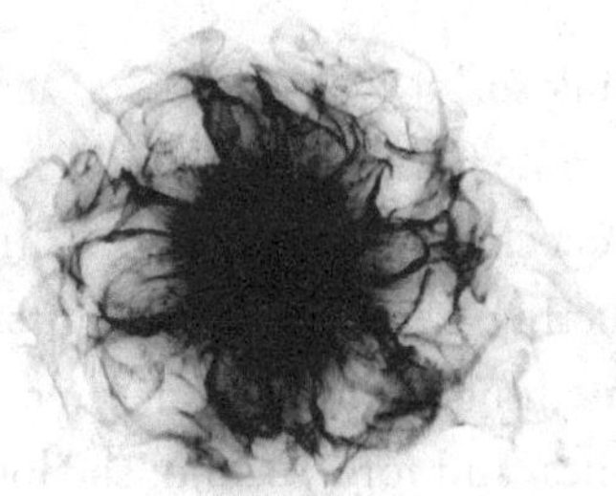

We burst into sunlight after so long in darkness, I've nearly forgotten that I belong to this world, not the tree's. When I bundle with Wyvern, I discover that we're already well east of the three rivers, heading back toward the Sensor village and the City of the Queens. The wyrm must have tunneled deep into the earth's crust to meet us, then found an underground shortcut to bypass the water and the canyon.

We cross the open plains east of the rivers at top speed, Wyvern moving so fast their body seems not to touch the ground. Peter and I cling to our bridles while we're awake, but Wyvern helps us when we're asleep with the skin-sticking trick. Sarah and Leah keep to themselves, the low murmur of their talk going deep into the night. I can't make out what they're saying, but whatever it is, it doesn't do much for Sarah's mood: she won't say anything to me or Peter, won't smile even when I hear the playful lilt in Leah's voice. I thought she'd be excited or at least pleased when she learned about my bargain with the tree, and I was sure she'd be thrilled to be back on speaking terms with Leah. But I'm beginning to understand that, whatever happened to her over the past ten years of self-imposed exile, it's going to take more than a few days of human company to bring her back.

After three days on the plains, we reach the western edge of the great forest that leads to home. I try to bundle with Wyvern as they plunge into the shadows beneath the heavy canopy, but this is one of the rare times they don't respond, I guess because they need to focus on dodging close-packed trees. With Peter too busy holding on for dear life to talk to me, I send my Sense outward toward the woods, and I'm surprised by the answer that comes back. Before, I always accepted the world for what it was; now, with the tree's power flowing through me, I see what the world *could* have been if not for the Ecosystem. Everything around me shows signs of pollution: things growing out of control, species mingling that should have stayed apart, newborn mutations crowding out older creatures that didn't get a fair chance to survive. I'm surrounded by trees I've known all my life, ache and hexlox and pain and sickenmore, but now they look diseased, twisted and unnatural. I wonder how it all happened—how oak trees turned to aches and hemlocks to hexlox, how pine trees became filled with pain, how tall, graceful sycamores developed the venom to sicken more than just us. I understand why the Dawsons named their daughter Dominique, and why they called the hive-child that carried her genes *Apis impunita*, the invincible bee. After they left *edinnu*, they used their power over life and death to make a monster that grew up to dominate the whole world.

Maybe, I think, that's what they wanted. Maybe they were hoping to destroy everything so they could return to the garden they loved. Except before they could get back home, their creation killed them, too.

My morbid thoughts are interrupted when a shadow drops from the trees. Peter flings up a protective arm—mostly around me—but Wyvern comes to their first dead stop in days while Sarah lets out a cry of pure joy.

"Archie!" she coos, and I look behind me to see the quetzalopteryx perched on her arm, preening its feathers the way a fell-cat licks its fur. Sarah's eyes shine through the hair that won't stay in place no matter what Leah does to it.

"I told you he'd come back!" she exults. "Didn't I tell the silly people you'd come back?" she asks Archie in the syrupy voice grownups use with babies.

I stare at her, amazed by the change. Leah looks tickled too, though maybe there's a touch of sadness in her smile. Archie seems to take it all in stride; he nuzzles Sarah's face with his quivering nose, licks her cheek with a surprisingly long tongue. Quetzals, I remember from one of Peter's half-listened-to lectures, were insect-eaters, poking around in hollow trees to slurp flame ants and cicatrix.

"That's my good boy," Sarah gushes.

"How did he find us?" Peter pipes up, the first words either of us have said to Sarah since we boarded the wyrm.

As quickly as it came, her jubilant mood ends. She looks at Peter darkly, but instead of having the sense to turn away, he stares right back.

"I told you he's smart," she says.

"Yes, but that's *really* smart for a bird, even a hybrid," Peter says. "The expression 'bloodbird-brain' wasn't invented without reason, since it signifies the underdevelopment of the cerebral cortex and the prevalence of the brain stem in the primitive reptilian ancestors of old-world birds."

"Archie's no reptile," Sarah says. "He knew where to find *you* when I told him to track you down, didn't he?

Didn't you?" she repeats in the baby-talk voice, squeezing Archie's cheeks while he slobbers all over her.

"That may be true, but taxonomically speaking—" Peter begins, while I dig a finger into his ribs to shut him up.

"I don't care about his taxonomy," Sarah says. "I designed Archie to be better than anything he came from, and all you need to do is look at him to see the result."

She raises her arm, and the quetzalopteryx takes flight. Wyvern starts moving at the same time, but somehow, Archie keeps pace with the speeding wyrm.

"If he's not smart," Sarah says to the rest of us, as if we need more convincing of how special Archie is, "then explain how he knew what to do at the river crossing. He got you all across, and then—"

"Is that what he told you?" Peter asks.

Sarah looks at him as if she doesn't understand the question.

"He didn't get us *all* across," Peter says. "Simon and Catherine died, and Leah almost did, too. If Archie told you anything different, he's lying."

I can't believe even Peter would be stupid enough to say that, but he pays for it a second later when Sarah grabs him roughly and brings her face close enough that she could bite off his nose.

"Archie doesn't lie!" she shouts at him. "I've taken about all I can from you, and if you don't apologize this instant, you can find your own way home!"

She snatches Peter partway from his seat-bucket while Leah tries to grab her arms and I struggle to hang onto him atop the racing wyrm. Sarah's strength is like a raging beast's, and I'm convinced all three of us are about to end up as piles of broken bones on the forest floor.

"Apologize!" she says again.

"I'm sorry," Peter says, but without the panic I expect to hear in his voice. "I shouldn't have doubted Archie."

"Tell *him*!"

Peter looks up at the flying quetzal. I'm sure he has no intention of apologizing to a bird, but I'm wrong again.

"I'm sorry, Archie," he says calmly. "I don't know what I was thinking."

Archie doesn't show any sign that he understands beyond a flick of his wings. Sarah, though, lowers Peter into his seat before letting go. She's breathing hard, and when Leah reaches out to touch her, she jerks away. Peter leans forward to put the bridle in my shaking hands, and as he does, he whispers a few words in my ear.

"Tonight. Don't go to sleep."

I look at him strangely, but he ignores me. My eyes roam over Sarah, who's scowling as she watches Archie dance above her head. She's muttering something, but the wind of Wyvern's headlong speed makes it impossible for me to tell what it is.

Peter's got nothing to worry about. My heart is pounding so hard, I don't think I'll sleep for a week.

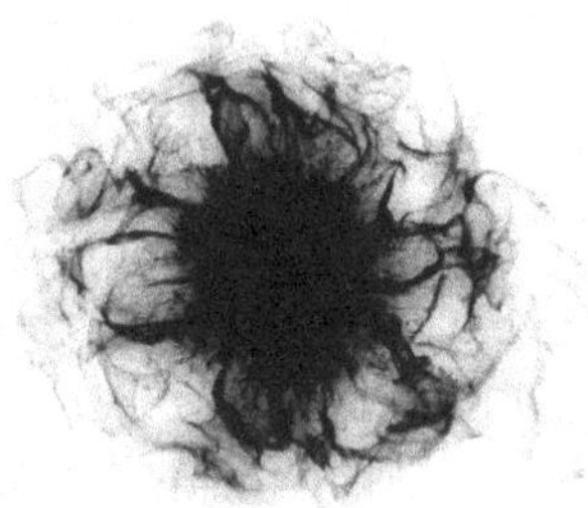

A HALF-MOON HAS turned the woods to silver when Peter jabs me in the side, much harder than he has to.

"Hadassah," he whispers. "Are you awake?"

"What do you think?"

"Good. Queen Sarah's asleep."

I glance behind me and see Sarah resting against Leah, so bundled in her thick furs she looks like a forest creature bedded down for the winter. Both of them are snoring softly. There's enough light to show that Leah's hand rests on top of her friend's, which strikes me as a hopeful sign after Sarah's rampage earlier today.

"What did you want to talk to me about?" I ask Peter.

He doesn't answer right away. I twist in my seat to find his nose not two inches from mine, his eyes pale and huge in the moonlight.

"I'm just basing this on the data," he says. "I don't have any unequivocal proof. But enough has happened that I thought you should know."

"About Sarah?"

He nods, bumping noses with me. "I think… I think she's…"

"Crazy?" I voice my worst fear.

"Dangerous," he says. "It's become obvious to me that she's hiding something. And people don't do that unless they're up to no good."

My heart starts pounding again at his words. "Hiding what?"

"I'm not sure," he says. "She suppressed her part in sending Archie to look for us, and that leads me to believe she's hiding something else. I draw that conclusion because there's no way she could have made contact with her quetzalopteryx if she was trapped in the world-tree's chamber, so she omitted that information to keep us from being suspicious of her."

"Maybe she sent him *before* she was trapped."

"That might sound like a plausible inference, but it doesn't fit the facts," he says. "I'm one hundred percent positive she wasn't meaning to let slip that she sent Archie to find us. If she wanted us to know, why didn't she tell us right at the start? She's totally in love with him, and she's only too happy to brag about him. But she didn't say a word until I pushed her buttons to get a reaction."

"You pushed them a little too hard."

"I know that," he says. "I only did it because I've felt concerned all along that she's..."

He lowers his eyes, and even in the bad light, I can see the redness creeping across his pale cheeks. "That she's what?" I ask.

"Under the tree's spell," he squeezes out in the barest of whispers. "The Dawsons weren't the ones running the show back there, don't you see? All that stuff about what a great privilege it was to be admitted into the presence of the tree was a big fat lie. This isn't Sir Thomas Malory, after all."

I have no idea what that means, so I don't even ask.

"They led us to the tree's chamber because the *tree*

ordered them to," he goes on. "The tree wanted us to come there, and so it must have convinced them—"

"Convinced them? I thought they were computers."

"Reprogrammed them, then," he says. "Tapped into their code and rewired them to serve its purposes. Remember that glitch we saw? I strongly suspect the tree did the same to Queen Sarah. It would explain why she's behaving so erratically, and it would also explain something else that doesn't make sense."

"Which is what?"

"You told me she survived in the tree's chamber for weeks," he says. "Did you ever stop to ask *how* she survived so long without food or water?"

"Queens can go without eating and drinking longer than most people," I say, but the excuse sounds weak even to me.

"Not for three whole weeks," Peter says. "No, the only logical conclusion is that the tree somehow sustained Queen Sarah for all that time and then released her to do its bidding. And here we are, heading back to the city as fast as we can go, with absolutely no idea what the tree commissioned her to do."

I stay quiet as his eyes flick over mine, reflecting a sheen of moonlight. "Maybe," I say, "you're jumping to conclusions. Because Sarah's been so mean to you."

"That's not the way I operate, and you know it," he says. "So stop trying to change the subject. Personally, I think the tree trapped Queen Sarah to get at you, because it knew you'd come running if she called. Which raises the question: what does it want from *you*?"

I should have known he'd figure things out without

my having to tell him. It's like *he's* the computer, always ten steps ahead of the rest of us. "I'm not under any spell," I say to him. "I'm making my own decisions, so you can stop worrying about that."

"But they're the decisions the tree wants you to make, aren't they?" he says. "Please, Hadassah. We were supposed to be a team, and now… now you'll barely say a word to me. And not only that, but ever since you left the tree's chamber, you've been… different…"

"How would *you* know I'm different?" I say, forgetting to keep my voice down. "You barely knew me before."

"I know you now," he says. "And I maintain that you're hiding something from me. I haven't been able to figure out what it is yet, but mark my words, I will eventually. You might as well save time and energy and just tell me."

I laugh. "That'll never happen."

"Then I'll have no choice but to conclude that you're under the world-tree's spell, too. That you're glitching as much as Queen Sarah. And that you're conspiring with her to—"

"What are the two of you whispering about?"

I freeze at the sound of Sarah's voice. She looms behind Peter, bulky in her furs, while Leah snoozes in the next seat back. Thick hair dangles over Sarah's face, but the bright glint of her eyes makes her look like a terror wolf stalking its prey.

"It's bumpy in this stretch of the woods," she says, speaking in a voice that sounds unnaturally loud in the stillness of the night. "Here, let me help you out."

Undeterred by the wyrm's speed, she lets go of the strap holding her in place and reaches for Peter. His eyes widen in alarm, but she merely lifts him from his seat and switches places with him, putting herself between the two of us. What frightens me most is how easily Peter comes free from Wyvern's sticky skin, which means the wyrm must have released their hold at Sarah's command.

"You'd better get some sleep," she says to Peter once everyone's settled. "You too," she adds, turning to me with a toothy smile that reminds me of the baneboo warriors, or the Dawsons.

I look away, trying to calm myself. The wind whips in my ears, and the wyrm's skin holds me in slime as sticky as tar. As if that's not enough, Sarah has a grip on my belt, right where my sword used to hang. She pulls me against her furs the way she was nestled with Leah, and I choke on the animal scent of her body.

"Your friend seems to think he's pretty clever," she murmurs, too low for Peter to hear. "Maybe you need to remind him that it's perilous for children to meddle in the affairs of queens."

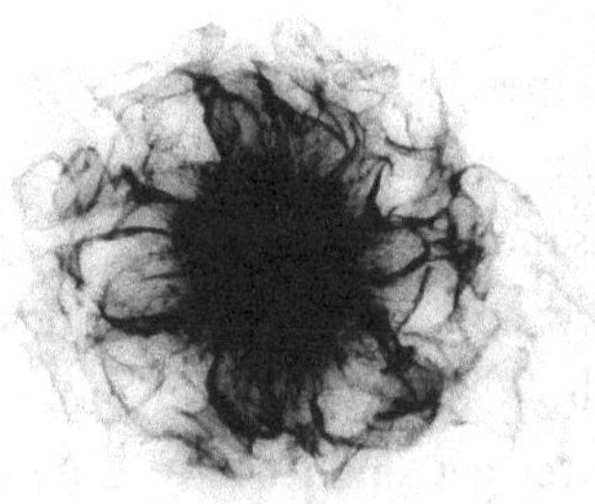

I DON'T KNOW who to trust.

Through the whole sleepless night, while Sarah's smell clings to me as tightly as her claw-like hand at my belt, I go over and over what Peter said, but no matter how hard I try, I can't convince myself he's not right. All I know is that I desperately want him to be wrong.

Sarah, under the tree's spell? Lying to me? Never in a million years would I have believed that.

But I'm starting to believe it now.

She *did* send Archie to find us. How could she have done that unless the world-tree let her? Based on my experience, nothing goes in or out of the tree's chamber without its permission—and Sarah is a queen, so it definitely wouldn't have allowed her to make contact with the Ecosystem unless it had a good reason to. What was one of the first things she said to me when I found her? *I knew you'd come for me.* At the time, I thought that was just the sort of thing Sarah would say. When I think of those words now, I have to ask myself: *how* did she know? Because the tree told her? Because it *made* her call for me, just like Peter said, in order to get what it wanted?

The more I try to tell myself *it can't be*, the more things I come up with that force me to answer, *yes, it can.* Peter's right: Sarah never could have survived that long without food or water. So was the tree feeding her its fruit—and its poison at the same time? Would that explain why she was such a mess when I found her, why she's still so different from the Sarah I thought I knew? And what about all those times I saw her looking at the tree, staring at it, nodding to it—was she listening to its voice, receiving its orders? Is *that* why she's been so unstable, because her mind is breaking under the power of the tree's spell?

And what does that say about *me*? I don't feel like I'm under a spell, but maybe that's the way spells work—maybe they make you carry out someone else's desires while you think you're acting on your own. If that's true, how do I know the tree will keep its end of the bargain? How can I be sure that, after I give it what I've promised to, the tree will save my dad and everyone else in the Queen's hive?

There's a simple answer, and it scares me to death: I can't.

But I also can't think of anything to do about it. Even if I had Leah's sword, I'd be no match for Sarah. I used to believe Wyvern would stand up for me no matter what, but now I'm afraid to bundle with them in case Sarah's gained control of them, too. Maybe Wyvern was part of the plot all along, helping me grow Sensitive to the tree so it could spring its trap. Maybe Queen Rebecca's most faithful servant was working for her mortal enemy from the moment Wyvern carried me to her brood chamber. Or maybe they've become the world-tree's puppet only now, taking orders from the former queen it ensnared.

Daybreak comes, but it doesn't shed light on any of my fears. Sarah's hand relaxes the tiniest smidgeon on my belt, and Wyvern slows as if they're responding to her command. We're passing through a stand of puny ache trees, with an open area in the forest just beyond. A sharp tingling in my mind tells me we've reached the site of the Sensor village. I felt nothing of the sort when we stopped here on the outward voyage, but as Peter says, I'm different now.

Sarah brakes Wyvern at the edge of what used to be her home. The crabapple grove is just as we left it, and Archie settles in the branches of one of the trees, where horrornets buzz around the tart fruit. My stomach rumbles at the tantalizing banquet; for the past three days, we've had nothing but water and a few bites of moldy bread Wyvern salvaged from Leah's pack. Sarah doesn't even glance at the trees as she climbs down. When Wyvern releases the rest of us and she helps me dismount, I realize she's not going to let me out of her sight from now on.

"Why are we stopping?" Peter asks her.

Her face twitches, and I can tell she's debating whether to answer or break every bone in his body. She chooses the first. Barely.

"There's something Hadassah and I need to look into," she says.

She holds a hand out to direct me onto the circle of black cinders that used to protect the village. I head where she's pointing, while Leah stays behind with Peter. When I hear the noise of Wyvern tunneling into the dirt, the thought pops into my head that Leah might be guarding Peter, which would mean she's in on the world-tree's scheme, too. If the tree could infect Sarah with its fruit, could Sarah have infected Leah when she healed her?

I glance at Sarah's face, hoping to catch a hint of what she's thinking, but she gazes over my head, not acknowledging me at all.

The tingling in my mind grows steadily stronger as we crunch across the gem-like grit. By the time we reach the mossy rocks that Leah told me used to be the town hall, the feeling has become so intense it's as if we're back in the tree's chamber in the heart of *edinnu.* Sarah takes hold of my belt to stop me. Of all the things that are upsetting me right now, I don't know why it should hurt me so much that she refuses to lay a hand on my actual skin, but it does.

"Leah told you this is where the gathering-hall stood," she says, not a question but a statement. "What she probably didn't mention is that it's also—"

"The place where my parents were supposed to get married."

That seems to surprise her. "Miriam told you?"

"She told me something went wrong at the wedding. She didn't tell me what."

"And I'm not going to tell you, either," she says. "If your mother chose to keep it a secret, she must have had her reasons. Eventually, though, she'll have no choice but to tell you. She'll want you to know before…"

"Before I do what the tree asked me to do?"

"That would seem like the right time, wouldn't it?" she says with a humorless smile.

"Sarah," I ask, "do *you* know what the tree's bargain is?"

She looks out over the site of the village, where I see Archie leaping from branch to branch of the crabapple trees. Her mouth moves without speaking, and I wonder if, during all her years on the road, she got into the habit of talking to herself just to hear another human voice. I wonder, too, if when her dream-self visited me in my room, her real self could hear in my voice how much I loved her.

"I know the tree's bargain," she says at last.

"And you're okay with it?" I ask. "Even though you know?"

"Whether I'm okay with it or not is beside the point," she answers. "I'm a queen of this land, and I know the force of the queen's compact with the Ecosystem. I gave up… many things when I accepted that compact years ago. The tree's bargain is no different. A being that ancient knows far more than either of us, and it knows that for there to be healing, there must be payment. That's the way it's always been, and the way it always will be."

I watch her face, hoping to see a sign of sadness, but there's nothing. She's a stone, a star, a tree. My words can't reach her, and neither can my tears.

I shed them anyway.

She lets me cry, and when I'm done, she smiles. Not cruelly. Not even coldly. Just like she always knew this moment would arrive.

"Come with me," she says, and this time, when she holds out her hand, she lets her fingertips brush across the token I wear at my throat. "There's something I need to show you."

A hole opens in the ground before us, and she leads me down into darkness.

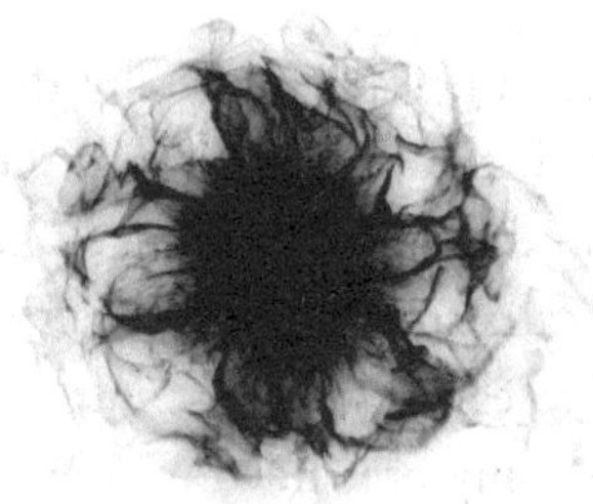

THE CITY OF the Queens rises before me in the predawn mist.

It's totally quiet. No voices, no clatter of hand-carts carrying fruits and vegetables through the lanes, no pounding of hammers or whining of saws from the work crews. There aren't even any songs from early morning birds. When I look past the gate, I see the same buildings as the day I left: the guard station, the Cathedral memorial, the houses on the outskirts of the city center. But as far as living things go, the Queen's sickness might already have turned the entire city into a ghost town.

"Where is everybody?" I ask in a whisper.

"I'd guess they're inside," Leah says. "Under quarantine."

"But Mom said quarantine wouldn't work."

"People do what's familiar to them," she says. "We've used quarantine before when there were outbreaks, so possibly they were hoping the same procedures would save them now."

We climb down from Wyvern, who promptly vanishes underground, probably headed for the tunnels beneath the Queen's house. Archie takes wing from Sarah's arm and disappears into the mist, but when I look at her questioningly, she merely shrugs.

"Wild things have to roam free," she says, and I wonder if she's talking about herself.

With Leah in the lead and Sarah bringing up the rear, we creep through the front gate into the silent city. My legs shake with exhaustion and hunger; Leah picked a few apples from Sarah's trees before we left the village, but I was too scared to eat them. Peter must have felt the same way, because he only pretended to nibble his. Starving as I am, I'm glad I didn't give in. My stomach is drawn so tight with dread, I don't think I'd have been able to hold anything down.

We pause when we reach the first group of houses. All the windows are shuttered, but I keep thinking I see shadows moving behind them. No one opens a window or their front door, though. As we continue toward the city center, I keep expecting to turn a corner and find bodies piled in the streets, the way I've heard it was during the War of the Queens. Only then there was shouting and the sound of explosions and running feet, not this deadly quiet that seems to weigh on my shoulders like a shroud.

At the central crossroads, Sarah takes the fork to the left. "Where are we going?" I ask her.

"To the Queen's residence," she says. "Right away."

"I want to see my mom and dad first."

She glowers. "There's no time, Hadassah."

"It'll take fifteen minutes," I say. "If the Queen is already dead, fifteen more minutes won't matter."

I see the impatience in her face, but I'm not about to back down. She was the one who said Mom would want to have a talk with me before I tended to the Queen. If this is going to be my last chance to have that talk, then Sarah can find a way to fit fifteen minutes into her busy schedule.

"What about you?" she asks Peter. "Feeling the need for a house call?"

"My mom will be okay," he says. "She doesn't have any more of the *Apis impunita* genes than I do. I'm with Hadassah."

Sarah glares at the two of us.

"Very well," she says. "We can check on Isaac's condition, and Miriam can come with us to the Queen's house. But we can't delay," she adds in her talking-to-herself voice. "The bargain must be kept."

"It will be," I say, and she looks at me as if she's startled to realize she said the words out loud.

We turn east and make our way to the home I haven't seen for almost three weeks. With each step, my stomach pulls tighter at the thought of what I might find. There's been no news from Mom since her last bird; for whatever reason—maybe because we were traveling so fast, maybe because of something I'm too scared to name—Leah didn't send any more birds even when we got back within range. Though the empty city seems to shout at me that my worst fears have come true, a tiny corner of my heart keeps alive the hope that Mom's blood-cure worked, that my dad and the Queen have recovered and I won't have to carry out the tree's orders after all.

That hope dies when I see what's become of my home.

The windows are shuttered like the others in the center of the city. No light peeps through the slats, no sound of movement reaches my ears. The garden that Mom and Dad have always kept in such perfect condition has undergone a horrible change, with a handful of plants grown wildly out of control and the rest nothing but brittle brown stalks. I'm startled that so much has died so quickly; the Ecosystem cares for its own, and most of the growing things in our garden should have been fine for three weeks even without human help. Unless…

Unless the Ecosystem itself is starting to die.

Peter reaches for my hand when he sees what I see, but I pull away from him and run up the path to my house.

"Mom! Dad!" I call out, and I don't stop calling until I reach the front door and throw it open.

The house is empty. I know it the second I step into the darkened foyer and hear my feet echoing through a vault that feels like it's never been lived in a single moment. Though my heart wants to tear through each room in hopes that I'm wrong, my head won't let me. I turn and race back to the path where Leah and Peter are waiting.

"They're not here," I say. "They're not here!"

Neither of them says a word, but I know what they're thinking.

"Sarah?"

She's at the end of the front walk, just outside the gate. As if she can't bring herself to come close to the house that used to belong to her friends, even now that they're gone. Fury grips me, and I scream at her like I never believed I could.

"I trusted you!" I say. "I believed you when you told me there was still a way to save the Queen! But it was all a lie, wasn't it? The only reason you brought us here was so we could see that the tree had already won. So you could enjoy returning to the city and finding everyone dead!"

She doesn't respond. I push past the others and charge through the gate, grabbing Sarah by the furs and shaking her as hard as I can. She doesn't try to fend me off, which is the only reason I'm able to move her at all.

"No one forced you to leave the city!" I shout at her. "No one made you lose the people who loved you. You *chose* to leave them, because you couldn't love them back the way normal people can. Because all you care about is your cursed tree! Now you've both got what you want. Are you happy?"

I slap her face, a sharp blow that echoes in the empty city. I'm winding up to do it again when my legs give out on me and I fall to my knees, covering my face with my hands. There's no point in attacking her, no point in anything. All that's left for me to do is wait for death to take me, like it has everyone I love.

Strong hands clutch my shoulders, pulling me upright. Thick furs scratch my face, while a musky odor fogs my mind. I'm too weak to struggle, and I wish she would squeeze me in her arms until all my breath is gone.

Her lips are beside my ear, her voice a rough whisper.

"There's more than one kind of love," she says. "Remember what you felt in the world-tree's chamber, what I showed you beneath the village. Remember those things when the time comes, and don't be stingy with the payment that kind of love calls for."

Fingers as coarse as sandpaper brush my forehead. My mind spins, and I feel myself falling into a swoon. *A queen's trick,* I think, as Sarah's grimy face blurs and I whirl off into the dark.

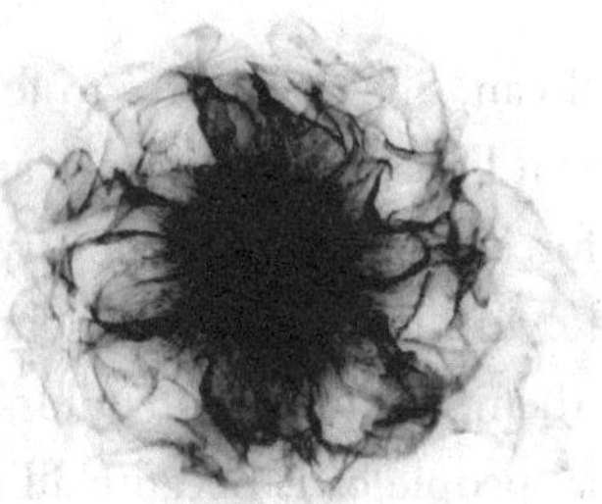

I WAKE TO a world the color of ash.

It's a minute before I realize I'm inside, lying on a floor as hard and cold as stone. Another minute, and I see the low ceiling, the six-sided walls pressing close. I'm in the Queen's brood chamber, but the golden light I saw when I found Rebecca three weeks ago has faded, leaving the room dead and gray.

I turn my head, and find that I'm not alone. The woman who lies beside me is recognizable as the Queen only by her pink dress and doll-size legs. Her thick curls are gone, her hair reduced to a few sparse patches on a scalp as gray as the room. Her breath, if she's breathing at all, is too shallow for me to see her chest rise and fall.

Two other people share the room with us. They're much bigger than Rebecca, stretched out on the floor with their faces turned from me. A feeling of horror shoots through my chest as I raise myself on an elbow and see the long legs and healer's outfit of the one, the black hair and Sensor's robe of the other.

"Mom! Dad!"

I rush to them. Their faces are as rigid as Rebecca's, their eyes closed. Their brown skin is paler than it should be, which accentuates the black slime-trails covering their arms. They must have been brought here by the wyrm I used to know as Wyvern. When I lay a hesitant hand on their foreheads, I find that Mom is as hot to the touch as Dad. That must mean they're both alive, but I can't understand how Mom caught the Queen's sickness when she seemed immune before.

"It was the transfusions," a voice answers my unspoken question.

I spin to find Sarah crouching in a darkened corner of the brood chamber, bundled in her thick furs. The room's gray light shadows her face, but I can see her eyes glinting like hard black coals.

"Your mother shared her Sensor's blood with Rebecca," she says. "Time and again, she bled herself to keep the Queen alive. It was a last-ditch effort, and it wouldn't have worked in the long run. The short-term result is that her anemic state overcame her natural resistance to the tree's blight."

"Then why did you bring her here?" I ask. "Why did you force me to see her and Dad like this?"

"I thought you would want to," she says. "To remember *why* you're here."

She stands and steps over Rebecca's body as if the Queen is nothing more than a dead branch lying on the ground, then squats beside me. A hand emerges from her furs, brushing my dad's hair away from his closed eyes. She leans down to press her lips against his forehead, keeping them there for what seems longer than she should before pulling away.

"I know you don't trust me," she says. "And I know that, in the absence of trust, you doubt whether keeping your end of the tree's bargain will save the ones you love. But trust or no, you're going to have to decide, and quickly.

The Queen is very near death. The light has already faded from this chamber, the place where she meets the Ecosystem face to face. Feel the floor; the wax has hardened, and the tendrils that would have reached out to her have withered below. If she dies, all living things that share her genes will soon follow. In a day, an hour, a minute, it will be too late for you to act."

I look at the Queen's face, and I know that I'm seeing the very face of death. Her skin seems to have pulled tight in the few minutes since I woke, showing me the skull beneath, the sockets of her eyes. I try to meet Sarah's gaze, but the eager flame dancing in their dark depths is too much for me. "What do I need to do?"

She reaches under my arms to raise me to my feet. Her hands are careful not to touch exposed skin, which isn't easy considering the state of my clothes. My knees tremble so much, she has to help me to the ground beside Rebecca's body.

"The world-tree's genetic code lies within you," she says. "To restore the Queen, you'll have to let that code flow from your body to hers. It will require a greater expenditure of energy than you've ever attempted—much greater than with Peter, for his genes are nowhere near as closely linked to the Ecosystem as the Queen's. You'll feel as if you're being torn in two, and the feeling will get much worse the longer it lasts. But understand this, Hadassah: if you waver, if you change your mind partway through, it will be ruinous for both of you. Once you've made the connection, you must continue until the tree's code has been transferred from you to Rebecca. Only when that process is completed can you rest."

Rest. The way she says the word, it sounds almost pleasant. "But when it's over… when the code has left my body and entered hers… then I'll…?"

"Yes," she says. "Then you will die."

Though I've known this since the moment I accepted the tree's bargain, hearing it spoken out loud makes my throat tighten with tears. "I never… I never got a chance to say goodbye to them."

"I'm sorry, Hadassah," Sarah says. "Our wishes can't always be fulfilled."

My tears flow even harder at the coldness in her voice. "Could… could you at least tell me the thing my mom was going to tell me?"

She pauses as if she's considering it. Her answer comes quickly, in the form of a shake of her head.

"There's no time," she says. "The Queen's body is growing cold."

I touch Rebecca's face with my fingertips. She's not cold; she's freezing. I take a long, shuddering breath and look at Sarah.

"Tell Mom and Dad I loved them," I whisper. "Promise me."

Again, she pauses. This time, she answers with a nod. "You can hold my hand," she says. "If you think it'll help."

I don't think it will, but I take her fingers in mine and squeeze as tightly as I can.

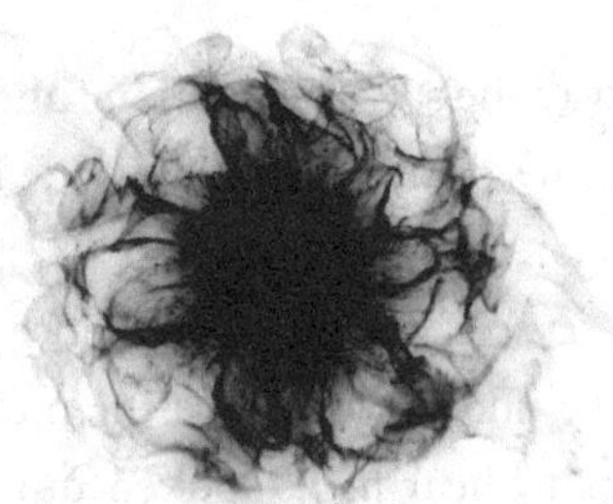

THE MOMENT I touch Rebecca's icy forehead, the pain begins. But it's nothing like Sarah said.

It's worse.

I don't feel like I'm being torn in two. I feel like I'm being torn into a billion pieces, each of them a sliver of the elder code, each sliver as sharp as glass. My skin rips open first, then my muscles, my veins, my bones. My teeth start from their sockets, and my eyes bulge from my skull. My hair, my stupid ugly hair, is pulled from my scalp strand by strand. Fingernails, eyelashes, tongue—parts of me I've hardly ever thought about—are all under assault, stripped or peeled or sliced from my body. I expect to see blood filling the brood chamber, but there's no blood. It's all in my mind, I tell myself, all in my mind.

But it's *not* in my mind. It's in my cells, my genes, the threads that bind me together. As the elder code spills out of me to enter the hollow vessel that is Rebecca, I feel like I'm being sucked dry by an army of vampire bees. By the time they're done with me, I'll be a husk, a shell, a dry seed pod that's fallen from its branch to wither and fade into the dust.

I want to let go. To stop the pain. I want to see my mom and dad again, to tell them I'm sorry, though I don't know what for. I want to run away from this ashy gray room and bask in the sunlight, to feel its warm rays caressing my skin. I want to hear Wyvern's voice inside my head, to bend down and smell a flower, to take a drink of cold, clear water and feel it trickle down my throat. I could even stand to be tormented by Peter, laughed at by my entire Sensor class, if that meant one more second of life. I want the world, everything in it, and I don't ever want to leave it behind.

But I know I must. If I stop now, Mom and Dad will die, and so will Chaim and Tovah and Peter and Leah, and so, in time, will everyone. Everyone and everything. No one can live if the Ecosystem dies, and even if they could, I would never wish such utter loneliness and despair on anybody.

The pain is an all-consuming fire; there's no part of me it doesn't burn. Soon I'll vanish in a puff of smoke to a place where there's nothing at all, no sight, no sound, no Sense. I almost welcome that; at least it will make the pain go away. Sarah promised that when I was done, I could finally rest, and that's the only thing that keeps me going, the only dream that seems possible to grasp.

The world has bleached to gray when I feel something stir inside me, some new life taking shape out of the nothingness. It might be Rebecca returning from the land of the dead, but there's no longer enough of me to be sure of anything. I wonder one last time if everything Sarah told me was a lie, if the purpose I'm giving my life for isn't to heal Rebecca but to kill her, and in so doing to fulfill the tree's desire. I'll never know, not now. I'm almost gone, and my last thought will have to be no more than a hope.

Hadassah, a voice speaks out of nowhere. *Can you hear me?*

I can't answer, can't talk, can't think. Can't wait to rest, to let go, to die.

Listen to me carefully, the voice says. *The code has been transferred. In a second, I'm going to tell you to release yourself from the Queen. You must do exactly as I say, no matter what you fear might be happening. Do you understand me?*

I don't, I don't understand anything, but the voice seems satisfied.

Now, Hadassah, it says. *Come to me. Let go.*

I let go.

The pain is gone, the fear, the doubt. I float in warm nothingness, without a body, without mind or will. A light grows out of the void, and I seem to be drawn toward it, as if I have no choice in the matter. It opens, widens, becomes a whole world in front of me, so bright there's nothing to see. I'm flooded with a feeling I can only describe as joy, and though I'm blinded by the rays of light, the first breath I take in this new place is so sweet it burns my lungs and brings tears to my eyes.

My mouth opens, and I release an aching cry.

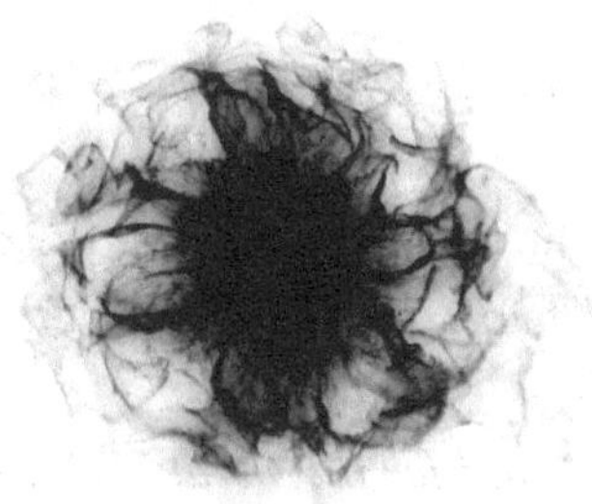

I'M ANSWERED BY the voice.

Hadassah, it says. *Don't cry, dear one. You've done it. You've succeeded. I'm so proud of you.*

I try my own voice, and find that it works, at least in my mind. *Am I… dead?*

You're alive, the voice answers. *You were at the very brink of death, but you survived. As did Rebecca. All worked out according to plan.*

I shake my head in confusion. *But the bargain…*

That bargain was between you and the world-tree, the voice says. *However, there was another bargain neither of you knew about. A bargain I kept secret lest one of you try to stop me from putting it into effect. I'm sorry, Hadassah. I never wanted to lie to you.*

Those words fill me with understanding, and with alarm. I know whose voice it is now. *Sarah!*

I'm here, she says. *But I won't be for much longer. Pretty soon, Rebecca's wyrm—Wyvern, is that what you call it?—will be coming for me. What's left of me, anyway.*

What do you mean? I ask, though I'm afraid I know.

Hadassah, she says. *I used up all the energy I had, and now…*

You're dying.

Something like that, she says, with a bit of her old laugh. *At least, I'm becoming… part of things. What Wyvern would call part of the bundle. Or what I prefer to think of as part of the elder code.*

Tears fill the eyes I haven't yet tested to the light. *You gave your life for me. So I wouldn't have to fulfill the tree's bargain.*

I did what I did for the world I love, she says. *But yes, you're a big part of that world.*

I squeeze my eyes shut to stop the tears, but they keep on coming. I know now why Sarah held my hand through the transfer. Not to comfort me. Not to make sure I didn't back out. To *heal* me, by substituting her life for mine when it was about to slip away for good.

And I know I can't give it back to her. It's inside me now, the life she traded. It's why I can hear her, though more and more faintly with each second. I keep talking, trying to hold onto her as long as I can, though I know that, in the end, I'm going to have to let her go.

How did you do it? I ask. *How did you hide what you were planning to do from the tree?*

I'm sneaky, she says. *I had to be. Tricking a being as old and wise as the world-tree wasn't easy, let me tell you.*

She laughs again, and I can hear how pleased she is with herself.

When I found the tree's chamber after all the years it had kept itself hidden, its first reaction was panic and rage. It wanted to destroy me, the Queen, everything. I convinced it there was another way: that we could save the elder code without condemning the people who were products of the Ecosystem. But the tree demanded proof of human fidelity, proof that one of our kind was willing to sacrifice everything to save the code. It was still so angry at the Dawsons, at what it saw as their betrayal. I offered myself in expiation of their acts, but the tree wouldn't accept. It wanted—

Me.

That's right. Can you guess why?

I can't think of any good reason, but I try for Sarah's sake. *Because the tree and I are… connected somehow?*

More than just connected. You're a product of the elder code, Hadassah. That's why you were able to carry the vision I sent you without threat of blight, and it's why you were able to communicate with the tree in its chamber. It's why you were able to heal Peter and Rebecca, too. The code has been inside you from before the day you were born. I just had to… wake it up.

But… does that mean Mom and Dad aren't my real parents?

They are your parents. That much I can tell you. The rest of it, I think, is for your mother to tell.

Is it… the thing she couldn't tell me before?

It is. Be patient, Hadassah. She'll tell you soon, I promise.

I'm not satisfied with that answer, but before I can say anything else, Sarah's voice continues. I can't help noticing that it's getting harder to hear.

I should add that I didn't realize any of this when you were first born. I knew there was something special about you, but I couldn't put my finger on what it was until the last time I visited the city, just before you turned four. I'd learned enough by then to understand where the power within you came from, but I was afraid your parents would resist the truth. I told them instead that you were ready to begin the Sensor training, which I had reason to believe would help your power to grow. And it did.

Not really. I told you I'm a bad Sensor.

Bad is too strong of a word. It's true you don't Sense in the traditional way due to the presence of the elder code within you, but the training gave you the foundation you needed to develop your unique skills. Without it, you would never have been able to bundle with Wyvern, to speak to the world-tree. The culmination of your apprenticeship came when I sent you the vision, which gave you knowledge of the tree as well as motivation to seek it out. All that remained after that point was for you to come to me as I was confident you would, and to do what I had faith in you to do.

I mull that over. I can hardly believe the chance she took, the trust she showed. What if I'd refused? She counted on me to love the world as much as she did, and even now, I'm shocked to realize she was right.

I wish you'd told me, I say. *Sarah, you scared me to death. I thought you were angry at me. That you wanted everyone to die so the tree could have the world back the way it was. I even worried that…*

I was under the tree's spell. I know. I heard what you and that smarty-pants Peter were talking about.

Then why didn't you tell me? Why did you… do the things you did?

She doesn't answer right away, and I think I've lost her for good, either that or she's offended by the question. Then her voice comes back to me on the outer edge of hearing.

I'm sorry, Hadassah. When I received the world-tree's approval to bring you to edinnu, one of its conditions was that you must act from what it considered pure motives, without human selfishness. This past week, I've heard its voice inside my head, urging me to test you to the utmost so it could be sure you were dedicated to your task, not to pleasing me. I couldn't say no to it. That would have broken our compact, and everyone would have died. To keep my true intentions hidden, I had to play along to the very end—I couldn't even touch you for fear of what you might perceive. I'm sorry I scared you, and I'm sorry for treating you so unkindly. But most of all, I'm sorry for…

What?

Having to say goodbye.

My heart goes empty at the sound of those words. Here I am being snippy with her when I'll never see her again, never hear the sound of her voice or feel the touch of her hand. Maybe she'll never even visit me in my dreams.

Sarah. I don't think I can make it without you.

Her answer's so soft I can barely hear it.

You don't have a choice. Your people are going to need you. I suspect things are going to be… different from now on.

Different how?

Listen to the world. Watch and ward it always. You'll figure it out…

Her voice trails off, and much as I wait for her to continue, there's nothing.

Sarah! I call out.

The faintest of echoes reaches my ears. *If you see Archie, tell him I said goodbye…*

Then silence.

Sarah. Can you hear me?

More silence.

Sarah. I love you. I'll tell Leah and Mom what you did. And I'll look for Archie, and… I'll look for you, too. In the water, and the clouds, and the moon at night, and in everything that grows. I'll never forget.

I listen once more for her answer, but there's nothing to hear. She's gone, and I feel as if the world's gone with her.

A hand touches my arm. I open my eyes to find my mom bending over me in the dusky dark, the color restored to her face, the shine to her hair. The look of concern leaves her brow when she sees me, and she smiles and smooths hair from my forehead. I try to smile back, but my lip trembles.

"Mom," I say. "Sarah is…"

"I know," she says softly. "And the tree?"

"It's still there. I can show you."

"There's no need for that just now. We have a lot to take care of first."

She helps me stand. Dad is starting to wake up, though he seems much groggier than her. The Queen is stirring as well, her thick lashes fluttering. Her cheeks glow with health, and even more amazing, her long curls cascade over her shoulders. Sarah's body is nowhere to be found. Seeing everyone else alive and well when she's gone brings my tears so close to the surface, I know it'll only take another word for them to pour out. But I guess that's what I want, because I keep on talking.

"Mom," I say. "When I… when I healed the Queen, something happened to the Ecosystem. It's…"

She stops me with a finger to my lips.

"I know," she says again, and gathers me in her arms.

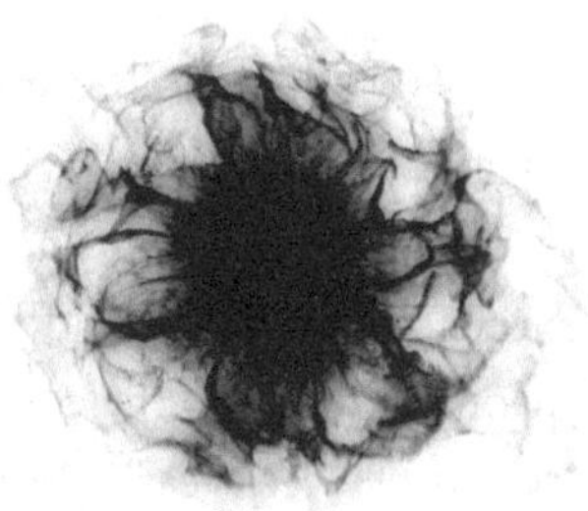

Mom wasn't joking. There's so much to take care of, it feels like we'll never see the end of it. So much we're going to have to do differently from now on, just as Sarah said.

The first order of business, though, is to help Rebecca and my dad out of the brood chamber. Both of them are weak and bleary from all the time they spent under the world-tree's spell, and Dad's not up to carrying Rebecca, so Mom and I form a chair with our hands and walk her to the end of the tunnel. When we reach the elevator, I wish I could call for Wyvern, but I know they wouldn't hear me. The wyrm's last job was to bear Sarah deep down below, where her body will start to become the soil-they-consume.

"What do we do now?" I ask.

"This way," Mom says, and leads me down a short side tunnel I didn't see when I was here before. There's a staircase at the end, with stairs made of dirt, not stone. It must be what the queens used before Master Gideon built the elevator for Rebecca.

"Do you think you can make it?" Mom asks.

I nod, and we start up the stairs with Rebecca in our arms.

It's not easy, and I have to rest a couple of times, but finally we get to the top, where Rebecca's wheelchair waits for us. Mom and I take her down the hallway and leave her in bed with a maid to watch over her, then send another maid to find Caleb. I wonder if Rebecca will ever visit the brood chamber again, if she'll keep living in the queen's cottage. If we'll still call her the Queen, or if that part of our past is gone, too.

I walk with Mom and Dad to the council house, where Mom spent the past three weeks caring for the sick, arranging for them to get transfusions so their fevers wouldn't climb too high. Caleb passes us on the way there as he sprints across the compound to Rebecca's bedside. All of the other patients are rising and stretching, but they're weak like Dad, and they're going to need time to rest. Even more than that, they're going to need time to adjust. To learn how to live in the world all over again.

I'm helping Angelica and Celestina from their pallets when Peter bounces up to me—which is a good thing, since Celestina, as always, demands the royal treatment. Leah's right behind him, and she registers Sarah's absence with a quick nod and a look of pain in her dark eyes.

"I think I knew from the start," she says. "Hints she dropped along the way, things she wouldn't tell me. That's how it's always been: when Sarah decides it's time to go, no one can talk her out of it." She smiles bravely. "At least I got to say goodbye to her this time."

We hold each other, then get back to work.

After a few hours of giving people water and helping them take their first wobbly steps with an arm over our shoulders, Mom lets me and Peter have a break. I try to give him the slip, but he pulls me aside to pester me about the fine points of the world-tree's bargain. I don't know why I feel reluctant to tell him, but once the words start to come, I find that it's a relief to say them out loud.

"It was like a… a reset," I tell him. "When I transferred the world-tree's code to Rebecca, it replaced the *Apis impunita* code. Which meant the clock went back to before the rise of the Ecosystem, before it learned to think and desire and dream."

"So the Ecosystem's gone?"

"Not gone," I say. "Just not aware, at least not the way it was. The creatures it produced are still here, and some of them are as dangerous as ever, but they're not able to organize an attack against us like they could before. They're just living their lives, the way they were meant to. The way the tree intended."

"Hm." I know before he says another word that he's figured out the rest, but I let him say it anyway, since he loves to observe and analyze so much. "Human beings aren't connected to the hive anymore either, are we?"

"No," I say. "The tree let us live, but only at the cost of losing our Sense of the wild. I guess it wanted us to learn to live in the world on our own."

He smiles. "That makes *sense* to me."

I roll my eyes. "Seriously? After all this time, that's the best joke you could come up with?"

"I could have said we're living in *Eden New*."

It takes me a second to get it. "*Eden,* that's the other word for *edinnu.* In ancient something-or-other."

"Akkadian," he says, shifting instantly to encyclopedia mode. "A Semitic language spoken at the dawn of human civilization, though most authorities agree that it was replaced by Old Aramaic by the eighth century BCE…"

I tune him out, keeping a half-smile on my face in case he's paying attention. There's an empty space inside me where there used to be something before, and when I try to reach out with what was once my Sense, I hear nothing but silence. I guess we'll all have to learn to be more like Peter: studying the world carefully, figuring it out a little bit at a time instead of expecting it to tell us everything there is to know about it all at once. Now if he could only learn to shut up for a single second, he might actually be able to help the rest of us.

I smile fully at him. Take a deep breath. And call out to the silence.

"Goodbye, Wyvern," I say.

Then I go with Peter to join the others.

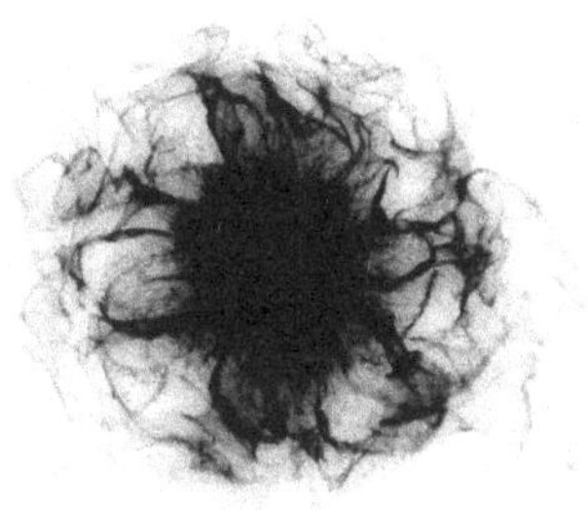

EPILOGUE

WORLD

The world was all before them, where to choose
Their place of rest, and Providence their guide.
They hand in hand, with wand'ring steps and slow
Through Eden took their solitary way.

—John Milton,
Paradise Lost (1667)

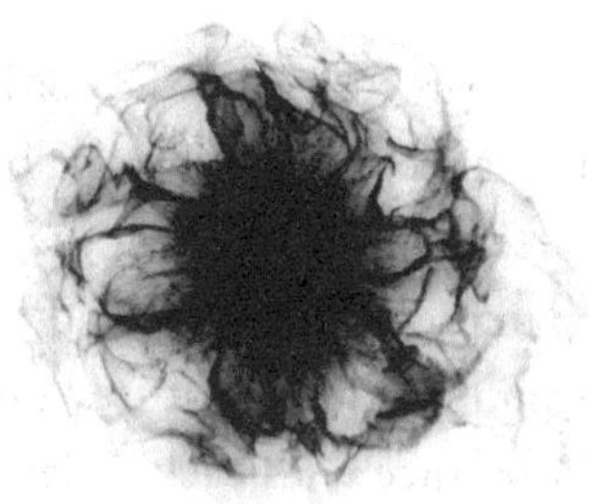

It's almost two months later when Mom and I set out for the village.

Those two months have been... well, something. Though Rebecca can't communicate with the wild anymore, she's stayed on as the city's governor, helping us adjust to our new lives. She's smart, and dedicated, and she knows secrets nobody else does—not even Peter—so she's been training us in everything from harvesting food to avoiding dangerous creatures to using the old-fashioned remedies Sarah taught her. Now that no one has the Sense, I'm amazed to realize how much we relied on it to get us through the day. There are times when I look out my bedroom window to watch the cardivores darting from tree to tree or the hollyhooks flashing their bright colors in our garden, and I feel an ache in my chest to know that all I can do is watch.

But there are positives to everyone being the same. There's nothing to stop people from choosing the jobs they like, nothing to put anyone over anyone else. Even though I sometimes miss the looks of respect I used to get for being a Sensor, it's much better just to be me, no different from anyone except in the ways I choose to be. It's better just to be Hadassah than to be the queen of the whole world.

And in some ways, it's better for me *not* to have the Sense. I can be surprised by the beauty of a newborn cicatrix crawling out of its shell, glistening a liquid green while it clings with tiny barbed legs to the garden wall. I can be brought close to tears by the swoop of a bloodbird across a sapphire sky, or feel my heart swell at the haunting call of a ghosthawk deep in the woods at night. I can be swept away by the simple wonder of life: creatures growing and dying, species living in balance with each other, everything from the smallest spider's web to the hugest burrowing wyrm part of a pattern too complex for me to grasp.

Still, I'll admit I find myself looking for Wyvern from time to time. I never see them, but I relish the feeling that someday I might.

*

It takes me and Mom two weeks to reach the village, just as we planned. Along the way, she shows me how Sensors used to hunt for food, and I'm impressed by how good she is at setting snares, tracking prey by footprints and scat, and finding places where edible plants like to grow. She's also good at not talking about things I don't want to talk about: what I'm going to do with my life now that I'm not a Sensor (I don't know), whether there's anything going on between Peter and me (there isn't), how my body's going to change when I finally have my period (which, believe it or not, I'm starting to get impatient for). She asks me about lots of other things—my sword-fighting lessons with Leah, my voyage upriver with Peter—but we manage to steer clear of conflict for the entire two weeks, which is way beyond a record for us.

Arriving at the village is the same as it was on the outward journey: we walk through a break in the trees and, without warning, it's there. Nothing has changed that I can tell. The flat black land, the mossy rocks that used to be the main hall, the grove of crabapple trees that Sarah planted—all are the same as they were on my return from *edinnu*. Thinking about that day brings back a flood of memories, each of them connected to Sarah in its own way. Mostly, though, I just miss her, keenly and deeply. I don't think that feeling will ever fade.

There's a flash of bronze among the crabapple trees, and I cry out in delight. When I raise my hand, he comes leaping toward me, feathers fluttering in the breeze.

"Archie!" I say as the quetzalopteryx lands on my arm.

"Archie?" Mom asks with an amused smile.

"Sarah's quetzal," I tell her, and grin when I remember what Sarah said: *Archie has a knack for showing up when he's least expected.* "He must have come back to live in the place where she made him."

"Sarah *made* him?" Mom asks. "Here?"

"I'll show you."

I take her hand and lead her across the crunching soil until we reach the site of the village hall. Archie seems to understand what we're about to do, because he takes flight as we duck our heads to enter the tunnel Wyvern opened for me and Sarah the last time we were here. Mom lights a torch to show the way, her grip tightening on my hand as if she's afraid of the shadows that flicker across the earthen walls. I squeeze back, trying to reassure her. We're going deep underground, far below the hall where she and Dad were supposed to be married. This is all according to the plan we agreed on before we set out for the village, but I can't be surprised if she's unsettled now that we're actually here.

The tunnel descends slowly, in a long spiral that Wyvern made sure wasn't too steep for human feet to walk. The smell of earth becomes overwhelming the deeper we go, and the air grows so cold I'm thankful for our torch. Mom's eyes flick warily from side to side. I grip her hand even tighter, the way she did the first day she led me to Sensor's training.

And then, all at once, we're here. The tunnel opens into a spacious vault, stone-walled and dirt-floored, and there's no need for our torch any longer. The radiance that fills the room is so strong it's as if a silver star has fallen to earth. Mom's violet eyes widen to reflect the perfect light.

The light of the world-tree.

It floats there in the vault, anchored to the ground by fine silver roots. It's not as big as the original tree, only about four feet tall, which Sarah told me is because it takes a long time for this kind of tree to grow. In all other ways, it's the same as its parent: the golden corona, the shining core. And the song—that much I can still hear. When I see Mom mouthing the notes, I know she can hear it, too.

"How…?" she whispers.

"Sarah planted it," I say. "Ten years ago, right before she came to the city for the last time. The village must have been a college before the rise of the Ecosystem, and this was one of the vaults where the Dawsons stored the world-tree's code for safekeeping. But this place was special, because it was never found by the *Apis impunita* hive. They raided all the other vaults and broke into the elder code, which is how they gathered the genes to make the Ecosystem."

"So this tree holds the code?" Mom asks. "The same code you carry inside you?"

"Carried," I say. "I passed it on to Rebecca. But yes, this

tree's code is pure and uncorrupted. It's where Sarah got the genes to make Archie, and it's why she brought me here two months ago. She wanted to show me that, even if I failed, the elder code would survive." I look into my mother's eyes, see the silver light shining there. "It's the same code you carry, Mom. The code you got from…"

"Delilah," she says with a gasp. "Then you knew?"

"Sarah explained to me where Delilah's web came from," I say. "She told me that when the lost queen was exiled from the city, she reached deep into the earth beneath the village for a power as strong and deadly as Queen Leonida's. The Ecosystem wouldn't listen to her because it was ruled by her cousin, but the elder code heard her plea and answered. That's how Sarah figured out that you and I were carrying the world-tree's code, because she felt the same power in this chamber that she'd felt in us. The same power she'd fought against during the War of the Queens."

Mom nods shakily, then lowers herself to the dirt floor. I sit beside her, both of us gazing into the branches of the world-tree, whose light seems to grow stronger and brighter every second we watch.

"I was… attacked at my wedding," she begins. "By a fellow Sensor who believed our kind should never marry. I was near death, and I… I fell. Into this vault, I assume, though I have no memory of it. Delilah's web—the seed of it—had taken root inside me days before, and in this chamber, it must have been given the freedom to grow. To bring the dark queen back into the world."

"Through you."

She closes her eyes, draws a deep breath. "I've tried ever since not to think about it. The things the dark queen did—the things *I* did, or at least, saw her do through me. I thought if I lived a… a blameless life, a life of service to my people, then I could… atone for what I'd done. What I'd been. But I…"

I lay a hand on hers. "It wasn't you, Mom. It was the tree, and it used Delilah's grief and rage to lash out against its true enemies: the Ecosystem and the one who ruled it. But that's over now. The elder code doesn't need to fight anymore. Sarah gave her life so it could be at peace. So it could be… healed."

She falls into my arms, and I hold her while she cries. I think about her as she was then, only two years older than me, alone and scared. Carrying the seed of the world-tree inside her without knowing what it was she carried—carrying it through darkness, and despair, and the agony of war. There must have been times when she felt it was too much for her strength, times she wished she could let it go. But she carried it, and passed it on to me. So that I could be the one to fight the final battle, with her old friend and teacher at my side.

"You were brave, Mom," I say.

She turns her teary face to mine. "No braver than my girl."

I hold her tight, and she's not the only one crying now.

"Sometimes," I tell her, "it feels like a dream. All of it. The tree, the Ecosystem, the journey. Like I dreamed it all from my bed at home, and when I wake up, I'll be ready to start the new day. The only part I know for sure was real is…"

"Sarah."

"I miss her."

"I never told you this," she says. "Before she left the city for good, Sarah said something to me I didn't understand. She said she was leaving, and that we'd never see her again. But she also said that a time would come when she'd call for you, and you'd need to seek her out. I asked Leah if she knew what Sarah was talking about, but all she could tell me was that Sarah had been restless and unhappy for a long time, that she felt there was something missing from her life. It's only recently that I've come to understand what that was." She touches my cheek, takes one of my tears onto her fingertip. "What she was looking for was you. Once she found you again, she could die complete."

That makes me cry even harder. The tears I shed are cleansing, and I know they'll water the world-tree and help it to grow strong. And one day, maybe, I'll look in its branches and see Sarah's smile.

When both of our tears have dried, we stand and make our way from the chamber. The uphill climb is slow, especially since neither of us really wants to leave. For a long time, we stand at the exit to the tunnel, watching Archie perform backflips against the bright sky. I think I hear a voice, one I've heard many times before in my dreams. It comes from deep inside the earth, and though I can't make out the words, I understand what it wants from me, as well as what it offers in return.

Mom kisses my cheek, then touches the token at my throat. "Happy birthday, my darling," she says.

I smile at her, and take her hand as we start the long walk home.

THE END

GEOGRAPHICAL NOTE

The following artist's rendering is based on an original warhog-hide map currently housed in the museum of the City of the Queens. The map depicts a portion of what was once the southwestern corner of the state of Pennsylvania (itself an administrative unit of the former United States of America). Despite the seismic changes occasioned by the rise of the Ecosystem, general features of this region have been preserved, including the confluence of three rivers and the densely forested terrain. To convey the approximate relationship between the area embraced by the map and the other regions referenced in this chronicle, the artist has included details of the estuarine system to the north and the village-city complex to the southeast.

It is worth noting that despite repeated voyages to the lake pictured herein, *edinnu* island has thus far eluded discovery.

THE WILD

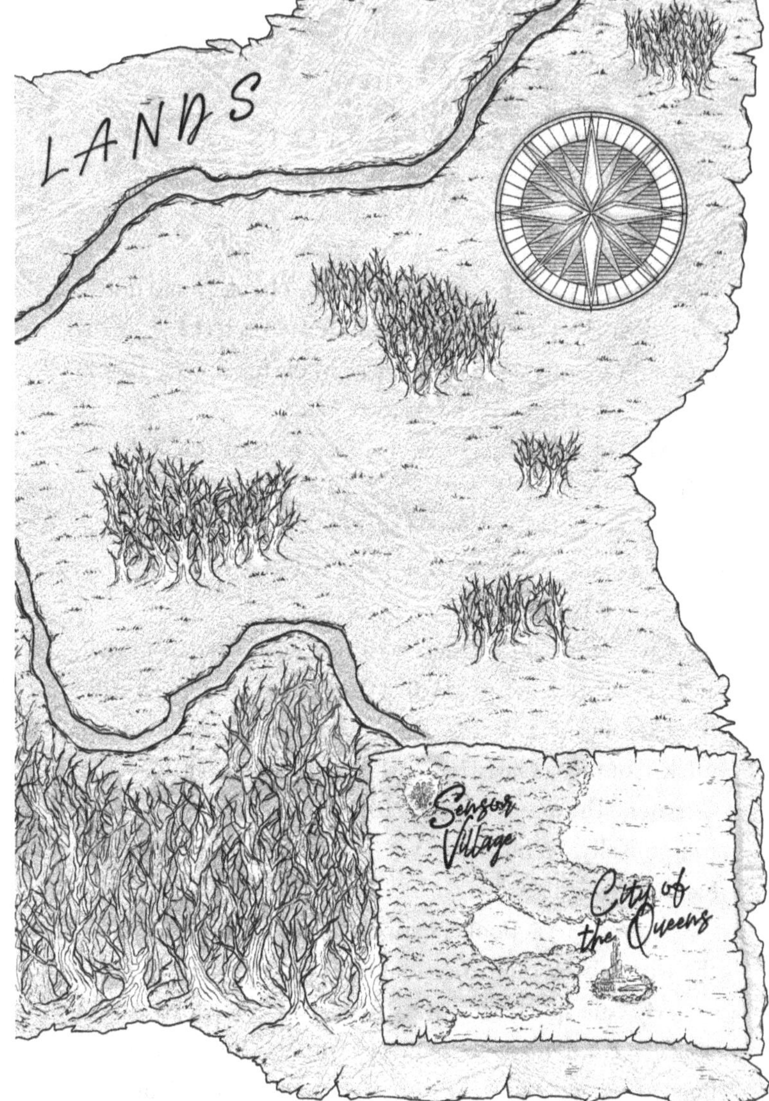
LANDS
Sensor Village
City of the Queens

ACKNOWLEDGMENTS

I wasn't sure I had one more Ecosystem book in me until I started writing, but now that I'm finished, I feel I've finally brought the story cycle to the place where it belongs. Thanks to those who helped me find that place.

My agent, Liza Fleissig, and my editor, Christa Yelich-Koth.

Cover designers par excellence Damonza, mapmaker extraordinaire Jessica Khoury, and booksellers to the stars Riverstone Books.

The many fellow writers who have inspired, encouraged, and supported me, including Jonathan Auxier, Jennifer Bardsley, Barbara Barrow, Jenny Birch, Jamie Beth Cohen, Nick Courage, Christina Farley, Sabrina Fedel, Caroline Gessner, Thomas Hallock, Tom Isbell, Larry Ivkovich, Margo Kelly, Stephanie Keyes, Leah Pileggi, Kat Ross, and Sarah J. Schmitt.

Lauren of YA Bookers, for loving and helping to spread the word about the Ecosystem books.

My colleagues, students, friends, and extended family, who have attended my launch parties, tweeted about my books, and generally treated me like a bigger deal than I am.

And last, my wife and children, to whom I've made a promise. Like Hadassah's, it will be kept.

ABOUT THE AUTHOR

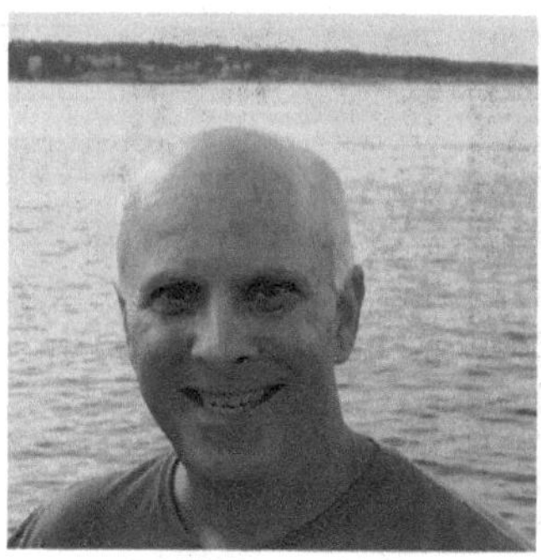

Joshua David Bellin has been writing novels since he was eight years old (though the first few were admittedly very short). He has published numerous works of fantasy and science fiction, including the four-part Ecosystem Cycle (*Ecosystem*, *The Devouring Land*, *House of Earth*, *House of Stone*, and *The Last Sensor*), the Querry Genn Saga (*Survival Colony 9* and *Scavenger of Souls*), and the deep-space adventure *Freefall*. His next book, *Scarred City*, will appear in 2021.

In his free time, Josh likes to read, watch movies, and spend time in Nature with his kids. Oh, yeah, and he likes monsters. Really scary monsters.

To find out more about Josh and his books, visit his website and sign up for his e-newsletter. He promises not to send it to you more than once a month!

joshuadavidbellin.blogspot.com

ALSO BY JOSHUA DAVID BELLIN

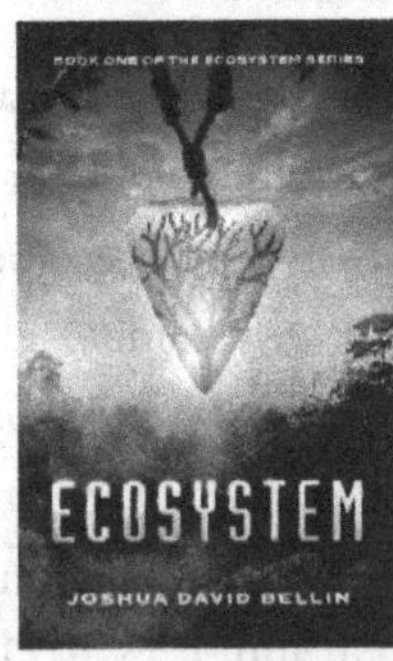

Ecosystem (Ecosystem Cycle, #1)
The Devouring Land (Ecosystem Cycle, #2)
House of Earth, House of Stone (Ecosystem Cycle, #3)
Survival Colony 9 (Querry Genn Saga, #1)
Scavenger of Souls (Querry Genn Saga, #2)
Freefall

Available from online retailers and selected booksellers

www.ingramcontent.com/pod-product-compliance
Lightning Source LLC
Chambersburg PA
CBHW011443170626
46816CB00008B/2502

* 9 7 8 1 7 3 2 1 8 5 9 7 5 *